FOR ONCE IN MY LIFE

SIÂN O'GORMAN

Boldwood

First published in Great Britain in 2024 by Boldwood Books Ltd.

Cover Design by Head Design Ltd

Cover Photography: Shutterstock, iStock and Alamy

A CIP catalogue record for this book is available from the British Library.

Paperback ISBN 978-1-80483-013-0

Hardback ISBN 978-1-80483-014-7

Large Print ISBN 978-1-80483-012-3

Ebook ISBN 978-1-80483-010-9

Kindle ISBN 978-1-80483-011-6

Audio CD ISBN 978-1-80483-019-2

MP3 CD ISBN 978-1-80483-018-5

Digital audio download ISBN 978-1-80483-016-1

Boldwood Books Ltd
23 Bowerdean Street
London SW6 3TN
www.boldwoodbooks.com

For Ruby

Tell me, what is it you plan to do
with your one wild and precious life?

— MARY OLIVER

There is a crack in everything, that is how the light gets in...

— LEONARD COHEN

1

Merrion Square, in the heart of Georgian Dublin, was by far the most lovely area of this beautiful city. It was the first day of June and the square was at its resplendent best on this Friday afternoon: the trees in the park at the centre were in their full green glory, the flower beds a haze of colour, the playground full of children squealing, the benches filled with office workers, their faces to the sun, their coffee photo cups and sandwiches beside them.

High above the square, in a conference room on the top floor of advertising company Mulligan O'Leary, Kitty O'Sullivan glanced down at the verdant oasis below. Beside her, Alex was in full flow, pitching to the Department of Health a potential new fitness campaign for children. Kitty watched as hand-holding children, from the small Montessori which occupied one of the houses, dressed in boaters and striped shirts, snaked their way across the centre of the square. People were picnicking on the grass, sandwiches bought from the cool basement café. There was a fiddle player in the shade of a cherry tree, the sun dappling grass around him, the music wafting heavenward, all the way to Kitty.

She was finding it hard to keep her mind on work and mainly thinking of Dave and how he didn't seem content with his life. Just that morning, he had been lying in bed, as Kitty had raced around getting dressed, tidying the house quickly, because she knew that Dave wouldn't bother, when he had announced he was unhappy and wanted to find a new job.

'Unhappy?' she'd queried, momentarily taken off balance.

He'd nodded. Or rather his nose, which poked out from the duvet, had moved up and down, which she'd taken to be a sign of acquiescence. Was he depressed or just down in the dumps?

Dave hadn't been his old self for a long time and had retreated into early middle age, the grumpy young man who didn't like socialising or having any kind of fun. He'd lost his father three years earlier which understandably had only compounded his decline. He needed something to get his mojo back and Kitty had begun to wonder if they needed to make a more definite kind of commitment. Would getting married be something that might help him feel more secure?

Kitty tuned back in to the conference room. Alex was still talking confidently, explaining their idea for the Hop To It campaign. She was the chief copywriter in their team, and Kitty was her junior. Kitty had worked at Mulligan O'Leary for the last five years, her skills lay in the honing of an idea and its essence, finding the perfect word and the sentence that would bring it to life, and she was quite content that Alex took the lead, being so much better at public speaking than she was.

Alex was tall, cool and queenly, her hair cut in a bob almost as sharp as her cheekbones, with heavy, perfect make-up and not a hair out of place. Kitty was smaller, blonde with straight shoulder-length hair, her suits a slightly more high-street version of Alex's, but a softer face, blue eyes and small features. She was pretty to Alex's beauty.

On the other side of Alex sat their newish team leader, Mary Rose, who was still on her three-month probation. She nodded along, interested in everything Alex said, as though this was her first time hearing it all. Hughie, their graphic designer, was sitting on the other side of Kitty. He caught her eye and with only the slightest twitch of his eyebrow nearly made her laugh.

In front of them were three grey-suited, sour-faced members of the Department of Health, one with a polished dome of a head which reflected the light from the large windows. The brief had been to encourage children to exercise and Hop To It was to be brought to all the junior schools in the country, linking up with sports days and summer camps. The mascot was a rabbit called Floppy Hopper – a character drawn by Hughie.

'Hop To It,' said Alex, managing to smile at everyone, 'will therefore be a perfect way to encourage children to move more and leave their phones behind.'

Kitty thought again of Dave, how things weren't working and what she could do to make a change. They'd been together for five years, but since his father had died, he hadn't been himself. Or perhaps he hadn't been himself before then. But whenever it was, she was finding it harder and harder to remember the lovely Dave from their early days. Then, he'd been sweet and fun, and although never outgoing or remotely gregarious, he had suited Kitty. Having someone to look after made her feel wanted and needed, and she felt nothing but affection for him. She planned to bring happiness from sadness, tidiness from disarray. Marriage, she thought, might bring him back to where he had been, and wasn't getting married the ultimate relationship tidying-up? He was in a life slump, dealing with the fact that he wasn't achieving all those ambitions he'd once reeled off when they had first met: his own company; a certain salary; his own house with gravel driveway. He'd been derailed and perhaps getting married would give him a solidity that would power him out of his slump. Kitty loved Dave and was determined to do whatever it took to make him happy... or at least happier.

Alex turned to Kitty and smiled. 'I'm just going to hand you over to Kitty, who will take you through how we believe the roll-out in schools should go.'

Kitty felt her stomach turn over with a lurch of nausea. Standing up and speaking had never become any easier over the years and she much preferred to let others take the lead and the limelight. Creating order in life, from words and sentences to tidying and cleaning, was what she loved, and standing up in front of people was her very definition of chaos. When things were tidy, she felt safe and secure.

Kitty got to her feet, somehow managed to smile and began speaking. Even though she knew their pitch was good, she felt exposed and silly.

Two of the Department of Health team were nodding encouragingly, but the shiny-headed man was looking unimpressed, his arms folded across his chest, his nose scrunched sceptically.

'It's a campaign which will make children feel they are part of a club,' Kitty said. 'And with the tokens and reward chart, they will want to run faster, for longer, jump higher, skip or even rollerblade even more.' Her voice sounded ridiculous. High and tinny, nothing like Alex's low, confident tones. 'Thank you for listening,' she ended. 'Any questions?'

The two encouraging Department of Health bods nodded.

'I love it,' said one. 'I like Hoppy...'

'Floppy,' said Hugh.

'Oh, so do I,' said the other.

But the man with the crossed arms shook his shiny head. 'It's missing something...' he said, a finger to his lips.

'Missing something?' Alex said as though to clarify that is what was said rather than asking what was missing.

'Yeah...' The man sat back in his chair, as though relaxing into the problem. 'I'm not sure what it is, but something is missing.'

Alex leaned into the table. 'We can work on it,' she said, smilingly. 'We can refine and re-present.'

The man looked at her. 'I don't know what it is,' he said. 'But it just doesn't grab me.'

Alex looked over at Kitty, her face utterly blank, but Kitty knew she was devastated. If he didn't like it, then they hadn't won the pitch. The campaign would go to one of their rivals. The problem was, Kitty agreed with him. Something was missing, and to be honest, there was always something missing, but that was normal. Kitty never produced a piece of work which she thought of as perfect. She had learned to just accept that she would never be 100 per cent happy with a pitch. She was a perfectionist by nature, but she had realised over the years that work and relationships would never be as easy to control as the inside of her wardrobe, which was perfectly organised, or her food cupboard with its alphabetised spices.

* * *

Later when all the goodbyes and handshaking were done and the Department of Health team had left, Kitty, Alex, Mary Rose and Hughie made their way back to their office.

Alex was almost incredulous as she sat at her desk. 'He didn't like it...'

'Only *one* of them didn't like it,' said Mary Rose. 'The other two did.'

'But...' Alex seemed unable to compute what had just happened. Just the previous month, she had won Gold at the

Irish Advertising Awards – her third such prize. She wasn't used to losing. 'He said something was missing.'

'Maybe some people can't see a good campaign when it is presented to them,' said Alex. 'We worked on that for six weeks... and I thought it was good.'

'I think it was a good pitch,' went on Kitty. 'And they loved Floppy...' She smiled over at Hughie.

'He could have been cuter, though,' said Hughie, adjusting his hair. 'I think the bow tie was a little too small...'

Mary Rose smiled at them. 'Let's see if we can use this as a learning experience, yes? Let's crack on and win the next one?' She paused, perching on the edge of Kitty's desk. 'And it's a big one. Right... drum roll... Hughie?'

Hughie drummed two pencils on his desktop. 'Brings me back to school orchestra,' he said. 'I was percussion. Until, of course, Cathal McGooly had a meltdown and got his mam up the school and said that if he was not given the drums, then he was going to have anxiety.' Hughie shrugged. 'And that is how I ended up on the xylophone. Just one tune a year, the bells just before "Silent Night". Still haven't got over it.'

'Very touching,' said Alex. 'But irrelevant to the fact we just lost a pitch. Something missing,' she muttered, looking over at Kitty again. 'What on earth did he mean?'

That was the problem, Kitty thought. Wasn't there always something missing and you just had to find it and fix it? Like the problem with her and Dave. Marriage was missing, and it would fix everything.

'Right,' Mary Rose continued, 'Mr Mulligan has emailed to say that we have been asked to pitch for a brand-new international campaign. We have exactly three weeks to work on it. And...' She paused for effect. 'The client is Welcome Ireland.'

There was a gasp from Hughie, and even Alex looked interested.

'I knew that would get you all excited,' said Mary Rose. 'It's a huge international tourist campaign, in every territory. We have to sell Ireland to the rest of the world. We're up against Jacinta Boyle and her team from DNG and Louella Murphy and her team from Elevation. They are both brilliant teams... we know that but this is a massive opportunity for us. Think you can do it?'

'If we can work out what was missing last time,' said Alex, 'then we might have a chance.'

2

Kitty sat on the commuter train, taking her towards her home in Sandycove, just a half-hour away from the city centre and travelled along the coast. She stared out of the window, at the glittering, sparkling sea, the flash of the yacht sails, the seagulls with their huge wingspan, those beady eyes as they swooped on the headwinds. Her mind was full of two things: that day's failed pitch and her unhappy boyfriend. How would she fix it all? And what was the something missing? It felt as though if she found the answer to that, everything might fall into place.

From Sandycove station, she walked through the village, with its small shops, past the pub where the Friday night drinkers spilled out onto the pavement, the noise of their chat drifting up in the air. It was one of the nicest villages in Ireland, she always thought, a busy, buzzy, beautiful place, with hanging baskets loaded with mauve and white lobelia and pink begonias. She knew most people and waved at Edith Waters who ran the haberdashery in the village and was Shazza's landlady. And there was Killian Walsh, the owner of the Sandycove Arms hotel holding hands with Flora, just back from their honeymoon. And outside

The Island pub, people were laughing and chatting, Aperol Spritzes in hands. There was a group of ladies with wet hair, who'd obviously been for a dip in the Forty Foot.

Dave wasn't a pub-goer, preferring to watch TV at home – 'Saves money,' he'd say – but Kitty looked with a pang of longing, sensing that prickle of anticipation that she remembered feeling before a night out.

When she'd met Dave, he'd worn such a long scarf that it had trailed on the ground, and for some reason, it had made her feel quite protective over him. He'd been funnier in those days, and told her he'd tried out in the university open-mic nights and had even won the 'Most Surprisingly Funny' award, which, as he reminded everyone, had been won by Dara Ó Briain back in the old days. Buoyed by his success, the world of comedy his oyster, he even planned a show to take to Edinburgh, but as the date to pay his deposit drew closer, his nerve seemed to fade, and the show remained unwritten. Instead, he dedicated himself to his studies and planned on dominating the world of engineering, setting his sights on a big job in the States. But, after graduation, those dreams faded, the scarves grew shorter, along with his ambitions.

Kitty had tried to help over the years, but he batted her away, content to stay in, commenting on the world from the comfort of their sofa. Maybe she would help him find himself again, the two of them together, Kitty by his side.

Her phone vibrated.

SHAZZA

How was the pitch?

Kitty texted back.

KITTY

We didn't get it.

SHAZZA

Really? But I thought it was great??????

KITTY

Something was missing. Apparently.

SHAZZA

You need a drink.

KITTY

Wish I could. But I said I would go home early.

SHAZZA

...

KITTY

Sorry.

SHAZZA

Don't worry. Have a nice evening. I have to go to a launch at the Sandycove Arms. A new local beer. It's a hard life!

KITTY

Love you.

SHAZZA

Love you too! Say hi to Dave xxx

Shazza had yet to meet Mr Exactly Right but had had several collisions with members of the male of the species who were either emotionally unavailable or unhinged or, in one case, addicted to his vape, which he couldn't remove from his mouth, even during meals or going to the bathroom.

'It's just so unhygienic,' Shazza had complained. And then she'd met a fellow journalist at the *Irish Independent* and they'd fallen in love. 'We're proper together,' Shazza had explained, 'as in actually together, accompanying each other to events. Finally, I have a plus-one.' But it turned out he just wasn't that into her. She'd told Kitty, tearfully, sloshing wine in her glass, that he'd decided to get married – and it wasn't to Shazza, it was to Arabella Scott-O'Brien who was in charge of the horse racing section of the paper and who hailed from very rich Kildare horsey family and was always photographed at some godawful race meet with a ridiculous fascinator on her head. Shazza had a penchant for leopard print, had long, unbrushed, highlighted blonde hair, and sometimes reminded Kitty of a stallion, its mane being blown in the wind. She had no time for prettiness or being quiet. She was loud and proud, in every way. Except after things had ended with her plus-one.

'You can't even tell which one's the horse,' Shazza had wailed, her lack of feminist solidarity excused due to extreme distress. In a fit of desperately needing to get far away from this man, now monikered Mr Unmentionable, Shazza had handed in her notice, refused the extra money she'd been offered to stay and walked out. She was now editor of the Sandycove Newsletter, dealing with community events, council happenings and the latest low-down in the local clubs and societies.

But marriage, thought Kitty, was the only solution to her and Dave's relationship stasis. It was either that or separate, which sounded so much more chaotic. After seeing Shazza's life being upturned after her break-up, Kitty really couldn't face the same.

3

'Hello... I'm home...'

Kitty stepped inside the hall as Romeo, her treasured black cat who had two white socks on his back legs, and a smudge of white on his face, bounded soundlessly down the stairs, making a beeline for her, winding his body around her ankles, purring delightedly, as though he'd been waiting for her all day.

She hung up her bag and linen jacket next to Dave's dead dad's winter coat, which he had taken to wearing, the collar up, looking like a man on his way to the betting shop.

After the wedding, she thought, they would go on a honeymoon somewhere too warm to wear old winter coats, where they could drink a few cocktails and relax and set a new course for their life. She felt buoyant at the thought. She would come up with an itinerary for the travelling, plan everything far in advance, and leave no room for mishaps or mistakes. Dave might even enjoy it.

In the living room, Dave was wearing another of his late father's clothes: a jumper which was so heavy and so scratchy that it made Kitty's skin itch all over. It had become Dave's comfort jumper, which he wore most of the time now, along – horrifyingly – with his father's old tweed cap. A couple of times, in the fading evening light, she'd walked into the room and almost had a heart attack, thinking it was the ghost of his dead father. Once, while wearing the jumper and cap, Dave had tried to kiss her, and it was impossible to explain without hurting his feelings why this was abhorrent. There was another time, one chilly evening during the winter, when the boiler wasn't working, that he wore them in bed – even the cap – and all night Kitty had slept on the very edge of the mattress, praying she wouldn't feel a wandering hand. She had thought that as the weather warmed, the hat, old cardigan and coat would be consigned to the wardrobe, but they still made their spectral appearance. But he was still obviously grieving and who was she to say what grief should look like?

But Dave and his father hadn't been all that close; he was much more of a mother's boy, taking her side when his father disappeared somewhere. Maureen, Dave's mother, was an intimidating woman, and Kitty often thought that she too would disappear from time to time if she was stuck with her for life. His mother was, in Kitty's opinion – an opinion she had never dared to breathe – an overbearing dragon, who hadn't liked Kitty from the moment she first laid eyes on her. She was a large woman, who seemed to like to juxtapose herself against small things, almost to make herself seem even more imposing. She always carried a tiny handbag and wore shoes which looked uncomfortably insufficient. And now she was to be Kitty's mother-in-law-to-be, then she would have to find some way of taming this dragon. Perhaps the two of them would discover that they had more in common than they first thought, perhaps they would end up being best friends.

Dave looked up, his face half in shadow from the peak of the cap. It was like something from a horror film. If she hadn't known it was Dave, she would have run screaming from the house. Instead, she smiled what she hoped was a soothing smile.

'I'll get your dinner on,' she said in a calm voice. Dave needed love and support and perhaps the old Dave would re-emerge.

He had zero culinary skills whatsoever, having had Maureen cater to every whim. He was clueless in the kitchen, frequently setting fire to tea towels or boiling pans dry or burning food so thoroughly the saucepan was rendered unusable. They had come to the agreement that Kitty would be in charge of feeding them both. He was a vegetable refuser and could only eat food with negative nutrients. It was a miracle he was still alive. But, before she began cooking, she wanted to broach the proposed wedding.

'Dave,' she began, 'look, I just wanted to suggest something that might be good for us... I just thought that perhaps we should... could... I don't know... perhaps we could discuss...'

He stared at her with glassy eyes.

'Anyway,' she stumbled on, 'I thought we could talk about getting married...'

Dave looked stunned, as though she had suggested listening to Ronan Keating's new album.

'I mean,' she blundered, 'it's just a thought... a change... it would mean that we would feel more committed to each other. Safer. More secure. I thought that you... After your...'

But Dave was shaking his head. 'No...' He looked up at her. 'God no!'

She hadn't planned on what to do if he refused her. But here she was, being refused by a man in his dead dad's jumper who hadn't ever eaten a vegetable in his life. And worse, so much worse, was how repulsed he was by the very thought of marrying her.

'Dave...' she began. And then she noticed her little rolling suitcase was packed.

'I've made a decision...' he said. 'I'm going to Mam's.'

At least he wasn't throwing her out, which was a relief. But when had she ever stopped him from going to his mother's, despite the fact Maureen had never liked Kitty and acted as though she and Dave were in a special club of two? 'How long will you be?'

His pale face reddened, eyebrows furrowed. 'There you go again! Controlling me! I'm going to Mam's to sort my head out. See what I want from life...'

Kitty wondered how exactly to respond. This was perhaps one of the stages of Dave's grieving process, except she couldn't remember which one. Was abandonment one?

'You keep pressurising me,' he went on. 'You keep going on about marriage...'

'I don't,' she said. 'I mean, once... once I brought it up, ages ago, and asked if it was something you would consider doing.'

'You proposed,' he said. 'That's a proposal! It's pressurising.'

'I think,' she said, 'that at the time you said we probably would. It definitely wasn't a proposal. More of a testing of the waters. Seeing if we are on the same page.'

'Oh, there you go again,' he snapped. 'Correcting me. Being superior. Talk about kicking a man when he's down. Which is why I'm going to Mam's. She's expecting me. Put my electric blanket on and everything.'

Slightly shell-shocked, Kitty tried to speak. 'Dave, listen, I'm sorry if you felt as though I put you under any pressure or—'

'Oh! Sorry if *I* felt the pressure! Not admitting you did!' He reached behind the sofa and pulled his old wheelie case towards him.

Kitty's brain was working overtime as she tried to catch up

with this turn of events. 'Go to your mam's if that makes you feel better... How long are you going for?'

'Not sure,' he said, stiffly, looking away, as though the sight of her offended him. 'It's just too much pressure,' he said in a plaintive voice, '*all* the time. Marriage. Tidying up. What's next? A child?'

'Well...' If she was honest with herself, she hadn't given it enough thought as it had always been something she'd always assumed was in the far-off distance.

'Jesus!' He slapped his hand against his forehead. 'There you go again! Pressure! I don't want to get married!' he shouted, wrestling with the telescopic handle of his suitcase. 'Or at least I'm not *sure* if I want to get married! Mam says I'm far too young! I'm thirty-two, for God's sake, and in *man* years that's really young these days!'

Kitty wasn't sure quite what he meant by 'man years' or why his mother was involved in any of this but she managed to remind herself to say focussed and that this was a serious discussion. Dave was struggling and needed love and support. She loved him, did she not? They had lived together happily for years, hadn't they? Well, not happily exactly. But wasn't happiness overrated anyway? Contentment was what was important and she and Dave had been content for a long time now, and she couldn't imagine a life beyond him.

Having seen *The Horse Whisperer,* Kitty knew the best thing to do was not to make sudden movements or speak too loudly. 'It's okay,' she said. 'You go to your mother's and...' She paused. How should she describe this situation without causing more offence? 'And sort your... sort your head out.'

'Yes,' he said. 'I need to go to Mam's, where zero pressure is put on me whatsoever...' He managed to pull up the suitcase handle, almost falling backwards as it snapped into position.

'Well, I think it's a good idea,' said Kitty, carefully. 'Give you a break... and you can come back when you are ready.'

There was a beep from outside before she could say anything else and Dave picked up his case and went to the door, taking his dad's coat from the hook and swinging it around his shoulders. 'There's Mam now,' he said, opening the door.

Maureen loomed behind the steering wheel of her tiny Renault Clio.

'When will you be back?' asked Kitty.

Dave shrugged. 'When I've decided what I want from life... Mam doesn't put pressure on me. She knows I can only eat chips and not much else. She doesn't buy own-brand ketchup and waits to see if I can tell the difference.' He glared at her.

'That was once,' she protested. 'Years ago. And you *were* able to tell the difference...'

'Exactly.' He opened his mouth to say something and then closed it again. He dashed off to the passenger side of the Renault Clio, and just as he pulled the door closed and even before he had managed to put the seat belt on, the car skidded off down the road, leaving just a pile of swirling dust.

4

The following morning, Kitty woke with a very clear sensation that all was not well with the world. It took her a few moments of anxiously sorting through her Rolodex of memories to recall what it was exactly. And when she found it, her heart sank even further. Dave was gone.

It explained the space in the bed beside her, the quiet of the house, the lack of someone snoring loudly or watching a blaring television. Everything felt eerily empty and quiet. It was better when Dave was around because there was something comforting about knowing that there was someone in the world who had shaped their life to fit yours, that they were your person and you were theirs and that your future was laid out like a yellow brick road for the two of you to skip along together to Oz. Or wherever.

But now, lying in bed, Kitty had never felt so alone.

She missed Dave. All of him. Even the awful bits such as his weird nostril breathing, the way he left his clothes on the floor or had breakfast in bed so there were always crumbs. And why were crumbs always so sharp? But he was a good person. Dave never harmed anyone, he was a sensitive man who was going through a difficult time, and she hadn't always been the most brilliant partner. Just the other evening, she had told him that she was fed up with picking up his clothes off the floor.

'What do you expect me to do about it?' he had said, grumpily, drinking the milk from his cornflakes straight from the bowl.

'Pick them up?'

'What's the point?' he'd said. 'They're only going to end back there soon enough.'

'Because clothes don't belong on the floor and they make the room look messy.'

He had shaken his head. 'But why worry about it? They are only clothes. They are not doing any harm. Stop being so uptight.'

Of course, he was right. They *were* only clothes. And she *was* uptight. When Dave came back, she would show him that she was willing to not put pressure on him about anything – marriage, clothes on the floor, his monochrome diet. Yes, he was somewhat flawed, lazy and a bit depressing to be around, but she couldn't abandon him or give up on him, not when there was still a chance to make everything better. She knew what it was like to feel abandoned and given up upon, and she didn't want to do that to Dave.

Kitty's parents' marriage had ended when Kitty was five and from then on her father, Billy, would take Kitty out every Saturday. They were usually boring days spent watching the local football team, the Sandycove Seafarers, and then they'd go to a shabby local café on the seafront for hot chocolate, which was always Kitty's favourite bit, but when he moved to the States to coach a local team when she was in her early teens, their contact lapsed, and they never quite found each other again. Billy moved back to Sandycove a few years earlier and lived in a cottage in the centre of the village. He was working at least three jobs, as far as Kitty could tell. There was his early-morning shift as a postman, then the morning sandwich-making session at the bakery, and then some evening coaching at the Sandycove Seafarers. Kitty felt a swirl of sadness that their relationship was so insubstantial. She loved him but they had little in common. It was complicated.

Her most loyal companion wasn't a human, it was Romeo. But he was nowhere to be seen. Normally, by this time in the morning, he had returned from his night-time prowl around the mean streets of Sandycove and had made his way through his cat flap, across the kitchen, through the living room, up the stairs, pushing open the bedroom door with his head, and then hopping, soundlessly, as though on strings, onto the end of the bed, where he would sleep off his night on the tiles.

Except he too was gone. The house was still, empty, with no heartbeat except her own. Kitty felt sick. She pulled on her dressing gown and in a few swift steps was heading down the stairs, barely able to call his name.

She pushed open the door of the kitchen and she almost cried in relief because there he was, curled up in the corner, on the warm patch over the hot-water pipe below. He was fine, just fast asleep, his eyes closed, looking just like the kitten she had brought home all those years ago, his small chest trembling with each breath.

'Oh, Romeo,' she said. 'You gave me a fright... why didn't you come upstairs?'

She began filling the kettle, thinking of Dave and that, soon, when he returned, she would be so much better. She would even make him his bowl of cornflakes and she wouldn't have to look away when he tipped the milk into his mouth. She had to change, she really did.

'I do, don't I, Romeo?' Kitty said. 'I have to change. Be a better person...' She went to the fridge for the milk. 'You see,' she went on, 'he knows me and I know him and...' She glanced at Romeo again and he'd shifted a little, revealing his right ear... but it was bleeding.

Kitty dropped to her knees to examine it. A bite had been taken out of Romeo's ear.

'Oh, Romeo...'

Kitty gently touched the area around it as Romeo looked back at her, his tiger eyes sad and baleful. Aged thirteen, he was an old-man cat and didn't deserve this kind of violence. There was only one cat who could be responsible. Timmy, the neighbour's terrifying tabby, which hissed and snarled at everyone – cats, dogs and humans. He'd attacked Romeo before, but not for a long time, and then Romeo had been sprightlier, far more able to dodge the claws.

'We'll have to go to the vets,' she said. 'I know you hate your carrier, but there's no other way.'

She usually went to one in Dún Laoghaire, but they'd been closed for the last few months while the owner was on sabbatical in Thailand. 'Seeing the world, Kitty,' she had told her when Romeo was last in for his shots. 'Life is short and I've had enough of this weather and this humdrum life. I'm off to have fun.'

Kitty found the number of the other vets and dialled.

'Good morning,' said the receptionist, 'Sandycove Veterinary Surgery and Day Hospital, your pet is our passion, how may I help you?'

'My cat has been attacked by another cat,' said Kitty. 'His ear has been bitten.'

'Let me see...' The receptionist seemed to talk through her

nose. 'We have a cancellation in fifteen minutes. Can you pop down?'

'Yes...'

'Name of cat?'

'Romeo O'Sullivan.'

'See you in fifteen minutes.'

* * *

Kitty carried Romeo in his special carrier, her arm aching, her heart almost as heavy as Romeo, and finally put him down beside the desk, where the receptionist chattered to someone with an energetic chihuahua who was twisting the lead around her legs as though maypole dancing.

'Prof Sweetman is such a great addition to the practice,' the receptionist was saying. 'We're so honoured to have him.'

The woman with the chihuahua nodded. 'He's magnificent,' she said. 'Cross between Pierce Brosnan and George Clooney in his *ER* days. It's the scrubs, I think. And the dark eyebrows. I am a sucker for eyebrows. Anyway, you know when he operated on Chicolito six weeks ago after he'd swallowed a sock belonging to my husband...'

The receptionist glanced at Kitty. 'Be with you in a second,' she said, before resuming her conversation.

'Chicolito, the poor thingeen, was at death's door,' carried on the woman. 'But the professor worked his magic.'

'We're just so lucky that he wanted to work in practice again after being in academia,' said the receptionist.

'I knew his brother,' said the woman with a sigh. 'The middle one. Patrick, wasn't it? Such a sad time for the family. The mother was beside herself.'

Kitty stared into the carrier at Romeo. He was still awake and staring out at her, looking not unlike an ailing Victorian poet. 'Poor Romeo,' she whispered in to him.

'He has one of those bedside manners that one could only dream about,' went on the woman. 'Honestly, little Chicolito adored him. And his voice... you could drift off to it. He should be doing those audiobooks...'

'Meditation apps,' agreed the receptionist, nodding. 'He'd be perfect.'

'I'll say goodbye and let you get on,' said the woman. 'Sorry to keep you.'

'You're not keeping me,' replied the receptionist. 'Sure amn't I just sitting here all day? See you, Noreen. Look after yourself, yes? Don't be rushing around like a headless hen like you always do.' Finally, she turned to Kitty. 'Take a seat in the waiting area, the vet will call you shortly.'

Kitty and Romeo – still in his carrier – waited on a long bench, where Kitty read the terrifying posters on the wall which warned of horrifying diseases, with images of the most horrific-looking parasites with teeth and the kind of legs which could scuttle about. It made being attacked by Timmy the tabby look almost benign.

'Romeo O'Sullivan?' called a voice.

On the back of the conversation she'd heard, Kitty braced herself for an Adonis to emerge. Except, Professor Sweetman was much, much older than she had imagined. Small, nearly elderly, with a white beard and a rounded stomach, he looked more like Santa Claus than George Clooney. But he knew what he was doing and he was so sweet and gentle with Romeo, who needed three stitches in his ear, a tetanus shot, and a course of antibiotics.

Professor Sweetman placed him gently back into the carrier afterwards. 'There you go, old man.'

Kitty smiled and shook his hand. 'Thank you, Professor Sweetman.'

The man laughed. 'Professor Sweetman? I haven't been elevated to that level. The eminent professor is at Trinity College today giving a lecture... we're job-sharing at the moment. I'm Joseph Kelly... I've had this practice for the last thirty years and when I had my stent put in and decided to take a step back, the stars aligned because' – he chuckled again – '*Professor* Sweetman said he missed working with the animals. He oscillates between here and Trinity while I oscillate between here and the golf course...' He picked up Romeo's carrier and brought it out to reception. 'Now,' he said, to Kitty, handing it to her, 'watch this little fella, won't you? A scare like he had can be traumatic for older felines. He needs to stay indoors and enjoy his semi-retirement, just like me...'

* * *

At home, Kitty placed Romeo in his bed, covered with her cashmere scarf, filled his water bowl and let him sleep it off.

'Just stay away from that Timmy,' she warned. 'You're too old to be off all night. Stay at home, okay?'

Her phone vibrated. Dave?

She bounded over, wondering if he'd changed his mind and he was coming home. But it was her mother, Catherine, on the family WhatsApp group, wishing her sister, Kitty's aunt Annie, a happy birthday.

MUM

Happy Birthday, Annie!

KITTY

Happy birthday to the world's best aunt!

ANNIE

Thank you, my lovely girls! Happy birthday to me! Have just exited the hot tub. About to join an online spin class and then for brunch with the girls! See you both later for champers!

Annie certainly had a far more fun life than anyone Kitty knew... even more than the levels of fun Shazza was proposing. It just seemed so unfair that out of two sisters, one was having all the fun.

5

Aunt Annie waved as she parked her duck-egg Fiat 500, reversing repeatedly in and out, edging closer to the pavement, at increments of what seemed like a millimetre at a time. Finally, Annie turned off the engine before exiting the micro-car like a model from the 1950s. Annie looked radiant, her gym leggings matching the colour of her car and her nail varnish, and she smelled of Britney Spears' Fantasy – her signature fragrance.

'I've just booked a girls' holiday to Ibiza,' enthused Annie. 'Have to celebrate being twenty-one again somehow!' Annie looked a full decade younger than her older sister, Catherine, Kitty's mother, even though there were only two years between them.

Annie always brought life and soul to family occasions, always insisting on a glass of something sparkling. Being unencumbered by husbands, children or even pets, she was a woman who seemed not to have a care in the world. Her job as a receptionist at the local Fiat showroom seemed to be a mere extension of her social life. Any time Kitty called in, Annie would be in deep conversation, emitting breathless utterances and gasps at the news being shared. She never asked how Kitty's life was going, and didn't seem interested in much beyond her own extra-fun, super-exuberant life. That was just the way she was. Not everyone could be bothered hearing how you were, not when there was gossip to impart, and today it particularly suited Kitty because she wasn't quite ready to try to explain away Dave's sabbatical.

Annie poked her arm into Kitty's and marched her through the small wrought-iron gate, up the path, to the front door. 'I'll leave the car here,' she said to Kitty. 'Pick it up in the morning. Need to celebrate my big day!' She rang the doorbell. 'What do you think of my brows?' She twisted her face so Kitty could get a good look. 'Hollywood Mega Brows... meant to define the face. Enhance my cheekbones and disguise the droopy lids. Magda in the salon says it makes me look as if I'm in my forties. What do you think?'

Kitty was about to agree when the door was answered by her mother.

'Happy birthday to me!' exclaimed Annie, giddily, making Catherine laugh, as she always did.

The two sisters were so different: Catherine who worked in a high-powered career, a single mother, who never went away with friends for alcohol-fuelled weekends; and Annie who lived in the here and now, whose only real concern was with having fun. Sometimes Kitty looked at her mother, who had risen at 5.30 a.m. every morning, gone to the office, returned at 6.30 p.m. to cook dinner and later resumed her work at the kitchen table, and wondered if she would have been happier if she too had disappeared sporadically to the Balearics.

For the last three decades, Catherine had worked for a bathroom warehouse firm, rising to the heights of deputy chairperson and now, with the retirement of the very head of the company, she had been given every reason to believe that she was next in line to take over. Finally, she would receive the recognition she deserved – a reward for her excellence and competence. Kitty was planning a little gathering when Catherine's promotion was official, which should be imminent.

Catherine looked at Annie and Kitty in turn. 'You look tired,' she said to her daughter. 'Have you been sleeping?'

'I'm fine,' insisted Kitty, smiling at Catherine, but she was thinking about what she could or would say to Dave. At work, she always chanced upon the right word, but she couldn't find them for Dave. What could she say to make him come back and give her another chance? How could she prove that she wasn't pressurising without pressurising him? It was impossible. Life without Dave seemed wrong somehow, they had been together so long that the thought of being on her own was terrifying.

Her only home comfort was lovely Romeo and she'd left him that morning with his head on his pink velvet pillow, blanket tucked around his little body, ear bandaged like Van Gogh and a look on his face as though to say, 'Sorry for all this trouble.' She'd kissed him goodbye, thinking that she would be far more lost if Romeo left her than if Dave did. And then she'd stopped, wondering if that was how she really felt. It was just, she reasoned, Romeo was so easy to love, and the fact that Romeo loved her back – which with cats was never a guarantee – made it even better.

'I'm fine,' Kitty now insisted to her mother, dismissing all those troublesome thoughts of Dave and Romeo. 'Anyway... hadn't we better get this party started?'

'Woohoo!' Annie pulled on an imaginary train horn.

They sat at the table in the small kitchen and sang 'Happy Birthday' to Annie and then clinked their glasses of champagne.

'So, you're nearly catching up with me,' said Catherine. 'Welcome to your seventh decade.'

'Seventh?' Annie looked puzzled. 'Don't you mean sixth? Anyway, I have the teeth of a much younger woman. Honestly, going to Budapest for my veneers was probably the best money I ever spent.' She glinted her teeth at Catherine. 'Well, your money. Which I will pay back, just as soon as I can.'

'No need...' Catherine brushed it away.

Annie began to tell them about her preparations for Ibiza. 'So, spray tan, extra dark. Three kaftans, of varying length. Full body hair removal.'

'Full body?' said Catherine, raising one eyebrow.

Annie nodded. 'Of course. And, well, I was thinking of getting another tattoo while I was there. Something which encapsulates my life's journey so far...' She took another sip of her champagne. 'Something like... Life is a Rollercoaster...' She stopped. 'Or maybe your names? Catherine and Kitty...'

Catherine laughed. 'Please do not,' she said. 'Have some silly phrase drawn on, but our names would be just awful.'

For a moment, Annie looked hurt. 'But you're my family...'

'Yes, of course we are... but we don't need to be tattooed on your leg.'

'It was going to be my forearm.' Annie was beginning to smile as well.

'What about some birthday cake?' said Catherine. 'That might take your mind off tattoos.' She picked up the cake knife and began slicing it into wedges.

'Does it have many carbs?' asked Annie, eyeing the chocolate icing. 'Because I'm currently low-carbing... and before you two say anything, fizz doesn't count.'

'I'll have a slice.' Kitty hadn't been saying very much, just trying to smile along and act as though everything was entirely normal. One thing she couldn't do was go low-carb. Sugar was going to be the one thing which might get her through the next few weeks – surely it couldn't be longer? – before Dave came home. She could feel a slight panic beginning to rise, but she smiled at her mother as she took the plate with a slice of the chocolate ganache.

'You know,' said Annie, 'I think I will high-carb today, as it's my big day. I'll have that one with the icing. That big piece there.'

Catherine laughed again, but Kitty found herself thinking that Annie never held parties for Catherine, or ever remembered her birthday. And as she never had any spare money, there were never Christmas presents either, but Catherine never seemed to mind, happy to just have her younger sister around.

'So,' Kitty said, 'you should get the news this week? Your promotion!'

Catherine nodded. 'I think there's going to be an announcement on Wednesday. Mr O'Neill has booked Thursday and Friday off, so Wednesday will be his last day.'

'My sister. The chairperson,' said Annie. 'Or are you CEO? Chief anyway. Who'd have thought it? You were always the chief of our family. Pick up my pieces, sort out my bits, the yin to my yang, the champagne flute to my fizz. I don't know what I would do without you.' She raised her glass.

'Thank you, Annie,' said Catherine. 'Now, more cake? And you can take some home with you if you're high-carbing.'

'I will be just for today,' said Annie. 'And then I am back in golden goddess mode. Just as soon as Magda aims her tan gun at me and fires.'

And Catherine laughed again, as though Annie was a small child to be indulged.

6

As Kitty cycled home, her phone rang and she pulled into the side of the road, fishing it out from her front basket.

'Drink?' said Shazza. 'The Island? I've been at the council meeting because there was a vote on the cycle paths and there was the ongoing issue with the ice cream van stand-off. Franco is now not allowed to park within 500 metres of Fro-Ro's frozen yoghurt. So, it's all happening. And I need a drink.'

Kitty didn't hesitate. 'Yes please,' she said, thinking that poor old Romeo would have to entertain himself, but if she went out with Shazza it would mean that she might be distracted enough not to think about Dave. But the most important thing was not letting it slip that he'd left because Shazza had never liked him and she would dislike him even more when she knew what had happened, and then it would be even harder for Kitty and Dave to get married without the full blessing of Kitty's best friend.

'You're coming?' said Shazza. 'I didn't think you'd actually say yes. You never come out on a Saturday evening. You always say you are staying in with Dave. I only asked you because I feed off rejection. I'm not comfortable when people actually want to spend time with me.'

'Of course, I want to spend time with you. You're my best friend. I love being with you. And I fancy a night out.'

'I don't believe you,' said Shazza. 'So what's going on?'

'Well...' Kitty hesitated. 'Dave's gone to his mother's... He says I'm controlling and pressurising him to get married... And that he needs to sort his head out.' Kitty was wondering whether she should or even *could* text Dave or not. They hadn't worked out the rules of engagement. When one is getting one's head together, does one want to hear from the person who they claim has added to the pressure of their needing to get their head together?

Shazza let out a long whistle. 'Well, I would agree with him there. His head needs examining. All of him needs examining. Not that I would want to examine him at close quarters...' she groaned. 'Are you all right, though?'

Kitty made a noise which she thought adequately expressed her feelings.

'You sound as though you need that drink,' said Shazza. 'The Island, 7 p.m. Okay?'

* * *

Kitty went home to change and feed Romeo. She kissed his fuzzy head, marvelling at his tiny paws and how he was the perfect encapsulation of feline beauty, and made sure he was tucked in his bed, and the cat flapped locked, before setting off for The Island.

The Island was one of the nicest of Sandycove's pubs, a cosy place, which was always lively, with music and a small courtyard at the back. It was busy on this Saturday evening, but Kitty managed to find a table in the courtyard and waited for Shazza.

'Quick! I need a drink before I keel over!'

Kitty looked up to see Shazza weaving through the tables towards her. She was dressed in a silver T-shirt and black biker jeans, her long blonde hair falling down her back.

Shazza slipped in beside her. 'And then you can tell me all about Dave the Rave and the pressure he's been under. The poor little dote...' She looked up for someone at the bar and signalled to bring her the same as Kitty's.

'Dave has been under pressure,' said Kitty, loyally. 'Work was asking too much of him. And I've been my usual controlling self. You know what I'm like.'

'Did you actually want to marry him, though?' asked Shazza, pulling a face, which she always did when she was utterly perplexed about something, such as social injustice or not liking chocolate. Obviously, someone wanting to marry Dave was as outlandish as those. 'It's a bit dramatic, don't you think? Not to mention unnecessarily drastic.'

'Yes,' said Kitty. 'Why wouldn't I? We fit well together, we accept each other's foibles...'

'What foibles of yours does he put up with?'

'My neat-freakery,' said Kitty. 'My controlling nature...'

'You're not controlling,' argued Shazza. 'Just organised.'

'I am,' replied Kitty. She sighed.

'Okay, so maybe you are a tiny bit, but not in an evil sociopathic way,' agreed Shazza. 'In a nice way. An efficient way.' She paused. 'But is he what you want in life? Do you love him?'

'Of course I love him...'

'But do you love-love him?' Shazza narrowed her eyes, peering at Kitty, looking for cracks in her argument, her journalistic bloodhound nose sniffing out inconsistencies.

'I've just said, haven't I?' said Kitty, as Michael, the barman, put down two fresh gin and tonics.

'Well, if you need me to have a stiff word with him,' said Shazza. 'Or duff him up. Or... I don't know... put cyanide in his tomato soup...'

Kitty laughed.

'I just don't want you to be unhappy,' said Shazza. 'You deserve more.'

It was the first time in years Kitty had been faced with such uncertainty. When her dad and mum had sat her down when she was very small and told her that they both still loved her but from now on she would have two homes, a gnawing had developed in her stomach, along with a sensation that her heart had slipped into an irregular pattern and was skipping every few beats, like a bad piano player. Change was excruciating. And now it was as though she'd been released into the wild after a lifetime of captivity. She'd seen those television documentaries with the chimpanzees being let go from their cages, clinging to their keepers. She wished she had a keeper to cling to. But for now, she had to hang in there until everything returned to normal.

'How's everything with you?' went on Kitty. 'Anything interesting going on?'

'Total disarray. My life is one long trail of destruction. My body has been trampled over by a stampede of wild stallions. The inside of my head seems to be scattered to the four winds. My heart shattered like a crystal glass dropped off the top of Liberty Hall. But apart from that, I'm grand.' She shrugged. 'You know me, just waiting for the next man to come along, behave abominably and leave me a husk of my former self...'

Kitty knew she was joking. Kind of. Shazza had always gone for the unattainable ones, the boys in school who loved themselves more than her.

'Being rejected and surviving is now my whole personality,'

said Shazza. 'One day I will write a book about it. When I am eighty and finally realise I am better off single.' She looked at Kitty. 'I would love to be more like you and less like me... But I think there's a middle ground... between my chaos and your perfection.'

Kitty was confused. 'You mean mediocrity?'

'No, just you being less perfect and me being more perfect.' Shazza put down her gin and tonic. 'I think,' she said, 'I have worked out what's wrong with us. Finally, after years of close research, I have deduced our problems. It's about frills,' said Shazza. 'Too few or too many. My problem is I have too many, a surfeit of frills, and yours is that you have too few. A deficit of frills. Not frills on shirts and whatever, frills in life,' Shazza went on. 'It's like a budget airplane. There is nothing fancy, no fripperies, no frills... there is nothing extra about the flight. They just get you from A to B. That's you.'

'I'm *no frills*?' Kitty was suddenly quite hurt. Of all the things Shazza could have said, she came out with this no-frills theory? 'So, I'm like a budget airline? Depressing, cheap and a weird smell of dubious origin?'

'Of course not!' said Shazza. 'You couldn't smell of anything except your Jo Malone pear and freesia... I may have taken my metaphor too far, but it's just that your life is completely non-frilly. Mine, on the other hand, is far too frilly. I always have that third cocktail, that second bottle of wine, the bigger bag of crisps. I spend too much on clothes which have sequins or shoes which are too high and only suitable for hobbling from a taxi to a bar. I fall for deeply narcissistic men. I stay up too late watching programmes that aren't good for me. I haven't read a decent book for years and yet I know every bit of celebrity gossip there is, even about people I have never heard of. I haven't done anything nourishing for my body, my brain or my soul in years. Neither of us is properly nourished in the good things in life, the fun things, the things that give life meaning. You're too good, and I'm too bad.'

Kitty was silent, taking it all in.

'I mean, you work. You go home. You work. You go home,' continued Shazza. 'Ad nauseam, to infinity and beyond, to hell and back. Now, are you having a morsel of fun in either of those two places? Work or home?'

Kitty shook her head. 'Not really,' she said. 'But you're not meant to have fun at work...'

'Au contraire, my little workaholic,' said Shazza. 'You are meant to have fun at work. You're meant to have fun everywhere... I mean, you are not meant to have it all the time. But in all the cracks and the spaces around the serious bits, you are meant to cram in as much fun as possible.'

Kitty liked fun as much as the next person, except the person next to her was usually Shazza and no one could like fun as much as she did. However, the concept of squeezing fun into everything was new and as such worth mulling over. Fun, she had thought, was something that perhaps just happened, if you were lucky.

'But moi,' she went on, 'sought fun a little too hard and crammed a bit too much in. I squeezed the orange past the juice stage and kept on going. Hence Mr Unmentionable. It's just you could perhaps add in more frills and I need to go on a frill diet.'

'And meet somewhere in the middle?'

'Yeah...' Shazza laughed.

'But there's no time for frills,' said Kitty, perplexed. 'It just makes life complicated, it means mess and chaos and craziness and I can't cope with that.'

'That's if you do it wrong,' said Shazza. 'Which is how I'm doing it, but there's a sweet spot, right in the middle, and neither of us is there yet.'

Kitty was silent for a moment, taking it all in. She wished life was as easy as Shazza made it appear. You lived hard, laughed lots, drank more... and lived as though life was a rollercoaster and you screamed as you went faster. Kitty's life was, she had to admit, like being on the teacup ride. But there was nothing she could do about it. And anyway, the rollercoaster looked out of control.

7

SHAZZA

Remember you promised to come to the Sandycove Community Hub meeting on Monday night? Be nice to meet some people. And there's free tea and biscuits.

KITTY

I thought we were meant to have fun. A community meeting?!

SHAZZA

Fun can be found in all sorts of strange places. You just have to leave the house to find it. So, you're coming? PLEEEAASE?

KITTY

I'll be there! Can't wait for all the incredible fun we're going to have!

SHAZZA

Oh, ye of little unfrilly faith. See you tomorrow evening. Love you! xx

Normally, Kitty's Sundays were spent preparing for the week and she usually managed to get through at least three loads of washing and batch cook a stew or two, as well as clean the house from top to bottom or have a very satisfying declutter. But today she hadn't felt up to doing anything like that, as though without Dave there was nothing to clean or corral. She thought about what Shazza had said about her being too unfrilly. The bed looked perfect. And not a frill in sight, just clean, crisp lines.

From the bedroom door, Kitty became aware of Romeo eyeing her. He looked concerned.

'I'm fine, Romeo,' she said. 'Don't worry about me. Yes, I probably had a gin and tonic too many, but it was only three in total. Shazza had six.'

* * *

The following morning, Kitty was relieved she'd survived the weekend and that she had managed two days without Dave. Yes, there was uncertainty about her current situation, but all in all, it hadn't been too bad. And this was now Monday morning and who knew? Dave could be home this week and all would be well.

At her desk, she scanned the printouts of the new protein bar campaign. The protein bar's slogan was wrong, boring and lifeless. Unfrilly, Shazza would say. What about Welcome Ireland? How could she come up with something that would encapsulate a whole country and its history, people and culture? What if she began to lose her ability to find the right words? What if her life continued to implode and she lost everything?

'Morning Kitty...' Hughie entered the office, a waft of Tom Ford and toothpaste about him. Hughie lived with John-Paul, a strapping Gaelic football player from Kilkenny who slept with his hurley under his pillow and went to the gym twice a day.

'Morning, Hughie,' said Kitty. 'You had an early start.'

'You know me, early bird and everything.' He sat down on his chair, spinning it to face Kitty. 'And how is Ireland's luckiest man?'

Kitty nearly laughed. Hughie had never met Dave, but he always called him this, with a slightly ironic tone in his voice. 'Well...' she began.

Hughie looked over at her. 'What?'

'He's left for a bit...'

Hughie narrowed his eyes. 'Define "a bit",' he said.

'Oh, I don't know... a week. Two. It's not permanent,' she insisted. 'He's just taking a break.'

'From you?' Hughie scrunched up one side of his handsome face, as though to suggest that the very idea of someone needing to escape from Kitty was impossible.

'Just from his life, the house... Romeo... and...' She sighed. 'And... me.' She didn't want to cry in front of Hughie. 'He never liked Romeo. But the feeling was mutual, really.' Luckily, Romeo would not be pining for Dave. 'So,' she said, 'how is John-Paul? Still flexing his muscles and popping steroids like Smarties?'

Hughie wrapped his arms around his chest. 'Actually,' he said, 'John-Paul and I are no more. It appears hurling is his one true love. Either that or the barman from Birchalls. His final straw came when he tried to explain the previous week the rules and my eyes glazed over and he got so annoyed he left. Last seen chatting to Sam... who is bleach-blond, Turkey-teethed, and tattooed.' Hughie shuddered.

'Sorry to hear that,' said Kitty. 'Hope you are okay.'

'Ah, you know me,' replied Hughie. 'Like a rubber ball. I bounce back from everything.'

'Maybe we both need to have more fun,' said Kitty. 'My friend Shazza says that's where I'm going wrong.'

'Fun?' Hughie emitted a hollow laugh. 'The last time I had

fun was when I was six and ate too many sweets at my brother's communion and bounced on the trampoline for four and a half hours until I collapsed.'

'Nothing since?'

He shook his head. 'Brief glimpses. Slight brushes with. But no actual, crying-with-laughter, filled-with-happiness, complete-and-total-joy type of fun. Now, all I want to do is comfort-eat.'

Alex had just entered the office and was hanging her coat on the hooks, before looking Hughie over. 'Actually, I thought you were looking thinner lately,' she said.

'Do I?' he preened. 'I was wondering when someone would notice.'

'You're not dieting?' Kitty looked up.

'I was,' he said. 'Just a little. Something John-Paul said.'

'But he's an athlete,' said Kitty. 'Never listen to athletes. They're not normal when it comes to food.'

'Exactly,' said Alex. 'I used to go out with this guy who played rugby for Trinity. Oh my God. He'd have fifteen eggs a day. The smell alone... Jesus...'

Hughie looked horrified. 'How long did you last?'

'About three days,' said Alex. 'I crawled out of there, gasping for fresh air.'

Hughie laughed. 'So, tell us, why are beautiful women like you two still single? I don't get it. There's Kitty here, pining for her mammy's boy...'

'I'm not!' Kitty interjected but knowing he was right.

Alex was nodding. 'I had one of those once,' she said. 'Used to ring his mother and ask her what he could eat.'

'Was this the egg man?' asked Kitty.

Alex shook her head. 'A different one.' She shrugged. 'I just haven't had much luck with men.' She turned to Kitty. 'So what happened with Dave?'

'He's just...' she began.

'He's opted out from all commitments, even to Kitty,' butted in Hughie. 'The man's a fool.'

'Unless he's having a breakdown,' said Alex. 'Is he having one?'

'No,' admitted Kitty. 'He just needs a break from me. He said he'd be back when he's feeling better.'

'And do you want him back?' asked Alex.

'Of course, I do,' said Kitty, but before she could say any more, Mary Rose walked into the office, looking serious.

'Right,' she said, placing herself between Alex and Kitty's desk, 'a few things... I was just in a meeting with the business planning department and Mr Mulligan and Ben O'Leary were both there. It was impressed upon us how important it was to win the Welcome Ireland pitch. Ben O'Leary has a great deal of faith in you, Alex. He said if anyone could win it, Alex Barry could.' She smiled at Alex, but Kitty noticed Alex's neck was turning red and she was looking away, embarrassed.

'Now there's a man who smells of eggs,' said Hughie, making Mary Rose laugh.

'I didn't get that off him... but he is very liberal with the expensive aftershave...'

'The kind of men who douse themselves in aftershave have something to hide,' said Hughie.

'His wife has just had a new baby,' remarked Mary Rose. 'He was showing us photographs. It looks just like him.' She mumbled something which to Kitty's ears sounded like 'more's the pity'.

Alex's head was down as she scrolled through her phone as though Mary Rose hadn't spoken a word, not even a polite nod of acknowledgement, making Kitty wonder if either Alex had temporarily lost her hearing or something else was going on.

* * *

At lunchtime, Kitty couldn't bear it any longer and dialled Dave's number.

'Good afternoon, David's phone...' It was Maureen, Dave's mother, pretending not to know it was Kitty calling. 'How may I help you?'

'Hello, Maureen,' Kitty said, trying to sound friendly. 'It's Kitty here. I wonder if I may speak to Dave, please?'

'Kitty...' Maureen sounded as though she was trying to place Kitty, searching for her in her mind. 'Oh yes, Kitty. Well, David's resting at the moment because as you know he's been under a great deal of strain and pressure lately. It's been building up for some time.'

'I understand that.'

'A great deal of pressure...'

'I haven't...' Kitty began, but Maureen interjected.

'You've done enough damage to that poor lad,' she said. 'Not supporting David when he's been so overwrought, making him marry you, forcing him to live with an animal...'

For a moment, Kitty thought Maureen was calling her an animal. Of all the things she could be called, surely it wasn't an animal. She was so tidy. But then she twigged. 'You mean Romeo...'

'Is that its name?' said Maureen sniffily. 'And having to deal with everything else in his life...'

'Will you tell him I called?'

But Maureen had already put the phone down.

Kitty wondered if Dave had been captured by his mother, his phone confiscated, perhaps locked in his bedroom, desperately hoping Kitty would come looking for him... but that was wishful thinking because she knew, deep down, Dave was where he wanted to be. It was almost as though he'd been looking for an excuse to move back in with his mother... and if that was true, then perhaps they were over.

Alex interrupted those unsettling thoughts. 'Do you want a quick meeting?' she said in a low voice. 'This Welcome Ireland pitch is freaking me out. I can't think of anything.'

Kitty followed Alex into the conference room which adjoined their office. Alex closed the door behind them, pulled out one of the leather and metal sling chairs and sat down.

'I'm having a few personal problems,' she said. 'We both are. Dave sounds like a pain in the hole. Obviously, if the two of you get back together again, forget I said that.'

Kitty smiled. 'I will...'

'How are we going to come up with anything for the Welcome Ireland pitch? I don't think I can even think straight, never mind come up with a decent campaign. I can't do it.'

'Nor can I,' said Kitty. Alex may have relied on Kitty's creativity and ideas, but she was the driving force of the team, the one who pushed hard for pitches.

'After last Friday, I've been spiralling,' admitted Alex. 'That man saying something was missing...'

'But we can't focus on the feedback of just one person...'

'No... but we don't have a clue what is missing. And nor did they.'

Kitty began to feel slightly panicky, as though all the skills and all the experience which she had been gathering over the years, everything she knew about life, were falling away. The last time she'd felt like this was when her dad would take her to a local football match and then for hot chocolate in a local café. She claimed never to want to go, but as soon as it was time to say goodbye, she'd start to feel panicky. It had all been so complicated. Life evidently still was.

'What are we going to do?' Alex looked even worse than Kitty felt, her face pale, real fear in her eyes.

They stared at each other soundlessly for a moment and then the words of Shazza came back to Kitty.

'Have you thought about having more *fun,* Alex?' said Kitty.

'Fun?' said Alex. 'I haven't had fun since I was a teenager...' She looked wistful for a moment. 'No, we need to work. Look, we've only got two weeks, so we'll just have to crack on and hope it all comes together.'

Kitty nodded. Alex was right. Fun would have to wait while they waited for inspiration to strike. Hopefully.

8

The Sandycove Community Hub met in the hall attached to the church at the end of the village. The room, which was the size of a badminton court, was heaving with Sandycovers, everyone talking in loud voices, while small children raced in and out of the adults' legs.

Shazza turned to Kitty. 'I've just seen Sandra Byrne, she's going for election for the council, next month. I've been trying to get a word from her for weeks... I'll be back in a sec.'

Through a hatch in the small kitchen, a red-faced woman was staring at the knobs on a tea urn as though it had defeated her. It was Edith Waters.

Kitty had been a Girl Guide years ago and had once won a tea making badge by making the most cups of tea which their leader had deemed 'drinkable' in an hour. She had made eighty-three of them and was proudly awarded her badge, which Catherine duly stitched on her sleeve that evening. Making tea was one way she thought she could effectively help out – the rest was too chaotic for words.

'Can I help?' she asked, stepping into the kitchen.

'My God, you'd think by my age I would be able to work out how to boil some bloody water!' said Edith. 'Why do they have to put knobs and buttons and you have to input your bloody vital statistics as well as star sign and dietary preferences before you can get anything to work these days? And I'm about to be strangled by my own scarf!' She wrestled a green silk scarf over her head and threw it to one side on the stainless-steel counter. 'There! Now, do you know how to work one of these tea things? What happened to just "on" and "off"?'

The tea urn was like something out of *Star Wars*, with flashing lights, timers and unnecessary buttons. Kitty pressed a few at random and, then, there was a slight rumble and the urn seemed to be on 'boil' mode.

The older woman smiled. 'Edith Waters,' she said, holding out her hand to shake. 'I have the haberdashery... but you're not a sewer or a knitter. You've never darkened my door, have you?'

Kitty shook her head. 'I'm not creative,' she replied. 'Well, not in that way. I work in marketing, so that's creative, but that's just words and thoughts. You take a sentence and work at it until it's perfect.'

'Sounds the very epitome of creativity,' said Edith, approvingly.

'I'm Kitty. Catherine O'Sullivan's daughter...'

'Ah! Catherine! I knew I knew you... you're just like her, so you are.' Edith looked straight into Kitty's eyes. 'And there's a touch of your father in you, as well, if I am not mistaken...'

'I'm nothing like him,' said Kitty.

The woman gave her a look.

'I'm Shazza Keegan's best friend,' Kitty went on, not wanting to talk about her father. She hated all these uncomfortable feelings, the gnawing sensation increasingly omnipresent these days.

'Ah! Sharon! Now there's a girl after my own heart,' said Edith approvingly. 'I hope she's moving on from that dreadful man. I remember once, many lifetimes ago, having to recover after the end of a relationship. I had to pick myself up, dust myself down and glue myself back together again... 'twasn't easy, I can tell you, but the things that matter rarely are. I'm only on tea duty to get away from the chaos,' went on Edith, now opening packets of biscuits and funnelling them straight onto plates, as Kitty quickly began arranging them in neat circles.

'So am I,' said Kitty. 'It's madness out there.'

'The problem with life,' went on Edith, eyeing the perfectly arranged biscuits, 'is that it's messy. You can't sweep it all up and smooth it out. You have to learn to love its rough edges and all the cracks and crevasses.' She turned to Kitty. 'Because it's in the cracks where the gold is hidden.'

Kitty laughed again. 'I prefer nice clean surfaces,' she said, taking a sheet of kitchen paper from the roll and quickly wiping away some biscuit crumbs. She turned back to Edith. 'Now, what about cups? Where are they hidden?'

'Over there,' said Edith. 'In the top cupboard.'

As Kitty opened the door, several cups dislodged and nearly fell out, as though the last person had closed the door on a Niagara Falls of crockery. And Kitty suddenly felt happy – here was something she could tidy. A problem so easily solved. And there weren't too many of those around. 'I'll have a quick sort out,' she said. 'Won't take me long.'

9

When the giant urn came to a boiling frenzy, Edith produced two outsized teapots, and she and Kitty made tea just as the swarm descended, heaping sugar into cups, snatching biscuits – one man held one between his teeth, and another three on his saucer – and sloshing milk into cups. Kitty kept trying to keep up with the wiping, as well as keeping the rows of cups in neat formations like a tiny, china Roman legion.

'Are you all right to keep the hordes watered and biscuited?' asked Edith. 'While I make my announcements... just a bit of general news, community ephemera, miscellaneous points of interest, or disinterest, depending on one's view.'

Kitty nodded, already planning exactly how she should start the washing-up – saucers first, so she could restack the cupboard properly. It was good to be busy.

Through the hatch, she could see Edith make her way to the front of the hall, just in front of the stage, beside the old, rickety steps.

'Ladies and gentlemen...' Edith boomed, smiling, as the room fell silent, everyone turning to face her, like sunflowers in the sun.

'Thank you for coming.' Edith glanced down at her notecards. 'Now just a little bit of business... which I won't dwell too long on, knowing how much we all detest such doodahs and dib dabs... Right... first up, as you know, we lost our stalwart organiser, Margaret Dooley, last month, who was last heard of sunning herself in Albufeira, so we need a new organiser... any takers? We've also lost Julie O'Flaherty to a creative writing master's, so she is now no longer available to us in the wide-ranging way she once was. So, any volunteers to be on the top table, as it were?' She looked around. 'Anyone?'

The once buoyant sunflowers kept their heads down or found a point on the wall suddenly fascinating or looked at their phones as though they had just received an emergency text that had to be responded to in that instant.

Edith beamed when a hand went up. 'Ah! Janet! I knew we could rely on you. Thank you.' She leafed through her notecards. 'Now, one more call to action. We need people to join the mixed five-a-side team at Sandycove Seafarers. This is football, soccer, the beautiful – so they say – game. The team's captain, Tara Gilhooley, is desperately looking for more members as she has lost four of her team to college courses, I think Veronica Flaherty-Joyce is about to give birth to a mini Flaherty-Joyce and Ciarán McGonigal decamped to Slovenia...' She peered into the crowd. 'Is Tara here? Ah! There she is. What else have your former team members succumbed to? Any plagues, pestilence or poxes?'

'We lost Aoife Murphy to a nursing job in Perth,' said a voice belonging to a tall, broad-shouldered woman, with cropped hair, in a sleeveless top and tracksuit bottoms, sliders and socks. 'And Rosie Egan-Maloney to her bar exams.'

'Thank you, Tara,' said Edith, 'so we need volunteers, please? Those who want to add a little fun in their lives... anyone whose life is a little on the dull side?'

At the word 'fun', Shazza flicked her head in Kitty's direction.

'Someone who needs adventure, excitement, fresh air and have Tuesday and Thursday evenings free? A few fun games of football, represent Sandycove against other local teams?'

Football? No way. Kitty, who had zero hand-eye coordination, had spent her school years desperately trying to get out of hockey by claiming to have a seven-year-long menstrual cycle and an aversion to showing her legs in public. Her father used to take her to the Sandycove Seafarers. Those Saturdays were always wet and cold, the seating in the rickety stands was uncomfortable and Billy would shout words of encouragement to those on the pitch, as the rain trickled down Kitty's back, and all she could think about was the hot chocolate he always brought her afterwards. Billy used to play himself and then he'd coached, even moving to the States for a time to work for a team over there.

'We're in,' said a man from across the room, who Kitty couldn't quite make out. 'Put our names down.'

Edith was smiling. 'I knew I could count on my nephews,' she said. 'Right, Tom and Rory it is. Anyone else?'

Kitty could still feel the heavy weight of Shazza's razor-sharp stare, but she refused to make eye contact, knowing it would be like staring into the eyes of the Medusa.

The last time she'd been at a football match was twenty years earlier with her dad. She'd hated it then, had no interest in football and knew next to nothing about it. There was no way she could or would volunteer, despite the terrible feeling her right hand was about to go rogue and shoot up. She'd last felt like this at a very expensive auction and had had to practically sit on her hands to stop herself from bidding on a priceless painting.

'Will anyone else respond to the plaintive call of their village?' said Edith.

Kitty was beginning to wilt under Shazza's telepathic pressure and finally looked over. 'Let's both join?' Shazza mouthed, eagerly, and then she turned back to Edith, her hand in the air. 'I'll do it,' she said. 'But on one condition. If Kitty O'Sullivan does it with me.'

Kitty's face flushed, and that feeling of panic, the fluttery, gnawing sensation, rose within her.

'I'll join,' she said, her voice dry. 'I'll join them too.'

Everyone turned towards her, with varying expressions of relief that they hadn't been strong-armed into making such a commitment.

Edith was all smiles. 'Wonderful,' she said. 'New blood.'

What have I let myself in for, thought Kitty, as Shazza elbowed her way through the crowd to Kitty.

'Our plan has begun!' she said, eyes shining.

'What plan?' said Kitty.

'The frills-no-frills one.'

Kitty closed her eyes. 'But I hate football...'

'Don't worry,' said Shazza. 'This isn't football, not in the true sense of the word. This is more like joining one of those clubs at university which are really about the drinking afterwards. No one will expect us to actually play.'

'Explain to me how joining a five-a-side football team is part of our plan?' asked Kitty.

'Because it's about you having fun...'

Kitty thought of Dave. *Please come home*, she said to herself. *It's horrible being on my own, knowing that I have to go and play football tomorrow night, knowing that there is no one at home*. She took out her phone. Maybe she would just give him a quick text, check in on him and see if he'd managed to get his head together again.

'Put your phone away,' ordered Shazza, sharply.

'I was just checking the time!'

'You weren't. You were seeing if Dave had called...'

Kitty shrugged. 'He might need me to contact him, just so he knows I don't hate him. And he might be fed up with living with Maureen... and just need gentle encouragement...'

Shazza held up a hand. 'Stop right there. Put your phone away. And promise me, never, ever, evvvverrrr, contact him. If he wants to speak to you, he knows your number, where you live, work... it's not going to be difficult for him to track you down. He's – and I can't emphasise it enough – absolutely grand.'

Kitty nodded, knowing it was probably true. But there was one male in her life who did care where she was. 'What about Romeo?' she said. 'He's only happy when I'm around. He likes me being there... what if he gets attacked by Timmy again?'

'I've said it before and I'll say it again,' said Shazza, 'that Timmy is a thug...'

'Who's a thug?'

It was a man's voice and Kitty turned to see someone about her age with dark, floppy hair, eyebrows which curved over his deep brown eyes, a strong jaw which made her think of Dave and his non-existent chin which was balanced out by an excess of neck, as though there was a bit of giraffe in there, going back a few generations.

'Just Timmy,' Shazza explained to the man. 'He rips off ears and leaves his victims broken and bleeding... I tell you, Sandycove is going to the dogs... or cats.' She winked at Kitty. 'Kitty, this is Tom Sweetman, he's the new veterinarian... I'm surprised you haven't met him.'

The name rang a bell. 'Sweetman?' said Kitty. Could he be the vet that had been such a focus of excitement?

'I know,' he said, smiling back. 'Stupid name...'

'No... not stupid...'

'It's a bit stupid,' said Shazza. 'I mean, you'd have to go around being sweet all the time. That's a lot of pressure on anyone. It's best to have non-adjective names, ones that don't suggest unrealistic personality traits.'

The man was laughing. 'It is a bit much to live up to...' He turned to Kitty, expectantly. 'I don't know your name,' he said.

'This is my best friend, Kitty O'Sullivan,' said Shazza, as Tom Sweetman shook Kitty's hand. 'She's a woman on the verge of a whole new life, one involving fun and frolics and... football. Kitty, Tom and his brother Rory are Edith Waters' nephews and are also brand-new members of the Sandycove Seafarers five-a-side team.'

So this was Professor Sweetman. He did look like a young George Clooney with dark eyebrows and a twinkling smile. Probably had women fawning over him all the time. But there was a sweetness about him, and unusually for a good-looking man, he didn't have that kind of arrogant aura of someone who is used to general swooning.

'Why are you on the verge?' he asked Kitty.

'Circumstances beyond my control,' replied Kitty, trying to sound evasive, but he was looking at her as though he wanted to know. So he was one of those men – the ones who were actually interested when you spoke.

'Ah, those,' he said. 'Circumstances, unfortunately, are rarely within our control.'

'Too true,' said Shazza. 'I'm all for not trying to control anything these days. Going with the flow, seeing what the universe has in store for us. I mean, who knew that we'd be joining a football team? And our first training session is tomorrow night.'

Another man joined them, a smaller version of Tom, his hair a little longer, his face softer. 'My brother, Rory,' said Tom.

Rory, who had a beard, an armload of tattoos and a 'Cher Turn Back Time Tour '89' T-shirt, held out his hand for Kitty to shake. 'How's it going?' And then he turned to Shazza. 'Last time I saw you was at the Sandycove festival...'

'Don't remind me,' groaned Shazza. 'I was a little tired and emotional. Thank you for being so nice.'

He shrugged. 'All I did was listen.' He smiled at her. 'Feeling better?'

She nodded. 'Much, thank you.' Shazza turned to Kitty. 'Rory caught me at a low ebb, just after the whole thing with Mr Unmentionable. But I am now determined to be on a permanently high ebb.'

Rory nodded at her. 'Good plan.'

'Are either of you any good at football?' asked Tom. 'Have you either played much?'

Shazza shook her head. 'I'm rubbish,' she said. 'I've never watched a football match in my life. I have been only peripherally aware of the concept of football and I know that it is popular with certain swathes of the population... but me, no. I may as well be attempting a spacewalk or Dry January. Anathema, in other words.'

Tom turned back to Kitty. 'What about you?'

'I've never played,' she said.

'Don't worry,' said Tom. 'Rory is better than me, but we weren't the type of kids who played on the street. Our older brother, Paddy, was the footballer in the family. He was eight years older than me and used to go for training at the Seafarers' ground.'

'Tidy-up time!' Edith was clapping her hands. 'Tom, you and Rory are on chair-stacking duty and then sweeping.' She smiled at Kitty and Shazza. 'What about you two on washing-up? Something tells me you would do a very good job of that?'

Kitty looked at Shazza, raising her eyebrows. Shazza laughed. 'Washing-up is all part of the plan,' she said, just loud enough for

Kitty to hear. 'There is method in my madness. Wait and see. Just put yourself in the hands of the universe... or me...' She grinned at Kitty. 'And all will be well.'

Kitty could do nothing other than hold up the tea towel. 'Wash or dry.'

'Dry!'

Kitty threw the tea towel at Shazza, making her laugh all the more.

10

Shazza spent most of the tidying-up time leaning on the hatch, jotting down some notes for her article, while Kitty washed up, rearranged the cupboard and gave the whole kitchen a good wipe down, feeling satisfied that everything was better than how she'd found it. She thought of Dave and how he always left crumbs on the work surface even when he hadn't been doing anything with bread. Once those constant crumbs had annoyed her but now, somehow, she missed them.

'Do you think...?' she began.

Shazza held up a hand to stop her. 'Don't even think about it.'

'But...'

'Let him go. The man's eejit central, let him go off and play with his toys.'

'He might be—'

'Remember, your new life is about to start.' Shazza pushed herself up to sit on the counter, her legs dangling down. 'This is the verge. Tomorrow it begins. For both of us. We're in this together.' Kitty moved to sit beside her. 'And there's no one I want to be on the verge of a brand-new life with more than you,' continued Shazza. 'Especially someone who can get a shine on a stainless-steel kitchen like you. It's gleaming. What is this? The Hall of Mirrors at Versailles?' She slipped her arm through Kitty's and gave her a squeeze. 'Seriously. You're going to be okay.'

'We both are,' said Kitty.

'I hope so,' said Shazza. 'Sometimes I wake up and wonder if it's going to be just me for the rest of my life. And that I may as well become an actual nun instead of just a virtual one and then at least I wouldn't have to worry about what to wear every day as I would just wear a grey cardigan and a giant crucifix and I would eat porridge and other wholesome things.' She brightened up. 'I might actually lose weight!'

Kitty laughed, just as a woman entered.

'Making tea for the troops,' she said. 'You'd think as a nation we'd reach saturation point... but, no, we are like those magic sponges you can buy on the internet. The ones for when your freezer defrosts... You go and sit down and I'll bring it out.'

Kitty and Shazza dropped to their feet, heading to the main hall.

'Strong, drop of milk, no sugar!' Edith was shouting from the steps beside the stage as Kitty and Shazza walked towards those who were left after the tidying up.

'Mine's the camomile,' said another woman. 'I'm convinced it's the only thing that is helping me sleep at the moment. I've been driven demented by the old insomnia.'

'Nescafé instant,' called an older man, sitting on the lower step, his legs pressed together, his hands clutched and resting on his knees. 'You know how I like it.'

Rory and Tom leaned against the stage, murmuring to each other.

Edith looked up. 'Aha! Well, if it isn't our new footballers!'

'I think the soubriquet "footballers" might be a bit ambitious,' said Shazza, making squiggles in the air, and sitting herself beside Edith on the steps. 'Kitty and I are useless at all sports... We're just people-pleasers.' She paused. 'Well, Kitty is, being so much nicer than me.'

Rory laughed. 'It's only meant to be a bit of fun,' he said. 'Don't worry about it.'

'Well,' said Edith, in her big, booming voice, 'I think you all are like modern-day Fionn MacCools, our great Irish hero, who listened while the spirits whispered, who chewed on his thumb and the secrets of the world were laid out for him...'

'Aunt Edith,' said Tom, 'it's just a five-a-side team... hardly saving the soul of Ireland, are we?'

'But we have to be ambitious, do we not?' said Edith. 'Dream big, live large and pan for gold, for ye will find it in the reeds of the river, for those who seek will be rewarded. Those who sit still will rot.'

The older man laughed again.

Edith turned to Kitty. 'Have you met my other nephew, Rory? My sister, Rosamund, is their mother,' explained Edith. 'And this is the one and only Carmen Kelly, accountant by day, belly dancer by night. Carmen may have the kind of hips that don't lie, but she's also got the finest mathematical brain this side of the equator...'

'You've got to make a living, haven't you?' said Carmen, smiling, and holding out her hand, first to Kitty and then Shazza. 'It's a joke, by the way,' she said. 'The belly dancing bit. Unfortunately, the accountant bit is very real.'

'She does my accounts for the haberdashery,' said Edith, 'and she's now also the comptroller-in-chief of the Sandycove community fundraising committee. She makes sure that all the dots are dotted and the t's are t'd. Isn't that right?'

'Right enough,' said Carmen.

'And this is Janet,' said Edith, just as the woman emerged from the kitchen with a tray of cups.

'I've made extra tea,' she said. 'For the stragglers. I think I heard the voice of the bold Sharon Keegan, did I not?'

Shazza was smiling at her. 'Good evening, Janet,' she said. 'I didn't get to say hello in the scrum.' She turned to Kitty. 'Kitty, this is the indispensable Janet MacNamara-Doyle, the real power behind the Sandycove Newsletter, our Rottweiler receptionist...'

Janet glowed under the flattery. 'This girl has done wonders with the Newsletter since she joined,' she said. 'It's proper journalism now. I keep saying it's like having Woodward and Bernstein in the office.'

'Aren't they the characters from *The Muppet Show*?' asked Shazza, making everyone laugh, especially Rory.

'Sharon is off men,' went on Janet, handing out the cups, including two very strong cups of tea to Kitty and Shazza, and giving Tom the packet of own-brand digestives to hand around. 'She was telling me this morning. I thought that was very sensible in this day and age. Girls can focus on their careers now, can't they? When I was young, it was all about finding a husband PDQ.'

'Well,' said Shazza, sitting down on the bottom step, 'when I say off men, I mean, I've joined a virtual nunnery and if it means my career, such as it is, benefits, then so be it.'

'Are you also off men?' Edith asked Kitty. 'Or is that an impertinent question?'

'Impertinent questions don't stop you, Aunt Edith,' said Tom.

'No,' said Edith, 'why should they? People don't have to answer...'

'Kitty should be off men,' replied Shazza, 'because she's been left dangling by her so-called partner, Dave the non-rave.'

Everyone seemed greatly amused by Shazza, as she held court.

'Joining my virtual nunnery is,' she went on, 'the only way I can guarantee a happy life. You see, I have spent my entire existence catering to the whims of men, putting my own needs second or even third... or fourth... and as Kitty and I have decided, men are not worth it... Anyway, I blame my mother...'

'Most people do, sadly,' said Edith.

'She wished she'd had sons, but she had me and my sister, Shona... and I must say if I had given birth to Shona, I too would have been disappointed... but she always said how much easier having boys would have been and how much trouble me and Shona were. I grew up with the idea that men were these idealised creatures who should be loved and adored. Well, it turns out that that's bollocksology.'

'Traumatising,' said Edith, making an amused face at Janet.

Tom leant back, sipping his tea. He was wearing long cargo shorts, and Kitty found herself wishing that Dave wore the same kind of clothes, instead of his navy blue, stiff denim jeans and those depressing shirts with the granddad collars.

Don't think about him, she told herself. *Keep busy. Keep going until life resumes.* At least, she thought, the football might fill in time until Dave came back.

11

In a previous life, the canteen of Mulligan O'Leary had once been the kitchen of the old Georgian house. There were still so many vestiges of the past, from the smoothed oak bannister which snake-charmed its way from the bottom to the top of the stained-glass fanlight above the door, or the stairs which had been worn away from 300 years of feet. But the building was also now firmly in the modern age, with neon signs and women and men in heavy-framed spectacles and geometrically precise hair.

Kitty was in the canteen, sitting at a large round table, beneath a high window, her coffee and tuna sandwich in front of her.

She took out her phone, checking to see if Dave had called. Nothing. Life, it seemed, was on pause and she was just waiting for it to start again. The uncertainty was agony. But, remembering Shazza's wise words – something about his general eejittery – she knew she couldn't call him... and she was just successfully slipping her phone back into her bag when she was possessed by her own inner eejit and, before she could stop herself, she dialled his number.

She held her breath, panic and anxiety mixed with shame, knowing that she was doing something wrong but desperately in need of reassurance. What if the phone just rang out? She would be back where she started. Limbo.

But, wonderfully, Dave answered. 'Hello?'

'It's me...'

'I know it's you.' He sounded irritated. 'Your name came up...'

'Sorry...'

There was silence for a moment before he spoke again. 'Yes?'

'Yes, what?'

'What do you want?'

'To see how you are, how you are doing... if you've... well, if you've got your... if you know, you're feeling better...?'

'Kitty, it's only been a few days... I explained. No more pressure, all right? I can't cope with it. Anyway, for your information I'm working from home and spending the rest of the time recovering.'

Recovering from what exactly, Kitty wondered. Recovering from her?

'That's good to know...'

She could hear Maureen's voice in the background – and what sounded like the *Countdown* theme tune. 'I've got to go,' he said. 'I'm helping Mam with something... Bye.'

'Bye...'

But he'd already put the phone down as humiliation seeped through her marrow. Shazza was right. Of course, Shazza was right. Never phone someone who doesn't want to hear from you. Rule number one in life.

Kitty took a packet of sugar from the bowl in the middle of the table, ripped it open and poured it into her coffee. And another. And another. One more, she thought. Anything to try to make her feel normal again.

She took a sip. Disgusting. She'd ruined her coffee as well as her life. Why hadn't she listened to Shazza? She must never call him again. From now on, she would have to not only listen to Shazza but act on her advice. Left to her own devices, she wasn't safe. And anyway, Dave still didn't sound like the old Dave, who was so much nicer than this new Dave. But perhaps the old Dave wasn't that nice? Perhaps she was misremembering. It had been so long now since things had been good between them, she couldn't quite remember.

She pushed her tuna sandwich away, ashamed with herself.

'Not hungry?' Mary Rose was standing with her tray beside the table. 'Everything all right?'

Kitty nodded. 'Grand, thanks...'

'Mind if I sit down?' Mary Rose pulled out the chair and sat down, placing her tray in front of her, with a sandwich which looked as though its filling was some kind of building material... 'This doesn't look too appetising,' said Mary Rose. 'It's meant to be egg and cress.' She picked it up gingerly as though it was a dead rodent. 'But I'm starving, so I'm going to have to go for it.' She nibbled at it. 'It's better than it looks,' she said.

Kitty tried more of her coffee. If you pretended it wasn't coffee, then it wasn't too bad. Perhaps more sugar would mask the coffee flavour and you could pretend it was another drink entirely. She added another sachet. And then another.

'How are you doing after the last pitch?' asked Mary Rose. 'I know Alex is still upset about it.'

'She doesn't like losing,' said Kitty.

Mary Rose nodded. 'No one does... well, some people hate it more than others. Some don't mind because they get used to it.' She smiled at Kitty. 'I'm not one of life's winners, you know? And that's fine. It's just the way things work out. They probably won't extend my contract at Mulligan O'Leary. My three-month probation is nearly up and if we don't win the Welcome Ireland pitch, then I would say I'm gone.' She shrugged. 'It's grand... I'll find another job. There's one going in the local further education college. I'm going to update my CV and send it off.'

'Do you want to leave?' asked Kitty.

'No... of course not,' said Mary Rose. 'I love it here. And working with you three is great. You're all so creative and full of ideas...'

'We were,' said Kitty. 'We're all a bit stuck at the moment.'

Mary Rose nodded. 'Being creative is not like turning on a tap, and out it comes. You have to be in the right frame of mind for it to flow.'

'Perhaps the three of us are in the wrong frame of mind at the same time.'

Mary Rose nodded, picking up her cement sandwich again. 'But it's good to change. Maybe it would be good for me... who knows? I'm learning not to worry about everything and be happier.'

'My friend Shazza was saying the same thing,' said Kitty. 'She reckons you should be happy in everything you do. Including work.'

'Happiness is something we forget to prioritise,' agreed Mary Rose. 'We keep everything going, mind other people, stay healthy, force ourselves to go to the gym, drink green smoothies, send thank you cards, smile at people and show up at events we don't want to go to.' She shrugged. 'But when I was going through my divorce, one thing that kept coming up was the fact that I had forgotten how to be happy, and joy and pleasure are like muscles we need to exercise but rarely do.' She smiled at Kitty. 'In the depths of my despair, I didn't think I could be any more unhappy. But then, I thought, surely the only way is up. And so, I've been trying lots of things to increase my general happiness, working that muscle. Sea swimming. Sunrise walks. Getting a dog, Peaches. She's adorable. Wearing more colour. That kind of thing.'

'Why were you in despair?'

'My husband left me last year and... well... that was something of a blow. And I can't afford the mortgage on my own and my microwave blew up and... a few other bits and pieces. But as my mother always said, isn't it great we're not dead? The problem is my mother is actually dead. But at least I'm not.' She gave a little laugh.

'It sounds hard,' said Kitty. 'And I'm sorry about your mother.'

'Thank you,' said Mary Rose. 'Sylvester... he was my husband...'

'Sylvester?'

Mary Rose nodded. 'It was a family name,' she explained. 'He was a fourth-generation Sylvester. Anyway, Sylvester decided he was better off without me and went off with one of my friends. Sandra. They're now living in her house in Skerries, but he left me with a broken heart and a massive mortgage. I love my house. I'd done up the kitchen, papered the hall myself, stripped the stairs... and then this. I'll either have to get two lodgers in or sell it.' She sighed. 'I'll have to sell. I don't want to live with strangers.'

'Not when you get to a certain age...'

'Exactly.' Mary Rose shrugged. 'When I was a child, I used to cry with laughter with my friends, even in my twenties. My friend, Ailish, used to make me laugh so much that I would collapse to my knees, tears rolling down my face. You know?'

Kitty nodded. 'My best friend Shazza does that to me.'

'Still?' Mary Rose looked surprised.

Kitty nodded. 'I don't know what I'd do without her.'

'She sounds like a great friend to have,' said Mary Rose.

'What about Ailish? Where's she?'

'We lost touch,' said Mary Rose, with a shrug. 'She moved to Galway. There was a job going in Shantalla as a teacher and I'd met Sylvester...'

And then Kitty remembered something said by Edith Waters the night before in the kitchen of the hall. 'Life is messy,' she said, 'and you can't sweep it up and smooth it out. You have to learn to love the rough bits and all the cracks because it's in the cracks where the gold is hidden.'

'It's true,' said Mary Rose. 'That's exactly it. If life was nice all the time, it would be boring. And you wouldn't learn anything.'

'I'm one of life's tidy-uppers,' said Kitty. 'But you can spend far too much time tidying and not enough time having fun.'

Mary Rose looked up, just as Ben O'Leary, the chief financial officer of Mulligan O'Leary and son of one of the founders of the company, walked past.

'Ladies,' he said, his blond hair falling over one eye as though he was a bohemian artist, rather than the public-school posh boy he was.

'Hello, Ben...' Mary Rose gave him a polite nod.

He moved away, just narrowly missing a collision with one of the girls from reception.

'Oh so sorry, Mr O'Leary,' she giggled, as they sidestepped each other.

His hands shadowed her waist for a moment, as he flicked his hair back and moved on.

'He reminds me of Sylvester,' said Mary Rose, in a low voice. 'There's something slippery about him. He can't look people in the eye. Have you noticed? Once you've witnessed a cheater up close, you can spot them everywhere. Your antennae are always twitching.'

'It's a great life skill,' said Kitty.

'It twitches *so* much,' said Mary Rose. 'That's the problem.

You realise the world is full of liars and cheats. The only good thing is that when it doesn't twitch, it's such a relief.'

'We all need a twitchometer,' agreed Kitty. 'It would save a lot of time that is wasted on relationships that go nowhere.'

'We'll need to invent one,' said Mary Rose. 'We'd make a fortune.' And the two of them laughed and Kitty thought how much she hoped Mary Rose would pass her probationary period. You needed people on the same wavelength, if you had any chance of enjoying your work. And even having fun at work.

12

Pearse Street train station at rush hour wasn't a place for quiet contemplation: the pigeons fluttering in the roof above, the commuters staring at their phones, the shafts of early-summer evening sunlight making spotlights on the platform. Kitty stood, thinking about work, about Dave... and whether it was possible that one could be washed up at thirty-two.

'Kitty! Kitty!' She looked behind to see her aunt, Annie, barrelling towards her. Annie was the colour of a freshly oiled teak cabinet, the smell of fake tan in the air. Her fingernails were bright pink. Her hair highlighted. 'Just getting my bits done,' she said. 'We're off to Ibiza in the morning.' She reached up and threw her arms around Kitty. 'We're so excited. We're heading straight to the bar in the airport for 8 a.m., few little Proseccos to get us going...' The train pulled into the platform and they waited their turn, while Annie talked about what they had planned to do while there – 'tanning by day, drinking by night' – and what she still needed to sort out before departure. 'I couldn't find my passport earlier,' she said. 'Tore the flat apart. High and low. In the end, had to phone your mother to sort it out. Was sobbing down the phone and who else but your mam to sort out my problems…?'

They took their seats on the train, Kitty beside the window. One of the posters that she had designed was on the wall at the end of the carriage about calling out antisocial behaviour on public transport. It was from last year, and she looked at it wondering if it too was missing something.

Annie was still talking. 'She phoned the passport office for me and they organised an emergency one for me…' Annie groped around in her capacious bag. 'It's here, somewhere. Just picked it up. The man was so nice. Now, where is it?' She groped around again. 'It was here just a moment… aggh.' She looked up at Kitty. 'It's gone. I've lost it!'

'Let me look…' Kitty took the bag, slipping her hand straight into the inside pocket, and retrieved the passport. 'Voila!'

Annie was all smiles again and flutters as she clasped her bag and passport to her chest. 'Cinderella is going to the ball! What would I do without you two? I couldn't face a life without balls and parties. Ibiza is going to be a ball.' She beamed at Kitty as the train pulled into Sandycove, and they both stood up, moving towards the doors. 'Now, by the way, your mother didn't get that promotion… whatever it was she was going for, chief thingamajig?'

'She didn't?' asked Kitty, confused. Surely she was a shoo-in?

'I was only half-listening,' said Annie, 'so didn't get all the details. I was running late for my bedazzling sessions and was so stressed about the passport. You know I was thinking of getting my toes done. Do you think diamanté on all the nails or just one or two… I don't want to overdo it…'

But Kitty was thinking of her mother. 'What did she say? Was she upset?'

'Who?'

'Mum!'

'Oh, you know your mother... never gets upset about anything!'

She was right, Catherine didn't get upset about anything. Kitty couldn't remember the last time her mother was anything other than her cool, calm self. And yet, this was something she had worked for, something she wanted... something she deserved.

They walked to the top of the steps of the station, and through the ticket barrier and stood for a moment outside, ready to go their separate ways.

'I'm going to go over and see her...' began Kitty, as Annie delved into her bag. 'See if she's all right.'

'Who?' said Annie, her head still inside her capacious bag. 'My purse... It's gone... ah! No! It's here! Thank God. Panic over.' She looked up, fixing Kitty with one of her little smiles. 'I don't suppose you could lend me some money? Just a little bit... tide me over...' She smiled even more winsomely. 'I'll pay you back! You know me... always good for a debt. Don't want to fall out with my favourite niece...'

Annie had never paid her back, but Kitty was thinking of her mum. She could pop over now and then home and then to the five-aside.

'Kitty?' Annie gave her a poke in the arm. 'Please? I'm just running low and I need a few spends for the old holliers, you know how it is...'

'Yes, yes, of course...' How could she say no to Annie, her mother's only sister? 'How much?'

'One hundred euros? Two? Two fifty would be better, obviously.' Annie put her head on one side. 'Or more. Only if you could spare it. Three hundred, final call. Or... well, whatever you can spare.'

Kitty felt herself being herded by Annie towards the bank machine on the outside wall of the station.

'Promise I'll pay you back...' Annie was saying. 'It's just there's been a bit of a cash-flow logjam... you know how it is and you know me... clueless I am with money. It comes in and it goes out... I never hold on to it for long enough...'

Kitty's fingers hovered over the keys and then inputted €300. Annie was family. And she was her favourite aunt, her favourite relative, and if you couldn't lend some of your money, then there was something wrong with you. 'Here you go...' She handed over a sheaf of crisp €50 notes as Annie's eyes gleamed.

'You are the best niece anyone could have.' She beamed at Kitty. 'The best and the sweetest and the world's most amazing niece. I will remember you in my will!' She gave a wink, grabbed the notes and vaguely kissed the air near Kitty's face. 'Now, bye-bye, sweetie! Must dash and fling a few bikinis into a bag! See you in a few days! I'll need another holiday to recover!' And she was gone.

Kitty made her way to her mother's house, more concerned about Catherine at that moment than the fact that she would probably never see that €300 ever again, but to her relief when she opened the door, her mother was looking her normal, composed self.

'Hello, darling,' she said. 'How lovely to see you...' She smiled at Kitty, hugging her. 'How was work?'

'Fine...' Kitty stepped into the house, following her mother through the hall and into the kitchen. 'I just met Annie...'

Catherine turned around. 'She's all excited about her trip...'

'She told me about your promotion... or lack of it... is it true?'

'Oh, that.' Catherine stopped in the hall.

'What happened?'

'Well...' Catherine shrugged. 'Someone else is going to be CEO. It was stupid of me to presume it might be me.'

Kitty was silent, trying to think what to do and to say. Her mother was more upset than she had at first assumed, and they walked into the kitchen, Catherine sitting at the table.

'I just thought that the right person always gets the job,' her mother was saying, as Kitty filled the kettle. 'You work hard and you are rewarded.' She smiled at Kitty. 'I had forgotten about the old boys' club and the powers of a game of golf.'

'What are you going to do?'

'Carry on,' said Catherine. 'Isn't that what we do? Never give up?'

'Even when you feel like it...?'

'Especially when you feel like it.' Catherine nodded, as though the moment of upset had passed. 'Anyway, enough about me...' She smiled at Kitty. 'How's everything with you?'

'Fine,' Kitty replied.

'Have you heard from...?' Catherine drifted away.

'No...'

Catherine opened her mouth as though to say something and then stopped. 'Well...' she said. 'I don't... I mean... it's...'

'My sentiments exactly,' said Kitty.

'How is everything at Mulligan O'Leary? Everything going well?'

Kitty wasn't ready to tell her mother that the team had lost their groove and that she felt sometimes as though she had suddenly forgotten how to swim, mid-length of a pool, and chlorinated water and panic were starting to fill her lungs.

'It's all fine,' she said, firmly.

'At least one of us is working hard and seeing the results,' said Catherine. And then she laughed. 'Annie was in earlier, looking for spending money. She's always running out at the end of the month.'

Kitty looked up. 'How much did you give her?'

'Five hundred euros.' Catherine shrugged. 'She's having enough fun for the two of us.'

'And why can't you have fun?' said Kitty. 'Why shouldn't you be off on holiday?' She immediately felt irritated with Annie, taking advantage of Catherine who was stuck at home, after not receiving the promotion which should have been hers. And, worse, Annie had duped them both for money and they all knew she wouldn't ever pay them back, she never did.

Catherine shrugged. 'Holidays mean so much more to her than they do to me. I've never been good at switching off.'

Life, thought Kitty, wasn't fair. For the first time, she understood what Shazza had been trying to say. Some people had all the fun, and others not very much of it at all. It was time for some fun before life slipped by, unnoticed. And where better to try out this new theory than at the five-a-side football?

13

The Sandycove Seafarers' stadium consisted of a few run-down terraces with broken seating on four sides of a pitch. And there wasn't a pitch as such, as in the large manicured green vistas, with grass which had been cut with nail scissors, sprinkled with spring water and minded with the attention you might give to a prize-winning orchid. This was a farmer's field type of pitch, with unearthed sods, sparse grass and an undulating topography more suited to an upland slice of Connemara, perfect for scraggly sheep and not much else.

Kitty was wondering what she had agreed to. Yes, it was true, she had agreed to have more fun in her life, but perhaps agreeing to play football had been rash. Kitty's new football boots, which she had bought hastily from a sports shop in town, felt like circus shoes, as she tottered out of the changing room and then sank into the soft grassy mire.

'I don't care what I look like any more,' Shazza had told Kitty, as they changed in the grotty little building beside the field. 'No one is looking and I have to say, it feels fecking marvellous.' She'd put one leg up on the bench beside Kitty. 'Feel it,' she'd ordered. 'Go on.'

Kitty had brushed her hand across the sharp stubble.

'Haven't shaved in weeks,' Shazza had explained proudly. 'No more hair removal, no more uncomfortable shoes or undergarments, or anything that pushes me up, straps me in or restricts my right to be a chest-thumping, flag-waving, bra-burning feminist. I'm so au naturel, I'm practically fully compostable.'

They walked out to where Tom and Rory were standing on the sidelines, neither of them looking particularly professional in their faded T-shirts and the kind of shorts you might wear on the beach in Alicante, but they were both smiling and waved to Kitty and Shazza.

'Lads,' said Shazza, 'if anyone can enlighten me why exactly we've found ourselves inadequately dressed, in an environment to which we are unused, and about to partake in an activity in which none of us has ever bothered partaking before, then please go ahead.'

Rory laughed. 'Well, I'm not that unused to football. Played it at school. Was never on the team... but our brother...' – he gave Tom a half-smile – 'our brother Paddy and I used to play. He was good. This brother here... he was always reading.'

Tom shrugged. 'I used to play with Paddy and Rory,' he said. 'Rory has just forgotten it or blocked it out. But he's right... I'm not the world's best player.'

'So why are you here?' asked Kitty. 'Why did you volunteer?'

The two men looked at each other again. 'We're here because...' began Tom, and then there was a voice.

'You made it!' It was Tara, the woman from the community hub meeting, jogging towards them, dressed professionally in white shorts and a football top in blue and yellow, a whistle around her neck. 'Sorry I'm late,' she said. 'Work was crazy.

Had to get changed in the car, which was not easy, I can tell you.'

'Tara,' said Tom, 'have you met Kitty and Shazza properly?'

'Briefly,' said Tara, reaching out and shaking Shazza's hand, then Kitty's. 'What's your experience?'

'What do you mean?' said Shazza. 'Regarding what?'

'Football!' replied Tara. 'What else could I have meant?'

'I don't know,' said Shazza. 'Could have meant anything.'

'But it's all about context, is it not?' said Tara. 'We're all dressed ready to play football. You have special boots on. We're in the Sandycove Seafarers' stadium...'

Shazza was nodding. 'Yes, of course. Context is everything.'

'I think,' said Kitty, 'that we just don't believe we're here...'

Shazza was nodding. 'It's like an out-of-body experience. We don't play football. We're not the type.'

'So why are you here then?' asked Tara, incredulously, her hands on her hips, staring at Shazza and Kitty as though they were mad, which, Kitty felt, they were. 'No one forced you to volunteer. Your lives did not depend on it. You raised your hands.'

'For fun,' said Kitty, as Shazza nodded in agreement.

'To keep us off the streets,' continued Shazza. 'Metaphorically, anyway, just to clear up any confusion. Anyway, my experience of football is zero. But I'm mainly here as part of my healing journey.'

Tara was trying hard not to show utter bemusement as she turned to Kitty.

'No experience whatsoever,' said Kitty, trying to manage expectations. 'I can't play.'

'Right...' said Tara, letting the word hang in the air. She blew the whistle around her neck. 'Come on, let's have a kick around. See what skills anyone has. Maybe we have an undiscovered Roy Keane in our midst?'

'Keen? Who said anything about being keen?' said Shazza, as she jogged onto the pitch behind Tara.

It was like being back in school, those awful games periods where you had to hang about outside in all weather, being shouted at by a bossy woman in a tracksuit, her whistle piercing your eardrums. Tara soon had them jogging up and down, or passing the ball to each other, or practising firing it at the goal. Kitty did her best, running after the ball, and trying to kick it in the general direction of the goal or to a team member.

At last, Tara blew her whistle for the final time as Shazza and Kitty collapsed in a heap, the two of them groaning.

'Fun, Shazza?' managed Kitty.

'I may have got it wrong,' said Shazza. 'I think we are looking for fun in all the wrong places.'

Afterwards, they joined Tara and the two lads in The Island, the pub in the village, Kitty and Shazza crawled onto the benches and then listlessly tried to stay upright. Rory was wearing a faded and slightly holey Take That T-shirt. He was one of those people who floated through life, thought Kitty, who was effortlessly charming and likeable, who were always assets to have around because they made everything more pleasant. Tom was taller, broader and darker. The same affable charm, but he was more serious than Rory, he smiled less, but there was a relaxed air about him, as though... Kitty couldn't quite work it out, but it seemed as though he had nothing to prove, he was just him.

Tom bought a round and placed a gin and tonic in front of Shazza and Kitty. He and Rory both had pints of Guinness, Tara was drinking sparkling water.

Tom held up his pint of Guinness in a toast. 'So, to our first five-a-side meeting,' he said.

'I can't stand meetings,' said Rory. 'I make it a rule never to have one.'

'Except for now,' replied Shazza. 'Not much of a rule if it's broken while you're doing it. It's like saying I don't smoke while smoking. Or I'm on a diet while stuffing one's face with cream cakes.'

Rory laughed, taking zero offence. 'What can I say, I'm a tangle of contradictions?'

Shazza rolled her eyes again. 'Like all men,' she said. 'Say one thing and do another.'

'Still off men?' said Tom.

'Yes, forever,' said Shazza. She sighed. 'I mean, it's not your fault, Tom, or yours either, Rory... it's just for my sanity, I have to put myself in a women-only zone. I was listening to this podcast called Healing After Relationship Trauma and they said that you had to consciously remove vestiges from the patriarchy from your zone.'

Tara nodded. 'Sounds like good advice...'

'Exactly!' said Shazza. 'So that's what I'm doing...'

'But why don't Rory and I count as vestiges of the patriarchy?' asked Tom, glancing at Kitty and giving her a half-smile. 'I feel I should be insulted.'

Shazza laughed. 'I'm doing my best. No one ever said healing after relationship trauma was easy.'

'I find the best way,' said Rory, 'is to get into another traumatic relationship. No two bad relationships are the same. It's endlessly fascinating. I'm on a trauma loop when it comes to girlfriends. I just can't seem to find the right person.'

'Join the club,' said Shazza. 'A needle in a haystack would be easier.'

'So, what about you?' Tom turned to Kitty. 'Any traumatic relationship stories?'

Shazza snorted as Kitty answered. 'Not at all... all very boring...'

'Boring to the point that it should be a cure for chronic insomnia,' said Shazza, darkly.

Kitty looked at her. 'Better boring than traumatic.'

'I think I'd go for traumatic,' said Shazza. 'At least trauma is exciting.'

'By boring, you mean safe and dependable...' asked Tom.

Shazza made another sound of derision. 'If you call dependable someone who's gone back to live with his mother!'

'He's under a lot of pressure...' explained Kitty to Tom. 'Thought I was trying to marry him off...'

'To whom?' he asked.

'To me,' she said.

'He should be so lucky,' said Shazza.

Tom turned to Shazza. 'I take it that you don't approve of this man...'

Shazza shook her head. 'Kitty is too good for him,' she said, giving Kitty a look, one eyebrow raised. 'Only she doesn't realise it.'

Kitty spoke to Tom. 'We've been together for a long time... we're happy... well, we're not... currently. And he's just going through something and I'm supporting him...'

'Hence she has more free time,' explained Shazza.

Kitty thought again about if she and Dave had ever really been happy. They had been content, she thought. But it had always been her smoothing the way, organising everything, ensuring life ran along relatively easily for the two of them. But since his father had died, he'd almost resisted her efforts, making it harder to smooth things over.

Tom was frowning slightly, listening, and Kitty felt it necessary to jump in and further elucidate. Or, rather, defend herself because Shazza wasn't helping with her snorts, sighs and eye-rolling.

'Dave needs me,' Kitty said. 'He likes me to have everything organised for him, and make sure he's got everything he needs. We work well like that. I'm like his... I don't know... his PA or his secretary...'

Tom's eyes widened slightly and even Rory stopped fiddling with the coaster to look up. Tara had a look of abject horror on her face.

'But in a good way,' Kitty quickly assured them. 'We love each other...'

'Each to their own,' said Shazza. 'But what do I know? I'm in my virtual nunnery, wearing my virtual wimple, my virtual giant crucifix swinging from my neck...'

'You look very fetching,' said Kitty. 'Pity it's all virtual.'

'Have you girls ever thought about getting out of your virtual lives?' said Tara, rolling her eyes. 'Shazza here lives in some kind of dystopian fantasy world and Kitty is hanging around waiting for someone who prefers his mother to her. Neither of you is in a real relationship but neither of you is single. You're both in love limbo.'

Shazza was nodding. 'That's exactly it. Except love limbo is part of my healing journey...' She held up her gin and tonic. 'Well, that and also the mysterious powers of this essential ancient medicine of the gods and goddesses.'

Tara gave her a look. 'If the Sandycove Seafarers are going to win any matches, then you have to cut out the alcohol, the chocolate, the sweets... the fast food...'

Shazza was looking at her open-mouthed. 'You mean not self-medicate? Do you have any idea what might happen if I go off my meds? The hounds of hell might be released. The River Shannon would start to flow backwards. St Patrick would return to reintroduce snakes to this rain-benighted island. I am only just hanging in there. I have to remain slightly medicated at all times.'

'You'll be fine,' said Tara, drily, before turning to Kitty. 'What about you? Do you eat properly? Do you follow a regime? Protein? That kind of thing.'

'Salads, mainly,' said Kitty. 'Chicken…' She tried to think what else she ate. 'Porridge. Tuna and mayonnaise sandwiches. Eggs.' As she spoke, Kitty had a flash of realisation that she had the most boring diet in the history of diets. She was even no-frills when it came to food.

'I'm a big believer in protein,' Shazza was saying, earnestly to Tara. 'Like major believer. They are the building blocks of our bodies… and, I don't know… our hair?' Shazza started to look a little uncertain. 'Nails? And… well, biology was never my strong point. But the problem is, sadly, proteins don't agree with me as much as carbs do. Carbs are my true love.'

'Lion bars are my snack of choice,' Rory said. 'And Chunky KitKats. Toblerone.'

Shazza nodded, enthusiastically. 'I love all of the above… although I bought a giant personalised Toblerone for Mr Unmentionable for Christmas with his name on. Turned out he didn't like them. Should have known then. Never trust a man who doesn't like Toblerone.'

'That's a long name to fit onto one bar of chocolate,' said Rory.

'I just put Mr Unmensh,' said Shazza.

'You did?' said Rory.

Shazza laughed. 'Of course not. I put his name, which is, of course, unmentionable.'

Tara didn't look impressed. 'Sounds like boot camp is what you need.'

'As long as it involves sugar and alcohol, sign me up,' Shazza smiled.

'That's called a holiday,' said Tom.

'Well, book me a flight,' said Shazza.

'No,' said Tara. 'We have to be serious. We have our first match this Friday evening. That's precisely three evenings' time and I have absolutely no faith in us at all. I know it's meant to be fun...'

Shazza poked Kitty in the ribs.

'But,' went on Tara, 'I am worried we're going to be a shambles. We need to be less embarrassing.'

'That's my motto in life,' said Shazza. 'Be less embarrassing.'

'No, I'm serious,' said Tara, intently. 'The other teams have been training for months. And just because we've lost most of our members recently, we're starting from nothing. What's the point of doing something if you're not going to do it properly?'

'Exactly,' Kitty said, before realising that Tara was asking her to play football properly. She liked doing everything other than football properly.

'I'm only doing it because Tom is doing it,' said Rory.

'I'm doing it because I need a distraction from Mr Unmentionable,' said Shazza.

Tara turned to Kitty. 'What about you?'

'I'm here because I have a bit of spare time and I'm trying to have more fun.'

'Did you have fun out there today?' Tara scrutinised Kitty, her eyes narrowed.

'No, not really,' admitted Kitty.

Tara tossed her head. 'Jesus! I'm playing with amateurs and out-of-condition fools!'

But Shazza and Rory started giggling.

'I want us to be less of a shambles from now on,' said Tara.

'We can try,' said Shazza.

Tara turned to her. 'Try?' she exploded. 'Try? You'll do more than try. You'll play bloody brilliantly or you will bring the whole of Sandycove into disrepute. Right, we practise again on Thursday and then our first match is the following evening.'

'I thought you said this was going to be fun,' said Kitty to Shazza, in a low voice.

'I may have been hasty,' replied Shazza, looking scared. 'I think the word might have been misused. But there's nothing we can do about it, except get on with it.'

'I'll leave your strips on the benches in the changing rooms,' continued Tara. 'As long as you don't mind second-hand? We don't have the money to buy brand new strips for everyone.'

'I'm all about second-hand,' said Shazza. 'Reuse and recycle. That's me. Except when it comes to relationships.'

Rory laughed but stopped when he caught the beady eye of Tara.

'And it will mean, Rory,' she said, 'you will be wearing something other than your T-shirts. Think you can lower yourself not to look cool for fifty minutes?'

'I don't try to look cool,' said Rory, with a shrug. 'I just am.'

Now it was Shazza's turn to laugh. 'So deluded,' she said, with a sad shake of her head. 'So incredibly deluded.'

14

How was it possible for your legs to ache so much that you couldn't even lift your foot to step on to the train to work? Or for you to not even be able to cross your legs without not just wincing but wanting to make the kind of noises women make in childbirth? Or to wonder if perhaps you had been unwittingly steamrollered the night before? Kitty had somehow managed to get herself dressed, out of the house and to work without fainting with pain, but at every step, she half-hoped she might collapse in a heap and some kind passer-by would call an ambulance and then – bliss! – she would be placed on a stretcher by two burly men, never to move again. It was going to take an intensive course of massage, warm baths and a month laid gently on a mattress to be back to her previous un-aching self.

Who knew football was so strenuous? Who knew that a low-key, low-stakes, low-energy game of local five-a-side could be so hard? Every molecule in her body ached. It hadn't even been like this that time Shazza had made her go along to a Body Pump class because she fancied the instructor. And of course the reason why her whole being ached was because of Dave's absconsion.

The previous evening in the pub, she'd managed to forget all about him, but this morning, when she was lying in bed trying to work out which muscles hurt the least, she'd remembered that her life now consisted of waiting for him to come back. She had to spend this time wisely, she thought, and learn more about herself and work out how to be a better partner. Hopefully, the old Dave would return – a jokey, intelligent man who was good company and liked to go to the cinema and had ambitions involving dog ownership and camper-van holidays... instead of the more recent Dave.

In the office and at her desk, even typing was proving difficult because holding up her arms was hard. She shifted her legs, wincing in pain. She'd done what she said she'd do, she'd introduced more 'fun' into her life. She just hadn't thought that so-called 'fun' could equal pain. If Dave would just call her or come home or say he loved her, she would feel less at sea. Being with him gave her life solidity and structure. Without him, it was unsettling, like floating in space.

She stared at her phone, knowing that she could just phone Dave again, and perhaps he would answer, and perhaps he would be pleased to hear from her. And then, just as she was staring at it, it rang. Finally! Telepathically they were connected and Dave had relented and would be coming home, and all this nonsense of football and frills could be shelved forever.

But instead of Dave, it was her father, Billy.

'Kitty? How's the form?'

'Hi Dad... fine...' She tried not to sound disappointed.

'Grand, grand...' said Billy. 'So, any craic?'

'None whatsoever. You?'

'Ah, you know how it is. It's to be found somewhere, so it is, you just have to be alert for it.'

Kitty's father had never been lacking in the hunting down of craic. He was a man unsuited to family life, someone who found the responsibilities of fatherhood and marriage to be like a noose. Kitty could never understand how he and her mother had even managed to make it to just after Kitty's fifth birthday before they both agreed that life would be easier if they separated.

'Did I hear my daughter was now a footballer?'

The Sandycove grapevine was in fine fettle, she was unsurprised to hear.

'It's just a bit of fun,' she said. Except it hadn't been. At all.

'The mixed five-a-side is meant to be fun,' said her father. 'Even though Tara Gilhooley doesn't see it as such.' He chuckled. 'I'll see you at the ground some evening... maybe we could go for a hot chocolate? You used to like them? You'd chat about school and all the other things you liked to do... I think there was a Tiny Pony thing...'

'My Little Pony,' said Kitty, mechanically.

'Yes! That was the yoke. And you'd take an age to drink your chocolate...' He gave another laugh. 'Your favourite bit, you used to say, was the froth on the top and you'd scrape it off with your spoon like one of those Buddhist monks raking one of those gravel gardens. And you'd tell me about the books you were reading. And you'd tell me the plot in great detail... you were quite the storyteller...'

'I was?'

Billy had lived in the States for most of her teenage years and the contact had become too sporadic, the bond they once had stretched too thin. Sometimes she wondered if her need to fix things with Dave had something to do with trying to have at least one dependable relationship with a man. Being on the other side of the Atlantic for so long, her father had lived a pretty carefree life, and when he was around, he'd been unreliable, turning up late, forgetting dates or missing events. He was the least dependable person she had ever known. He used to have to pick her up from school every Wednesday and he was always late and Kitty would have to sit on the kerb, being unofficially minded by the lollipop lady. Or there were the birthday parties, painstakingly organised by Catherine, that he would forget about or turn up on the wrong day. Or Kitty's college graduation, where he arrived halfway through, pushing his way along the rows of knees. Growing up, she had cried herself to sleep when he let her down. She'd reached the end of her rope with him a long time ago. When, a few years earlier, Billy had returned to Sandycove, he would ring Kitty often, but she rarely called him back, or even accepted his calls.

Kitty felt her usual sadness that she and her father weren't closer, but this was one relationship which she'd long realised was too complicated to fix, the gap between them was too big to ever overcome. Somewhere between the hot chocolates and the My Little Ponies and now, they'd lost each other. As adults, there wasn't any common ground.

'Bye, sweetheart,' he was saying. 'See you at the club.'

'Which club?'

'The football club! I'll be down next time you're there.'

15

ANNIE

Ibiza is bliss!!! Dancing all evening!!! Tanning by day!!! You'd love it!!!

CATHERINE

Sounds wonderful!

ANNIE

Wish you were here!!!

CATHERINE

Definitely!

ANNIE

Back tomorrow!!! I'll be round for dinner! Need something that isn't tapas!

By Thursday, the day of the Seafarers' next practice, Kitty's body had recovered just enough, so she was able to move without wincing, stretch without crumpling in pain and cross her legs without whimpering.

Tara was already stretching at the side of the pitch when Shazza and Kitty hobbled out of the changing room and onto the pitch. Tom and Rory were making their way out of the men's changing room towards Tara. Rory was wearing a Celine Dion T-shirt over his regulation Seafarers' top.

'You're lucky,' said Shazza to Kitty. 'You've got the legs for shorts. And as you know, I'm not a leg fascist. The knobblier and the blotchier, the better... but yours are in a league above us mere mortals.'

'Really?' It had been a long time since Kitty's legs had been on display in public, and she had felt self-conscious about exposing them to the world.

'If I were to have anyone's legs,' said Shazza, 'I would choose yours. And your ears.'

Kitty laughed. 'My ears?'

Shazza nodded. 'Mine were once described as "characterful",' she said. 'Which I think means they are lopsided and one sticks out more than the other...'

'I have never noticed.'

'Well, proves how much time you've spent looking at me then,' said Shazza. 'I feel quite insulted.'

Kitty laughed again, just as Tara was making her way towards them, followed by Tom and Rory.

'Come on!' Tara shouted. 'What are you two doing just hanging about? It's not school, you know... jog on the spot, knees up, quick!'

Tom and Rory looked a little apologetically over at Shazza and Kitty, as though they were taking some of the blame for this truly awful predicament Kitty and Shazza had ended up in.

'Remind me again why we are here?' Kitty asked Shazza, out of the corner of her mouth, as they jogged up and down, knees up as high as possible. 'It's like some kind of punishment,' Kitty panted. 'Torture.'

Tara's phone rang and she went to answer it. 'Keep going!' she ordered.

'We wanted to get out of our comfort zones, remember?' said Shazza, breathlessly. 'Remember, meet in the middle? You lighten up, me lighten down?'

'I preferred us before,' gasped Kitty. 'I think we should go back to our old selves...'

'I agree,' said Shazza. 'I was wrong!'

'What are you two saying?' asked Tom, jogging closer towards them. 'Don't tell me you're thinking of giving up?'

'We have to,' wheezed Shazza. 'Otherwise, we might not make it out alive...'

'If you're going,' he said, 'I'm going. Even if Aunt Edith will kill me...'

'COME ON!' Tara shouted again, slipping her phone into her back pocket. 'KNEES UP! HIGHER! MORE ENERGY!'

Beside them, Rory was impressively bouncing up and down, his knees like pistons. It was like the birth of steam, thought Kitty. The Flying Irishman.

'That's it, Rory,' said Tara. 'Everyone, look at Rory. That's what it should be like...'

Still flying up and down, Rory managed to shrug awkwardly at them, to show that he was a reluctant teacher's pet.

Eventually, after sit-ups, a two-minute plank and forty star jumps, they began their kick around.

'Right,' said Tara. 'The aim is to kick the ball to the next person and then they kick it on. First, Tom, then Rory, Kitty, Shazza, and back to me... everyone spread out.'

They did so, Kitty feeling so far away from everyone that she had to squint to see Shazza. Tara blew her whistle as she kicked the ball towards Tom, who deftly managed to kick the ball towards

Rory, who then manoeuvred it around and jimmied it towards Kitty. She knew all she had to do was run faster than the speeding ball, get in front of it and stop it with her foot. Then she would just boot it to Shazza, the way she'd seen it done over the years, in the all-too-brief glances she'd had. But as Kitty took off in pursuit, the ball was skimming along the grass at the speed of a bullet, travelling over the painted white line, towards the stands, where it hit the hoarding. In an instant, the ball ricocheted back and flew into the air, and whacked Kitty in the face. The sound echoed around the pitch, and somewhere she heard Tom's 'Oooh!' and Shazza gave a yell and then all she knew she was on the ground, opening her eyes, and Tara was giving her a shake. 'Kitty? Kitty?'

Shazza was holding her hand, and up above were the worried faces of Tom and Rory.

'I'm all right,' Kitty said. 'I'm fine...' She wasn't though. She was humiliated, mortified, and appalled at what had happened. Her face was stinging as though she'd done a chemical peel bought off the internet.

'Kitty! Kitty!' Oh God. That sounded like her father. 'Kitty!'

Groaning, she closed her eyes and when she flickered them open again, there he was, looking down at her.

'I saw everything,' he said, his face a mixture of concern but also amazement and was that amusement? 'It was like you were hit by a cannonball,' he went on, 'lifted you right off your feet. Jaysus. Your face. You look like you've done a round with Tyson Fury...'

'Thank you, Dad,' she said. 'Helpful.'

'Why didn't you just move out of the way?' he said. 'Or, better yet, hooch it back?'

'I wanted to know what it would be like to be hit in the face,' she replied. 'Have to experience everything in life, don't you?'

Tom was kneeling beside her, his fingers on either side of her temples, looking into her eyes. 'How are you feeling, Kitty? Can you see normally? Is anything blurry?'

Tom was in sharp focus, his eyes fabulously blue, his fingers felt warm and soft. 'I'm grand,' she said. 'Fine.' She wished she was concussed because she wouldn't have been able to register the embarrassment. But Tom didn't look as though he was laughing at her, he seemed genuinely concerned. Gently, he pulled her up by one arm, while Billy pulled the other.

'You need to know where the ball is coming from and visualise its trajectory and then...' Billy was saying.

'Thank you, Dad,' Kitty intervened. 'But I just need to get changed... you can give me your top tips later...'

'I'll give you a call,' he said, as Shazza helped her back to the changing room, leaving him and Tom and Rory behind. 'I've got lots of top tips... I could even...' Billy's voice carried over the air, but Kitty didn't hear any more as her ears were beginning to throb along with everything else, as though a Garda siren had exploded in her brain. The humiliation was worse. To be smacked in the face in front of all those people... in front of her dad. And in front of Rory and Tom as well. For a moment, through the ringing in the ears, the pounding heart and the dizziness, she wondered why she cared about what Rory and Tom thought. At least, she told herself, Dave hadn't seen her or he'd never return.

Back in the changing room, Shazza insisted on wetting a towel and, after making Kitty lie on the bench on her back, laid it on Kitty's face.

'I can't do it, Shazza,' said Kitty, through the towel. 'I want to go back to the old me.'

Shazza lifted the towel from Kitty's mouth. 'What did you say?'

'I said, I want to go back to my old life, the old Kitty...'

Shazza replaced the towel. 'But was the old Kitty happy? Was the life of the old Kitty working? Did she have everything she needed and wanted?'

Kitty remained silent under the wet towel.

'To effect change, one has to completely change direction,' went on Shazza, as though she was giving an inspirational talk. 'You have to be brave. You have to strike out on new paths, different pastures... novel ventures... didn't we agree?' Shazza didn't wait for Kitty to answer. 'We have to keep going. I was nearly enjoying myself out there, once we'd stopped jumping up and down. A ball in the face is nothing if it means your life is changing.'

Kitty lay, her face throbbing, under the wet towel, water runnelling down the side of her face and neck, creating rock pools in her ears. *Right*, she thought, *I will pretend to Shazza I am willing to change, but really, this is just a holding position until my old life resumes.* And then she could go back to the old Kitty, where life was comfortable and she didn't get hit in the face with footballs. *Hurry up, Dave*, she willed. *I can't do this for much longer.*

16

Mary Rose stood in front of the whiteboard in the conference room and was about to speak when she caught sight of Kitty's face. 'Everything okay? Did you...'

'A football accident,' said Kitty. 'Just a small bruise.'

'It's the size of my arse before I went on that grapefruit diet,' said Hughie. 'I didn't want to bring it up, but are you sure it was a football accident? It sounds like one of those outlandish tales people tell to hide what they've really been up to. Since when have you been playing football?'

'Since Tuesday...' Kitty touched her bruise, which she hadn't thought was that noticeable this morning as she trowelled on the make-up. 'It was just training. Our first match is tonight. Anyway, I'm fine...' She kept replaying the moment the ball thwacked her right in the face, but it wasn't the stinging pain or the humiliation or even the threat of concussion, it was the way Tom had pulled her to her feet, his hand on hers. She was struck – not just by the ball – but by how gentle he had been.

'Right, to our campaign for Nutty Nut the protein power bar now...' said Mary Rose. 'Have we all eaten one? Feedback? What words came to mind? Did it trigger anything? Memories? Did it make you feel anything?'

'Nauseous,' said Hughie. 'There was a truly terrible aftertaste.'

'They weren't great,' admitted Mary Rose. 'I couldn't finish mine. The idea is to refuel, I think.'

'Refuelling is for cars,' said Alex, looking at her phone, something which she was doing a lot more of, Kitty noticed. Alex seemed permanently still distracted and thrown by the failed pitch. Unless, of course, there was something else bothering her.

'Aha!' said Mary Rose. 'Anything in that? Cars?'

'Planes, trains, automobiles. And other ways you can feel nauseous...' said Alex, as her mobile rang. 'Yes?' she said, quietly, and then, whispering, 'I told you not to...' She slipped the phone into her jacket pocket and looked up at Mary Rose, as though she hadn't just received a mysterious phone call and that Hughie was not making faces at Kitty. 'What about "Not Naughty, Nutty"?' Alex suggested.

Kitty nodded. 'Or, what about, "We're in the nutty corner"?'

Hughie laughed and Mary Rose smiled. 'Love it,' she said. 'Right... is that what you are going to work on? And are there any updates on Welcome Ireland? Alex?'

'Excuse me a moment,' said Alex, standing up. 'I have to just go and... sort something out. I'm still trying to think of something else for Welcome Ireland... I don't have anything at the moment. I know we have the camper-van idea.'

'Inspiration will strike,' said Mary Rose.

The door of the meeting room closed behind Alex as she left.

'I wonder what's wrong with her?' said Hughie. 'Someone didn't have their Sugar Puffs this morning. Or any morning lately.'

'Or she got out the wrong side of the bed,' said Mary Rose. 'Happens to me all the time.'

'A wrong side of the bed?' said Hughie. 'If only I had the luxury.'

'What?' Mary Rose looked confused. 'Anyway, we'll have to organise some fun... what about a night out?'

Hughie shook his head firmly. 'No... I can't do nights... not at the moment. And, anyway, the last thing I need is organised fun. I like my fun to be organic.'

'But you can't wait for fun to just happen, Hughie,' said Mary Rose. 'It's like dating apps. You could wait all your life for Mr Right to come along, but the apps organise it so much more efficiently.'

'But I never want to go on dating apps ever again,' said Hughie. 'After John-Paul, the only thing I want to swipe left on is the touchscreen in McDonald's.' The three of them went back to their desks.

'What about some music?' suggested Kitty. 'Is that the kind of organic fun you might sanction?'

'As long as it isn't heavy metal, Daniel O'Donnell or The Eagles,' said Hughie.

Kitty went over to the shelves in between the two large windows, picked up the dusty radio, plugged it into the socket on the wall and tuned into a local station. 'Freedom' by George Michael came on. 'Okay with everyone? Anyone object?'

'My all-time favourite song,' said Hughie happily, his mood lifted.

Kitty went back to her work and to the sounds of her colleagues singing to themselves.

After half an hour, Alex returned. 'Music?' she said. 'What fresh hell is this?'

'It's hell with a soundtrack,' said Hughie. 'Come on and join the fun.'

Alex rolled her eyes, flung her bag onto the desk and sat down with a heavy sigh. The radio continued, just softly in the background, but enough that when Kitty looked around, she could see Hughie's foot tapping along when Coldplay came on. Mary Rose sang along quietly to herself, and then when Celine Dion made an appearance, Alex mouthed the words as though she was on a Las Vegas stage.

Kitty stared at her screen. She'd been going through images of Ireland, hoping inspiration would strike, but any idea she had just seemed flat... as though something was missing. Now all she could see was the invisible missing bits, but she still had no clue what they were.

Perhaps, she thought, she needed a change of scene to think about the Welcome Ireland campaign. A trip to the library to read some books and magazines might help in the search for inspiration.

'I'm off to the library,' she said, picking up her bag.

Hughie immediately thought it was an excellent plan. 'I'm coming with you,' he said, standing up. 'I need to get out of this office. Sometimes I feel like I live here.'

17

The glass on the façade of the National Library shimmered in the bright sunshine, as Kitty and Hughie walked along the cobbled piazza towards the front door. It was a brand-new building and had been opened the previous autumn to great fanfare. The president of Ireland had turned up, a tiny white-haired man who was also a poet, along with Bono, who wore reflective sunglasses which matched the windows of the library.

'Look!' Hughie gestured to a large abstract sculpture, an elongated shape which twisted around itself at the top. 'It's Alex, having a conniption over the fact that one person – one! – didn't like her work.' He laughed to himself. 'My God. If only I was so emotionally fragile.' And then, in a quieter, more urgent voice. 'I mean, I am,' he said. 'I'm far more emotionally fragile than she is. I just hide it better.'

Kitty laughed as they walked into the main atrium, with the shop and café on one side, a swirling staircase sweeping around the reception desk. They went their separate ways: Hughie taking the lift to 'periodicals' and Kitty entering the reading room.

The walls were lined with books, and in the middle of the

room were rows of large tables where people were working, laptops open in front of them and research books beside them. There were two areas of soft seating, long, low couches, and smaller armchairs, which were filled by people reading newspapers. On one chair, an older man was snoozing, the *Irish Independent* open on his lap. No one minded or batted an eyelid and, in fact, someone had shut the large, modern shutter behind him, occluding the sunlight, creating a little haven. Toddlers were in another area, playing with toys or being read to, and there was a group of teenage girls in school uniforms, revising for their Leaving Certs at the tables at the edge of the room, their heads bowed low, writing furiously or scrolling through their phones.

Kitty had forgotten what amazing places libraries were, all those words and knowledge floating about, everything you could ever need to know at your fingertips. She paced the shelves for a few minutes, gathering a pile of books that she thought might stimulate her creative juices, and then sat down at a long table. As she scanned through them, she made notes in her trusty Moleskine.

After thirty minutes, she was pleased with herself so picked up a newspaper that was strewn on the table.

Kitty checked her phone for a message from Dave. Nothing. Her life was on hold. What about booking their holiday or his cousin's wedding they were meant to be going to next month? There were the tiles she was going to buy for the kitchen. She wouldn't have minded his input, although his stock answer was always: 'Dunno, you choose.'

There was a cough from someone sitting on the chairs immediately opposite her. Then another cough, and another. Kitty looked up to see that it belonged to Tom Sweetman, who was looking over with a funny expression on his face, one eyebrow up, which made her laugh. He signalled to his cheek and pointed at her. 'How's the face?' Kitty lip-read.

'Fine,' she mouthed. 'I'll live.'

He gave her a thumbs up. 'My mother,' he mouthed back, pointing to a woman sitting on the long sofa beside him. The woman's grey hair was the colour of a Connemara pony and was cut into a bob just lower than her jaw, and she was wearing loose black trousers and a pale blue linen blazer and sandals. She gave Kitty a smile and a wave.

Tom was near-unrecognisable in a suit, looking older and far more responsible, as though he was a proper adult, not like the pretend adults Kitty and Shazza thought of themselves. The suit also made him look even more handsome. His hair even looked different, neater somehow, and there was a delightful novelty about seeing him out of context. Perhaps he was thinking the same, seeing her in her work clothes, as opposed to her awful football shorts. For some reason, she wished she wasn't wearing her old silk blouse, with the small, rounded collar, that she always thought made her look as though she was going to Sunday school. But she'd paid far too much for it a few years before and wore it as often as possible just to relieve the retail guilt. Tonight, she thought, it was going straight in the decluttering basket. She didn't want to look like a good Catholic girl... not in front of Tom, anyway.

She felt herself blushing. What was wrong with her?

She glanced back at Tom and caught his eye again, and even more embarrassed, quickly returned to her books, trying to focus on what she was reading. The old man asleep in the chair stirred and shut his eyes again, the schoolgirls were now whispering loudly. And then Tom and his mother were standing up, and walking towards Kitty.

'Hello,' he said, smiling. 'Fancy meeting you here,' he went on. 'This is my mother... Rosamund Waters-Kennedy...' He flashed a grin at his mother, as though he was teasing her.

'I've been saddled with that mouthful since I was born,' she explained to Kitty. 'Roz is quite sufficient. When I had my boys, I was determined that none of them would have anything complicated.' She gazed up at Tom lovingly. 'Paddy, Tom and Rory. All very nice, simple names.' She turned back to Kitty. 'And you're Kitty...?'

Kitty nodded, shaking her hand. 'Kitty O'Sullivan.'

'Kitty has just joined the five-a-side team,' Tom explained. He turned to her and all she could remember was the feel of his fingers as he gently touched her face as she was spreadeagled on the ground. Instinctively, her fingers touched her face, which made Roz peer closer at her.

'Has your bruise anything to do with your new career as a footballer?' she asked.

Kitty nodded, reddening. 'I was hoping that it was going down a bit, but, yes, I had an altercation with the ball. Proves how terrible I am at football. I'm only doing it to fill in time...'

Roz was shaking her head, smiling, searchingly. 'Fill in time? Why would you want to do that?'

'Oh, because... well, I'm waiting for...'

Tom and Roz were both listening far too intently. So Roz was like Tom, then, actually interested in people's answers. Unlike Maureen, who was only interested in the words coming from her own mouth. 'I'm waiting for... someone...' she began.

'Don't tell me you're waiting for a man?' Roz's eyes widened. 'Oh my dear... they are the very last things you should wait for. They should be waiting for you, isn't that right, Tom?'

Kitty didn't look at Tom to see what his response was but blundered on, desperately. 'I'm not,' she began and then, suddenly, felt the need to unburden herself. Lying made life far too complicated. 'Well, I might be... just a little.'

Roz's face was one of kind concern, her grey eyes soft, as she listened to Kitty.

'He's gone, just for a break or to put the brakes on...' said Kitty. 'But it feels as though I'm on hold...' Oh God, why had she said that? Now Tom knew that she was pathetic and useless and had no feminist principles. They had gone too, along with her pride. 'And so, Shazza suggested I keep myself busy... she's my best friend...'

'She's also on the team,' explained Tom to his mother.

'Just until he comes back,' Kitty added. 'He said he needed to go and find himself...'

'Did he, now?' Roz looked distinctly unimpressed.

'We've been together for so long,' said Kitty, trying to make it sound as though everything was normal. 'He's just a bit down, I think. His dad died a few years ago and he's an IT specialist and he's just reached a crossroads in his life... a stumbling block... he's lost himself...'

She glanced at Tom to see what he was making of it all. He too was listening, a slight frown on his face.

'My sister...' began Roz.

'Edith,' said Tom to Kitty, 'who you know...'

'Well,' went on Roz, 'my sister Edith always says to never live someone else's life, live your own. We've only ever got one life, don't waste it living the wrong one.'

Kitty nodded, trying to smile and prove how normal she was. She carried on speaking in a light, breezy tone. 'This is just temporary, anyway... we've got a wedding to go to soon... and tiles to choose...'

'Of course.' Roz looked again at Tom. 'Right, I've returned my books. Are you heading back to Trinity now or do you have afternoon surgery in Sandycove?'

'Trinity. I am giving some tutorials this afternoon.'

'My son, the professor,' said Roz, giving Tom a playful elbow in the arm. 'People are so impressed with titles, aren't they? Have you noticed?'

'It's meaningless,' agreed Tom. 'It just means I lecture a little bit, that's all.' He looked at Kitty. 'What about you?'

'Back to the office...'

Kitty followed Tom and his mother into the main foyer, falling into step with them as they walked out into the sunshine, where people gathered on the benches, eating their lunches, soaking up an hour of daylight.

'Oh, isn't it lovely,' said Roz, her face turned up to the sun and the flowers. 'So warm after such a long winter...' For a moment, Kitty sensed something between her and Tom, as their eyes locked, as though thinking the same thing, and then he smiled at Roz, before turning back to Kitty.

'I need to head this way,' said Tom. 'Which way are you going, Kitty?'

'Merrion Square,' she answered.

'Well then,' he said, 'we're in the same direction.'

The three of them walked to the train station, where Roz stopped. 'Here's me,' she remarked. 'Back to Sandycove. The best thing about being retired is not having to go back to the office after lunch.' She held out her hand again to Kitty. 'Come for Sunday lunch,' she said. 'We always have a full house... Edith will be there, and Tom and Rory... and bring the other team members. Shazza, is it?' She turned to Tom. 'And Tara, as well?'

He nodded. 'I'll call her...'

'Thank you,' said Kitty. 'That sounds lovely.'

Tom kissed his mother goodbye and then he and Kitty began walking along Nassau Street towards Kitty's office.

'It's so nice being in town,' he said, 'but I love taking the train back to Sandycove. I'd forgotten how much I liked that feeling of leaving the city behind and watching the sea all the way home. I missed it when I was away. London's nice, but it's not home.'

'When did you come back?'

'About a year and a half ago,' he said. 'I was offered a role in Trinity but also there was a possibility of going into practice again and so I took up both, balancing academia with being a hands-on vet. There's nothing like it. I mean, I love lecturing, but there is something about taking care of an animal, helping the family, taking a small, defenceless creature who is scared, and making it better.'

Kitty smiled. 'I have a cat, Romeo... he's still going, aged twelve and three-quarters. I swear he's got more than nine lives. He's going to outlive me.'

They turned right towards Merrion Square. 'And you're a...?' asked Tom.

'A copywriter for Mulligan O'Leary, the advertising agency.'

He nodded. 'What are you working on?'

'Various things – health campaigns, a nut bar... trying to make that sound delicious with just words. And a new campaign for Welcome Ireland...'

'Oh yes?' Tom looked impressed.

'We haven't got it yet,' said Kitty. 'We're putting a pitch together. I mean, how do you sell an entire country? How can you distil everything about Ireland into one image?'

Tom shook his head. 'I have no idea...' he said. 'Except... isn't that the secret to happiness? Find the essence and forget everything else?'

'The essence of what?'

'Well,' he said, 'if you like something or someone, work out what it is you like about it or them and do more of it. So, if you like singing, do more of it. If you like someone because they make you laugh, see more of them.'

'And football?'

He laughed. 'It's not that I like football so much, but I like my brother and I want to spend time with him. And I like being out and about and busy... and... well...' He smiled again. 'It's good for me. And for Rory... and...'

Kitty stopped. 'Here's me,' she said. 'Go on, what were you saying?'

He smiled down at her. 'Look, you don't have to come on Sunday... sorry about my mother. She's very insistent when she likes someone.'

Maybe he didn't want her to come, she thought, suddenly disappointed.

'She's always taken a shine to some of my friends and she always invited them for Sunday lunch. It was always a tradition. And then when we lost Paddy... he's my brother who died... well, we stopped for a while, and then, a few months ago, Edith insisted Mum start up again...'

'I'm sorry about your brother,' said Kitty. 'What... what happened?'

'He just didn't want to live any more,' said Tom. 'He stayed as long as he could... but... ah... well... you know. It was hard for him. Life was hard.'

'I'm so sorry,' said Kitty.

'Yeah... yeah... thank you.' He smiled at her but there was a sadness to him. 'Paddy was an amazing person. The best of us, you know?' He shrugged. 'But I promise you the lunches are not maudlin affairs, full of sad songs and people crying into their parsnips... so you will come, won't you? And Shazza. Edith will be there as well. And Rory. Mum likes a full table.'

Kitty smiled at him, inordinately relieved and surprisingly happy to be included. At least, she thought, that was Sunday taken care of.

'And anyway,' he went on, 'I'll see you for our first football match this evening? We're playing the Shankill Killers. They sound terrifying.'

'We're going to be crucified,' said Kitty. 'But I think I am more scared of Tara than the Shankill Killers.'

Tom laughed, as she walked off, giving him a wave and then smiling across Merrion Square, thinking how nice it was of Roz to take a shine to her. Being taken a shine to was perhaps one of the nicest things to happen to someone.

Shine. There was something in that... something perhaps she could work with.

18

The women's changing room at the Sandycove Seafarers smelled of decades of stale sweat, blood and tears, and there was a top note of Harpic from the toilets. It brought Kitty back to school hockey, where they were shouted at by sergeant major-like PE teachers who were utterly confounded and therefore apoplectic when flinging balls accurately didn't come naturally to all the girls. There was one teacher, a small woman from Belfast, who would peer up at the girls and say things like, 'I've seen lesser atrocities on the Falls Road than you playing here today,' or, 'You have the hand-eye coordination of a blindfolded sniper.' She'd been terrifying. Kitty had vowed never to take part in organised sport ever again, but here she was, being transported back to her schooldays.

It was Friday evening and their very first match. A friendly, apparently, but Kitty thought there was nothing friendly about facing an opposing team. She wasn't a naturally competitive person and it felt a little like going to war. Especially as all she knew about football was that the point was to kick the ball into a net. Anything further than that remained a mystery. She needed someone who could explain some of the finer points and then she could surprise Tara, their captain, by being a tiny bit better.

Wait. Did she actually want to get better? Was she actually beginning to enjoy herself?

There were two football strips folded on the benches, which had been left by Tara. 'Blue and yellow polyester,' said Shazza, holding her set up between finger and thumb. 'I normally wouldn't be caught dead in polyester.'

'We're here to have fun, remember?' said Kitty.

'Hold your head still.' Shazza was examining Kitty's face with an air of expertise as though she was a fully qualified nurse. 'No bruising, good...' she was saying. 'Redness practically gone... brain damage... to be confirmed.' She let go of Kitty's chin with a satisfied nod and sat down beside her on the wooden bench, their backs against the wall. 'Mr Unmentionable turned up at the office today,' said Shazza. 'Janet, you know, who's on the front desk... well, I heard her saying in her posh voice, the one she puts on...' Shazza gently mimicked Janet, putting on an old-fashioned lady-of-the-manor accent, 'And whomsoever may I say is attending? And he said his name and she said, I'll just check if Sharon is in residence... and she rang through, but I was on the other side of the door... I mean, you've seen the office, it's a shoebox. So she rang through, and I didn't answer and Janet said, Sharon Keegan doesn't appear to be present currently... I will take your card.' Shazza laughed. 'And she did! She took his business card and said he looked shifty and suspicious because she said his eyes were crooked. And it's true, he does have a very tiny, little turn in one of his eyes which I've barely noticed, but then Janet prides herself on being Sandycove's very own Miss Marple. She never misses a trick.'

Shazza smiled, but there was something about her which broke Kitty's heart, as though her healing journey wasn't over yet.

'Why did he come?' asked Kitty, gently.

'I suspect his ego needs flattering. Maybe Miss Horsey Kildare has realised he's not the asset she thought he was. Or... I don't know.' She paused. 'Do you think I should have gone and talked to him? Asked him what he wanted? Maybe I should unblock him on my phone? Or... he might be ill. Dying. Ebola. Leprosy. Irritable bowel syndrome? Does that kill you? Something bad, anyway. So, maybe he needs to tell me something, like where he's buried his treasure or that... he loves me and he was wrong and leaving me for Miss Kildare and...' She stopped, her eyes big and sad.

'Shazza...' began Kitty.

'I know... I know...' Shazza looked away. 'If Janet wasn't such a good gatekeeper, I would have gone and talked to him. And... well, thank God for Janet or I might have been caught again. I mean, he's the reason why I've gone off all men, which has effectively ruined my life because it's his fault I will never get married or have children and will remain a consecrated virgin the rest of my life...'

'I've noticed you've shaved your legs though,' said Kitty, running her hands over Shazza's billiard-ball smooth legs.

'I had to,' said Shazza. 'It was becoming unmanageable. I'm going to knit a jumper or a scarf out of my shearings.'

Kitty laughed but took Shazza's hand in both of hers. 'He's such an idiot...'

'He is...' Shazza nodded. 'Why did I allow myself to get entangled with Mr Unmentionable? Every red flag was billowing in my face and I pretended not to see them. And he wasn't as clever as he thought he was. He thought eating seasonally was hot cross buns on Good Friday.' She covered her eyes with her hands. 'I am just determined not to be that stupid ever again. I love the Newsletter and working in Sandycove and being part of the village. It's surprisingly satisfying. And I'm covering Lola O'Hare's wedding next week. You know I've loved her forever.' Lola O'Hare was an international singing superstar who had come home to get married. Shazza took Kitty's hand. 'I saw Dave with his monstrous mother earlier, doing the shopping. I utilised my undercover investigative journalism skills and followed them around and saw that they were buying those heat-in-the-oven roast dinners... with the foil trays with the potatoes, gravy and carrots.'

For a flickering moment, Kitty wondered if this was the man she wanted to spend the rest of her life with. But yes... of course it was. Dave was still obviously yet to rediscover his former self and if his healing journey involved him eating pre-prepared roast beef and potatoes, then so be it.

'The two of them looked quite chirpy as though they had discovered the secret to a happy life.'

'The essence,' said Kitty.

'The what?'

'Nothing...' said Kitty. 'It's just that if you find something that makes you happy, do more of it.'

'Obviously.'

'But we don't,' said Kitty. 'We ration the fun things, the nice things, we do the hard things and forget about the lovely things. Like you spend your time mooning after men who make you unhappy... rather than men who make you happy.'

'Are you saying we all self-sabotage?'

Kitty was nodding. 'A lot of the time, yes...'

'I have a biscuit addiction,' said Shazza. 'It's as though they are in charge of me. I can't resist them. I am in a very unhealthy relationship with them and am being coercively controlled by custard creams.'

'I can't eat another tuna and mayonnaise sandwich,' said Kitty.

'I want to enjoy food again. And nice men again...' Shazza put her feet up on the bench across from her. 'When I leave this virtual nunnery, I'm going to follow your advice.'

'It's not my advice,' said Kitty. 'It's Tom's. I met him and his mother in town earlier. We've been invited to Sunday lunch at theirs.'

'Lunch?' Shazza's eyes gleamed. 'As in proper, home-cooked food?'

'I think so.'

'Tell them yes,' said Shazza. 'My new plan to eat widely and well has begun.'

There was a long, shrill sound of a whistle outside which hurt their ears, followed by a booming 'COME ON!'

'Oh God, Tara...'

'We'd better go...'

Their first match. Kitty's stomach churned, thinking of the time she was whacked in the face but also how out of her comfort zone she was. Literally. Wearing shorts, being injured, the horrible hobbly football boots... she was decidedly uncomfortable in every way.

'All right?' said Shazza.

'Fun, you said?'

'Fun takes all forms. It's not all Waltzing Chairs and helter-skelters, you know? Fun can be anything you want. Now, come on, Messi...'

'Messy?' That was the last thing Kitty was.

'Beckham, then. Come on and let's have fun!'

19

The Shankill Killers didn't look as terrifying as Kitty had feared. They were a mixed team of five very un-killer-like individuals who were all teachers from the local primary school, most of them bespectacled and seemingly not the fittest of specimens.

The Sandycove Seafarers might actually win, thought Kitty, because they had Tara and Rory. And Tom was pretty fit, and surely they were all enough to make up for her and Shazza.

Once the match began, Kitty managed not to get brained by the football and she even kicked it a few times, but mainly she missed, her foot kicking the air immediately above the ball.

The Shankill Killers were not only deceptively good but they also lived up to their homicidal name. They skidded and slid around, heading balls, slicing through their opponents' legs, high-fiving each other and screaming obscenities.

The Sandycove Seafarers lost 5-1, the one goal was scored by Rory, who celebrated by pulling his top over his head and running around the pitch like a headless chicken.

In the end, Shazza and Kitty hobbled off the pitch, two

broken women, leaning on each other for support, like survivors of the American Civil War making their way home.

'You need to get in front of the ball,' said a voice. 'Think ahead. You're both reacting. Take charge...'

Kitty's father, Billy, was walking towards them.

'Hello, Billy,' said Shazza.

'Good evening, Shazza,' he said. 'Hello, love...'

'Hi, Dad...' The last thing Kitty needed was to be dad-splained to, not when her body ached, and although Billy meant well, Kitty wasn't sure if he had a right to dad-splain to her, not after all these years. It had been Catherine who had done all the parenting and all the minding. 'We've got to go and have a shower,' she said, pulling on Shazza's arm.

But Shazza, always deferential to other people's parents, turned around. 'We have to try to get better...'

'I can go through things with you,' he said. 'It's no bother...'

He had waited thirty years to show an interest in her, but it was too little, too late.

'We have Tara,' said Kitty, tugging again at Shazza. 'But thanks...'

He nodded. 'You know where I am...' He smiled at them. 'Just remember the ball wants to be told what to do...' he called over, as they walked away. 'You're its master...'

'Or mistress,' corrected Shazza over her shoulder as she and Kitty went up the steps of the changing room. 'But thanks again, Billy.'

They showered in cold water and when they came out, towels wrapped around them, turbans on their heads, Tara was sitting, her back against the wall, her legs up on the bench across the way, her eyes closed.

'Sorry about this evening,' said Kitty.

'We were rubbish,' added Shazza.

'As in truly awful...'

Tara still hadn't moved and Shazza and Kitty looked at each other, anxiously.

'We were woeful...' said Shazza.

'The worst,' agreed Kitty.

Tara's eyes didn't even flicker.

'We're sorry...' repeated Kitty.

'Like, really sorry,' said Shazza.

'WILL YOU STOP SAYING SORRY!' Tara suddenly bellowed. 'Jesus! I'm just trying to take a minute and you two rabbit on about how fecking terrible we were out there and don't you think I don't know? I was there too! I saw it with my own eyeballs...' She jabbed towards her eyes with her two fingers. 'I know we were woeful, but you two ninnies being sorry isn't going to change that.'

'No, Tara,' said Shazza, sheepishly.

'Absolutely, Tara,' said Kitty, looking down, managing to stop herself saying sorry again.

Tara sighed, leaning her head back, and staring at the ceiling. 'I've realised in life the worst quality to have is to be competitive. People think it's a great thing, to want to win, to be that person who is always pushing for success, for more and more... but it's an affliction I could well do without. I wish I was born without it, someone who doesn't care if we lose. Someone who doesn't particularly care if we win. Someone who just floats through life on an even current, not bothered about anything much except staying out of trouble.'

Shazza and Kitty stayed silent, listening, both feeling dreadful.

'It would make my life so much easier if I wasn't the one who wanted to win the family board games, who didn't storm out of the room when someone – my brother' – she gave a little snarl at the memory – 'was cheating. Or playing hockey in school and the other girls were only there because they got to get out of history but spent most of the time giggling together and making up dance routines at the side of the pitch. Or even at work...' She looked at Shazza and Kitty. 'I have my own cleaning company. Offices, homes, that kind of thing. And my standards are too high. I want things better than clean. And cleaner than any other cleaning company. I mean, I can't sleep at night, my heart's racing so much, thinking of how I could do things better... how I can win at everything. I can't ride a bike any longer because I kept seeing every cyclist in front of me as a potential competitor and I raced to catch them up. Same with cars. I scare myself sometimes.' She sighed again. 'So don't say sorry. You're normal, the two of you... It's me who's not.'

Shazza went and sat down beside her. 'That's the nicest thing anyone has ever said to me,' she said.

Tara jerked her head towards her. 'Which bit?'

'When you said I was normal. No one has ever said that to me before. All I've ever wanted was to be normal.'

Tara suddenly cracked a smile. 'Well, congratulations,' she said, laughing. 'You've won.'

Kitty went and sat beside Tara's feet, which were still up on the bench, her football boots still laced on. 'I wish we were more competitive...'

'You know,' said Tara, looking at her, 'it's nice sometimes... you know, when you're winning or in flow, when everything is coming together and you know you've worked hard and done all the training and you are just in the moment, all you have to do is bring it home... My God, you wouldn't change that feeling for anything in the world. There's no greater feeling than being in flow, as though the whole universe is behind you, you are doing exactly what you were put on this earth to do...' She sighed again. 'But you're always chasing that feeling. Always.'

'We couldn't have been less in flow,' said Shazza. 'It was like a blockage in the pipes, there was so little flow.'

Tara laughed. 'It's about learning to live with disappointment, the universe being against you...'

'Tell me about it,' said Shazza.

'Me too,' said Kitty.

'And maybe my ban on alcohol is unrealistic. I mean, it's not as though we are professionals. This is meant to be fun... isn't it?'

Shazza nodded enthusiastically. 'We hear you, Tara. We appreciate and love you. But yes, this is meant to be fun. And whether we have a drink or not will have very little bearing on whether we win or not.' She shrugged. 'Wish it were more simple.'

'So do I,' said Tara, defeated. 'Anyway, the lads are going for a pint. Shall we join them?'

Shazza and Kitty both nodded. Kitty had been out more in the last week since Dave had left than she had been in years. It was as though she had forgotten that there was a world out there, that people socialised in the evenings, that they went to see films and plays and drank exotic drinks and told jokes and laughed at funny stories and went home feeling full and happy.

'Last one to the bar, has to get the round in,' said Shazza.

Tara laughed. 'Why did you have to make it a competition?' she said, wriggling out of her clothes. 'Now I have to win!'

20

Shazza ushered Tara and Kitty off to find Tom and Rory, while she tried to catch the eye of Mick, the barman. 'You go outside,' said Shazza, 'and I'll buy the drinks. Tara? Water and a slice of lemon? Or is the lemon too much?'

Tara laughed. 'I'll have a Diet Coke,' she said. 'Go mad.'

'Can we twist your arm, Tara?' said Shazza. 'Just a small twist. A tweak of your arm?'

Tara made a face. 'Oh, go on then,' she said. 'Choose me something nice.'

Tom came up behind them. 'I'm buying,' he said. 'What does everyone want? Shazza? Kitty?'

'What are you two having?' said Shazza.

'Just Guinness,' said Tom. 'We're taking it easy. Well, I am anyway... shouldn't speak for Rory... but he's working at a food festival in his van. Wheely Delicious.'

'Ah-ha!' said Shazza. 'So he's one of those trendy food-truck people. It all makes sense. The tattoos. The beard. The ironic T-shirt.'

Tom took their drinks order. 'Go and sit down,' he said. 'Keep young Rory company. He's not good on his own. Likes an audience.'

'I know someone like him,' said Kitty, giving Shazza a wink.

The small courtyard was filled with plants in pots and bench seating around the small, round tables, the space glowing with candles and from the fairy lights strung along the stone walls. The air was full of that sound of Friday chatter, so different to the sound of people on other evenings. A weekend stretching ahead, everyone happier and lighter than on any other evening.

Except... weekends were long, thought Kitty, wishing she didn't have to go to bed alone or wake up alone. Although, sleeping without snorey Dave did have the benefit of not being pulled from REM by his somnambulant sounds. She looked at her phone. Still nothing from Dave, obviously too busy with his microwavable roast while watching *Countdown*.

They found Rory, and Kitty went on one side of him, and Shazza and Tara on the other.

'So you're one of those,' said Shazza to him, knowingly.

'One of what?'

'The food truckers. The trendy food brigade. I long for the old burger van, the kind that would give you E. coli or clean out your insides after one bite. Or the fish and chip vans which never changed the oil.'

Rory laughed again. 'I like to think we've evolved as a nation,' he said. 'I mean there's still a place for E. coli and chips, but not everyone wants food poisoning. I mean, who has the time these days?'

Shazza laughed. 'So what's on the menu, Mary Berry?'

Rory began telling them about his plans: falafel wraps, tofu burgers, bean chilli and chocolate doughnuts – and then Tom arrived with the tray of drinks and handed them out, before slipping in beside Kitty.

Strangely, she felt a little nervous. Was it because he made her forget all about Dave? Or was it because, when she did remember him, all she could think about were his flaws?

'Still on for Sunday lunch?' Tom said. 'My mum is insistent on you all coming.'

Kitty nodded. 'Sounds lovely... anything other than my awful cooking.' She laughed a little awkwardly. 'I mean, I'm not coming for the food. Well, I am. Coming for the food, I mean. But it's not the only reason...' Would he think she was coming for him? 'I am looking forward to so much about it. Everything, really.' And now it sounded as though she had zero life and was just so desperate and grateful to have received any invitation at all, as though she had little else going on in her life which, while technically true, was not quite the aura of louche, successful woman about town she wanted to convey.

Tom smiled. 'Did you enjoy the match?'

'It was awful,' said Kitty. 'I mean, I was terrible. You couldn't call what I did playing. It was more being terrorised by a ball.'

Tom laughed. 'Didn't you see that woman tackle Rory? Took him down and stuck her studs into his shin...'

'I missed that,' said Kitty.

Across the table, Rory, Shazza and Tara were laughing together.

'And then when it was a penalty, they walked forward with the ball... and the referee didn't notice because one of the others made a noise which made him turn around...'

'Missed that as well,' said Kitty.

Tom laughed. 'Oh yeah, I forgot, this is you just marking time until your boyfriend comes back.'

'No...' began Kitty, thinking that was it exactly. 'I'm just not overfamiliar with the rules of football...'

He nodded. 'So, this boyfriend...?'

'Dave.'

'Why's he worth waiting for?' asked Tom, frowning.

'Because she's a fool,' said Shazza, leaning forward. 'She's too loyal. She needs to learn that relationships are like a war and you have to be a ruthless general.'

'Are you a ruthless general?' asked Rory.

'No,' admitted Shazza with a sigh. 'I'm one of those privates who gets shot on the first day. I too need to learn how to be a ruthless general. Eisenhower. Monty. Motors. One of them.' She sat back and picked up her drink again.

'By the way,' said Tom to Kitty. 'I didn't know Billy O'Sullivan was your dad. He was legendary as a coach. All the kids loved him.'

'They did?'

'He used to play for Shelbourne...'

Kitty nodded. 'A long time ago...' She wasn't that clear on the history – all she did know for sure was that he was a player, but once he was injured he'd moved into coaching, first in Ireland and America and then home again. 'I don't know too much about it,' she admitted. 'He was injured quite badly. Ligament or something. He still walks with a little bit of a limp.'

'Did he ever bring you to any matches?'

Kitty nodded. 'A few... when I was younger. I was bored more than anything and so it all stopped.' She felt bad, suddenly, as though realising for the first time how little she knew of him.

'Maybe you've inherited his football skills and you haven't realised it yet?'

Kitty laughed. 'No, we've nothing in common. I'm like my mother completely...' For some reason, she started telling him about Annie and how her aunt was now expecting her to look after her in the same way as her mother did. As well as managing to extricate €800 from the two of them. 'I mean, I love her,' she said. 'And I will always do things for her, but it's like she wants us all running about after her.'

Tom seemed to understand. 'Her needs trump yours and your mother's?'

Kitty nodded. 'It wasn't as though I'd ever thought that Mum and I had needs before, we're both very practical, just get on with things... but Mum had a disappointment at work, and Annie didn't even care about it...'

Tom nodded. 'Some people are all about them.'

'It's just that she could have thought about Mum – not that Mum needs it, but it was the first time Annie could have asked how she was...' It seemed so trivial when she said it out loud. 'I love Annie,' she said. 'Obviously, I do.'

She was enjoying talking to Tom, the way he listened as though he was interested and wasn't looking for you to take a breath so he could insert himself into the conversation. Dave always seemed irritated when she spoke, waiting for her to stop so he could start talking again.

She looked up to see Shazza smiling at her. 'Okay?' she mouthed.

Kitty nodded. She was okay. In fact, she was more than okay.

Shazza held up her mojito. 'Here's to us...' she said, smiling.

'Here's to us,' echoed Kitty, smiling back.

'What are you two cheersing about?' asked Rory.

'Oh, nothing,' said Shazza. 'Just celebrating our celibate lives.'

Rory laughed. 'How can you deprive the male of the species like that? It's so cruel!'

Shazza smiled. 'It's my revenge,' she said. 'You're all going to have to live with it.'

Kitty laughed with them and, as she turned to Shazza, she realised something momentous had happened. She was having fun.

21

Instead of dreading the long weekend ahead, Kitty woke up on Saturday morning feeling almost happy. She walked to the village to buy bread from Sally-Anne's bakery, which she hadn't done for years because of Dave's gluten intolerance. She might as well make the most of his absence because he vetoed all wheat, claiming his intolerance was airborne. Kitty hadn't questioned it, but now, as she walked along Sea Road, she wondered quite how severe his intolerance was because once she'd caught him eating a mince pie and often found biscuit wrappers hidden down the side of the sofa.

The bread in Sally-Anne's smelled properly yeasty, fluffy and gluten-y. Kitty bought a loaf, along with butter and jam.

Her phone beeped. Dave? But... surprisingly, it was Tom. She found herself smiling.

TOM

If you are still trying to fill in time, do you want to come sailing? My friend, Fergal, is taking out his boat and needs a crew. Meeting at the Dún Laoghaire sailing club at 10.30 a.m. I'll ask Shazza as well.

Kitty couldn't think of a single reason not to go. She did try, valiantly, thinking of her cupboard under the stairs which needed decluttering, or there was the grout in her bathroom tiles which needed scrubbing, and the weekend newspaper she had been going home to read. But going sailing in Dublin Bay was as good as anything to fill in time, wasn't it?

KITTY

Great! See you then!

The exclamation marks made her sound too desperate, she thought, too eager and too grateful he had taken pity on her. She deleted her message.

KITTY

Sounds good. See you then.

TOM

Great! Bring your swimsuit. We always go for a swim.

Still no text from Dave. Kitty was having a life without him which was not part of the plan. She felt guilty, for some reason, as though she was cheating on their pact. Except it wasn't *their* pact. It was his. And, therefore, could it even be classed as cheating?

'Good morning!'

Kitty looked up to see Edith Waters, aunt of Tom and Rory, standing in front of her.

'Isn't it a beautiful summer morning?' Edith tended to bellow a little, one of those people who were living a life they loved and exuded contentment. 'I've been up with the larks today, saw the sunrise, went for a dip at the Forty Foot with my tribe... and now I feel magnificent!'

'You look magnificent,' agreed Kitty.

'It's good for the soul is sea swimming...' Edith tapped her chest. 'And for the heart... not just for health reasons, but to remind oneself of the important things in life. We need to be connected, do we not?'

Kitty found herself nodding. 'We do...' Being connected wasn't something she'd ever given much thought to. She had friends, she had colleagues, she had relatives, but she had never felt part of anything before.

Edith was still smiling. 'I hear you're enjoying the football team...'

'Yes, I am... I love it...' And she did, she realised, she really did. Somewhere along the way, from being thwacked in the face to that sense of camaraderie with her teammates, she had started having fun. And it wasn't about winning or even losing. It was about having a shared goal, a purpose, it was about winning and losing with other people. It was about connecting. It was why as a species we didn't all live separately or compete on our own. We liked being around each other, learning from others, and sharing ideas, ideals and goals. And she liked her teammates. All of them... including Tom. 'I'm not very good at it, though...' she admitted.

Edith peered at her again, in that way she did, which made her look as though she thought you were either dense or daft, or both. 'But that's not the point, is it? The point in life is not to be good, it's to be. Just that. Be.'

'Be?'

Edith was nodding. 'Just be. Be you. Be brave. Be big. Be

small. Just be. Live. Feel. Breathe. All of it. Be fun. Be serious. All of it. Whatever it is. Just be.'

Kitty thought she understood what Edith was saying. It was entirely the opposite of filling in time. It was about living and getting out there. It was about making each moment count. It was about meaning.

'I'm going sailing now,' she said, hoping to impress Edith with her be-ing-ness and that she wasn't just filling in time on this sunny, summer Saturday. 'With Tom...' God. It sounded like a date. 'I mean, others are going. Shazza obviously... and Tom's friends...'

'He's a wonderful young man.' Edith smiled. 'His mother is very proud of him. And Rory, of course. They've been through a great deal as a family and... well...' She stopped speaking for a moment. 'It hasn't been easy.'

Kitty nodded. 'Tom told me,' she said. 'I am so sorry for your loss. Losing your nephew...'

Edith pressed her lips together. 'Well, my job is to support Rosalind and the boys. But I try to work out what we are to learn from such a dreadful thing. There's not much to learn, it turns out, except that life can be unnecessarily cruel. To Paddy, more than anyone. But loss teaches you a great deal, does it not? When you have lost something you thought was there forever, whatever it is, but worst of all, a person, especially a person you loved deeply, someone you relied on to give your life meaning and shape... well, it takes a long time to reconfigure yourself.'

She looked straight at Kitty as if she knew what Kitty was thinking and what Kitty needed before even Kitty knew it. For a moment, Kitty thought she would just give her life over to Edith, take her advice on anything, and do whatever she told her to.

'I wish...' began Kitty. 'I wish you could tell me what to do... I need someone to tell me how to live. Because, of course, I want to be me... but I'm not sure how.'

Edith laughed. 'It doesn't work like that,' she said. 'What makes life interesting is knowing it's a puzzle that you have to work out on your own. Find your own path. There are signs everywhere – you just need to not ignore them.' She smiled at Kitty. 'That's the wonder of being alive, don't you think?' She glanced down at Kitty's bag, with the bread in it. 'That's my partner's bread. Sally-Anne. She's a wonderful baker... she bakes it with love.' She smiled again. 'Goodbye, Kitty. Enjoy your day on the high seas! Give my love to Tom. And remember, live fully, loudly and just be!' And off she went, full of wisdom, passion and contentment.

22

Kitty and Shazza made their way to Dún Laoghaire, just a few minutes' walk from Sandycove. The sea, after a long grey winter, seemed to dance and glitter, like the floor of a New York nightclub, shooting out laser beams of sunshine.

They stood in front of St Brendan's Yacht Club, a pillared building with huge oak doors and neat hanging baskets and the kind of brassware which was polished to such a high gleam that you had to look away in case of being blinded.

'I hope Tom's friends are not annoying yachty types,' said Shazza. 'My only goal today is to stay alive long enough to get to that yacht club bar this evening. I've heard it's all mahogany and gold and they have superior bar snacks, things like wasabi peas and, I don't know... smoky bacon crisps. Those are today's priorities. And if I may say so myself, they are not bad priorities to have. I live in the now... And now, I need to find a loo and adjust my bra because the wire is about to sever my left breast. And then we'll find these annoying yachty types and get going.'

Except, it turned out, none of them were annoying and the boat wasn't some big posh yacht, it was an old, varnished wooden vessel with a turquoise stripe and *Pansy-Pearl* painted on the hull. Even Shazza looked quite pleased when she saw the set-up and shook everyone's hands, telling them how nice the boat was.

Tom was in his cargo shorts and T-shirt, as was Fergal – tall, with floppy sandy hair, freckled arms, faded pink long shorts and a backwards baseball cap.

'We have no sailing skills whatsoever,' Shazza announced loftily, making Fergal laugh.

'That's grand. We're not in the Olympics...' he said, before introducing them to his girlfriend, Sadie, petite and tanned, bare feet and a tattoo of a four-leafed clover on her wrist.

'What's the plan?' asked Kitty. 'Where are we going today?'

'No plan,' said Sadie. 'Just see where the wind takes us. Probably make for Howth Head and see where we end up. Why? Is there somewhere you would like to go?'

Kitty shook her head. 'I was just wondering...'

'Kitty's the kind of person who doesn't like to just end up somewhere,' explained Shazza. 'She usually has it all mapped out and planned to within an inch of its life. Every time we go on holiday together, Kitty has an Excel spreadsheet with our days itemised to the minute. I always need a holiday when we come home.' She nudged Kitty to make sure she wasn't taking offence and then added, 'I wish I was more like Kitty, though. I went on a weekend away last summer with another friend and it was so chaotic, neither of us had done any reading up or any preparation. We missed every museum opening, ate in bad restaurants and couldn't find anything nice at all... it was a disaster. I remember on the flight home, feeling a bit depressed, wishing I'd gone with Kitty rather than him.'

Sadie was smiling. 'He sounds useless,' she said.

'Oh he was,' said Shazza. 'But that's the past. I live in the now... and the future.' She beamed at Sadie. 'We're very much looking forward to a drink this evening in the yacht club... the one with the gold and mahogany?'

'And the smoky bacon crisps.' Kitty nudged her.

'Oh, we never go there,' said Sadie. 'Too stuffy and boring. We always go to the secret bar...'

'The secret bar?' Shazza and Kitty looked at each other in excitement.

'All will be revealed later,' said Sadie, grinning back at them.

Tom held out his hand to help Shazza aboard, making her shriek when she almost lost her sandal in the water. 'Tom Sweetman,' she said, 'if I lose one of those flip-flops in the sea, then you're going in after it.'

Tom laughed, glancing at Kitty's feet. 'You should be wearing shoes like Kitty is... ones that stay on.'

Fergal divvied out the life jackets as Tom propelled the boat away from the jetty and leapt aboard. The boat lurched a little as the motor puttered into life, and *Pansy-Pearl* headed out of the harbour, between the two lighthouses towards the open sea.

Fergal stood behind the large steering wheel, staring at the horizon, as *Pansy-Pearl* puttered away from land. Kitty could see Sandycove, the small golden beach, and the small figures of walkers and swimmers far away. There was the coffee van she walked down to and there was the bench she drank it on. She was struck suddenly with the sense of freedom, that life was what you made it. If you stayed in all the time and waited for someone else to do things with, living by their clock and their rules, then you weren't living.

Tom was perched on a pile of coiled ropes, leaning back on his elbows, his face in the sun, his long brown legs stretched out. Shazza was lying on her back on the roof of the cabin, eyes closed, sunbathing as though on holiday, and Sadie was at the front, her face in the wind, eyes scanning the horizon. Kitty leaned against the side of the cabin, watching the wavy white caps, the roll of the sea, the sparkling iridescence... and felt, somehow, happy.

It was strange, she thought, when you created a vacuum, it got filled with something else. It was impossible to do nothing because something always happened. When Dave came back, she would have to talk to him all about this. Perhaps he was thinking the same thing, perhaps he too was experiencing the same revelations about life and would want to go out more.

Life was for living... and, Shazza was right, for bringing fun in where you could. She had imprisoned herself in her relationship with Dave. It hadn't been fun. It hadn't even been enjoyable. And worse, she'd chosen it. She'd wanted to be imprisoned. But she liked her new freedom, she thought. The world had suddenly opened up in front of her and she felt a shiver of excitement about what on earth would happen next.

The sea was a glittering, shimmering wash of abalone green as *Pansy-Pearl* gathered up the wind. Even Shazza seemed to be ready for action, as Fergal shouted out orders and Tom and Sadie untied ropes and winched them tightly. The sails flapped albatross-like, catching a tailwind until it began to soar.

Kitty had done sailing courses at school, where they kept falling off the small boats and into the sea, developing hypothermia and having to be dragged into the rescue RIB and submerged under silver foil. This was better than anything and she felt invincible, as though they could go anywhere in the world. They could go to Sydney and keep going. The idea was impossibly exciting.

Tom was beside her, gesturing to the winch. 'Tighten this as hard as you can,' he shouted into her ear before he tied another rope beside it. 'Watch your head!'

She ducked as the boom swung around and then there was a

moment, as the sail paused, and then whoosh, *Pansy-Pearl* was off again, this time heading in the opposite direction.

'We're tacking,' shouted Fergal. 'Heading towards Howth.'

Kitty nodded, still thrilled, and gave her winch another turn for good luck.

Howth was the long headland which swooped out to sea, encasing the city of Dublin within its reach. They zigzagged their way into open water and then past Howth Head and its lighthouse, staring up at the beautiful gardens belonging to the mansions which tumbled down towards the sea.

Kitty and Shazza sat together, smiling.

'The word is "glorious",' said Shazza. 'Not that I ever use that word and if you ever do hear me using it again, you have permission to drown me at sea.'

'Deal,' said Kitty, looking out at the waves, and feeling part of something bigger than she could ever have imagined.

They spent the rest of the day cruising around the islands off the coast of Dublin, where seals basked in the sunlight and shoals of fish shimmered in the shallower waters. They glided towards a small green-grassed island, the sea lapping where it met its rocky edges. Sadie and Tom were tying up the sails, a rumble from the engine beneath them, as Fergal manoeuvred the boat through the shallow waters.

'It's beautiful,' breathed Kitty, holding on to the side of the boat, staring down at the golden sand.

Beside her, Tom smiled. 'We've been coming here for years... first in Fergal's parents' boat and now in *Pansy-Pearl*. We camped on the island once, me and Fergal. We were seventeen or so... lit a fire, and slept in just our sleeping bags.' He looked over at Fergal, whose face was contorted with concentration. 'Fergal was convinced the island was haunted, weren't you, Fergs?'

'What's he saying about me?' said Fergal, still focused on

guiding the boat. 'Because whatever he's saying it's a lie. He was the scared one.'

Tom laughed. 'We both were,' he said. 'One of the most magical and terrifying nights of my life.'

He and Fergal grinned at each other for a moment before the engine was silenced and all Kitty could hear was the slapping of the sea against the hull and the sound of the seabirds as the anchor was dropped.

'Swim then lunch?'

Tom pulled off his T-shirt and shorts to reveal his swimming trunks. His chest was lean and brown, his legs were slender and long. He looked, Kitty thought, even better like this, especially the way his… but she realised that her look might be lingering too long, and she managed – with Herculean effort – to look away.

Fergal was tugging off his life jacket and T-shirt and before Tom had a chance to jump in, Fergal shouted, 'I'm in first!' He launched himself off the side of the boat and into the sea, closely followed by Tom, and then Sadie did the same.

Kitty and Shazza looked at each other.

'Are we meant to get in?' asked Kitty.

'I suppose we should…' Even Shazza looked perturbed. 'I mean, it's June, but what if it's freezing?'

'We're going to have to,' said Kitty. 'Remember, we have fun these days?'

'Me and my big mouth,' said Shazza. But after a quick change, the two of them held hands, teetering at the side of *Pansy-Pearl*.

'I'll count us in…' said Shazza, and then, 'One, two…'

Sadie, Fergal and Tom joined in with the counting, and then, 'THREEEEE!'

Shazza and Kitty threw themselves in, and for a moment Kitty felt as though she was flying, and then the cold black of the sea, and she thought she was dying… She surfaced, the salt on her lips, the wet of her hair, the ice of her body... and she felt incredible.

She and Shazza paddled in the water, grinning wildly at each other and laughing at the crazy fact that somehow the two of them were in the Irish Sea, miles from home. How quickly life could change.

'Oh my God,' said Shazza. 'How are we here? How is this happening?'

'I have no idea... you said to trust the universe and I am so glad we did!'

The five of them swam around, floating on their backs, taking turns to climb back onto *Pansy-Pearl* and launch themselves off.

'Shark!' shouted Fergal suddenly.

Kitty's blood ran cold, and she began to swim manically for the boat, heart beating, and then realised that no one else was swimming, they were all laughing.

'Sorry,' said Fergal, giving her an apologetic wave.

'He always does it,' said Sadie. 'He's an eejit.' He and Sadie clung to each other. 'You're my eejit though,' she said, kissing his cheek.

By mid-afternoon, they all clambered back onto the boat and dried off as best they could as Tom brought up a large cool box from the cabin and they sat in the sun, eating chicken salad sandwiches and sharing crisps.

'Anyone fancy a drink back in Dún Laoghaire?' said Fergal.

'We thought you'd never ask,' said Shazza.

Tired, windburned and happy, they zigzagged back to port and to land. Kitty needn't have worried about filing the weekend. Somehow, she had had one of the most wonderful days of her life.

23

'Do you think we're going to go to that secret pub?' said Shazza to Kitty, as they stood on the boardwalk, watching Sadie, Fergal and Tom tie up *Pansy-Pearl*.

'Where can it be?' said Kitty. 'Surely we know every pub around here...'

'A secret pub, though,' said Shazza, excited. 'Like a hidden, underground place, full of spies and smugglers...' She clutched Kitty's arm as Tom, Fergal and Sadie walked towards them.

'Ladies,' said Fergal, 'are you ready for a drink? Fancy a little sundowner?'

They both nodded.

Kitty felt a million miles away from her house, and her old life, as though she'd stepped into another world.

'Right, onwards,' said Tom. 'To The Grace O'Malley!'

They walked along the wooden boardwalk, and the old granite wall of the harbour, but instead of turning left to the yacht club, they turned right, to where the old fish factory used to be, on the end of the old pier. As far as Kitty knew, the place hadn't been used for years and years, and from the outside, it looked disused and dilapidated, but as they drew closer, they could hear the sound of music and voices.

The door was on the far end of the building and there was a shabby, green-painted metal riveted door, with the hand-daubed painted words 'The Grace O'Malley'.

'Ladies…' Fergal stood to one side as Sadie, Shazza and Kitty entered.

It was like nothing Kitty had ever seen before, the place didn't seem like a pub at all, but a party. There were the old counters which were now used as a bar, with Guinness and beer being served straight from the barrel. A man in denim shorts and a sleeveless T-shirt was pouring shots for a group, all of whom had the same sun-kissed glow Kitty and her new friends had. The place was lit only by hurricane lamps which were hung from rope from the ceiling. Over in one corner, there was a DJ, and people danced or talked, or sat in groups on plastic garden chairs or old park benches.

Shazza and Kitty looked at each other. 'How did we not know about this place?' asked Kitty.

'Because it's secret,' said Tom, smiling back at them. 'But you're in on it now.'

'You passed your initiation,' said Fergal.

'Right, what's everyone having?' Tom took their orders and while the rest of them found somewhere to sit, he disappeared to the bar.

They found an old-school PE bench and Fergal balanced himself on an orange buoy. 'Good for the core,' he said, wobbling around.

Somehow, they had bonded and felt like old and the very best of friends, as though they had known each other forever, as though the sea had cast a spell.

'We've fallen down the rabbit hole,' said Kitty to Tom, when he returned with a tray of cocktails.

He nodded, immediately understanding. 'Like *Alice In Wonderland*. It's exactly what it feels like. Enjoying yourself?'

She nodded. 'I love it...' The place was filthy and smelled of long-ago fish and the bench they were sitting on was dirty and probably had mould and woodworm and all sorts of lurking things, and back in the real world, away from The Grace O'Malley, Kitty would have been disgusted and demanded something to wipe it down, but for some reason it didn't matter. She smiled at Tom.

'Not a bad way of filling in time...' he said.

Kitty didn't mind him teasing her. She liked it. There was no edge to him, she realised. 'No, it's not a bad way... I could fill in my time very easily like today...'

'Well, then it would be called living,' he said.

Sadie and Fergal began dancing together and for a moment Kitty watched them, wishing Dave was the kind of man who danced with her, but she pushed the thought away as she didn't want to think about him and everything that was wrong with them, not after this glorious day.

'I like it here,' said Shazza. 'I'm going to come all the time...'

'But it doesn't happen all the time,' said Tom. 'It only happens when you want it to... when you need the secret pub, it appears.'

Shazza couldn't quite work out if he was joking or not. 'Well, I needed it.' She slightly drunkenly tugged the sleeve of his T-shirt. 'Thanks for inviting us,' she said.

'My pleasure... it was only to get Kitty out of the house...'

Kitty could tell from his body language that he was teasing her again.

'We don't want her going mad while her life is on hold.'

'God knows why she is waiting for him,' said Shazza. 'I'd have kicked him out years ago… you know what Kitty's problem is? She's too nice…' Shazza rested her head on Kitty's shoulder. 'It breaks my heart to see it because she deserves so much better…'

'Shazza…' began Kitty.

'And it breaks my heart to think of your brother,' Shazza carried on. 'When did he die?'

'Five years ago,' Tom said, looking at her steadily. 'He was everything I wished I could be. He had brains to burn and could charm the birds. Everyone loved him. He was my hero, you know? I looked up to him… and he looked after us. He was the best.'

'You poor things,' Shazza said. 'You and Rory… you must be devastated.'

Tom nodded. 'We are… we'll always be…'

'Sorry for making you talk about him…' said Shazza, teary-eyed. 'The world is so cruel…'

'Sometimes it is…' said Tom.

'It's full of good people like Paddy who die… and then people like Mr Unmentionable who lie…'

Tom nodded again. 'It's called humanity…'

'Yes, but it's not fair…' Shazza said. 'I'm sorry. I was having a nice evening and then I started thinking about everything again. The best thing is not to think…'

'But if you don't think, how will you learn? Thinking is part of the process… thinking means you are alive.'

Kitty looked at Tom, hoping he wasn't upset, but he seemed amused more than anything, and concerned for Shazza. She stood to buy another round and as she stood at the bar, waiting to give her order, Tom stepped in beside her.

'Thought you might need a hand,' he said, shouting over the music and the noise.

She nodded. 'Thank you…' They stood there, smiling at each

other, Kitty taking Tom in, and Tom taking her in, as though wanting to remember and recall exactly what the other looked like.

The barman began lining up the drinks on the counter behind her, and as they both reached for them, Tom's hand brushed Kitty's and then, somehow, he was holding her hand and she was holding his, his eyes momentarily on hers, and she felt as though she had landed at the bottom of the rabbit hole with a thump, everything slowed, the music deadened, just his eyes on hers. And then, they were carrying the drinks back, her following Tom through the bodies and the people, back to Fergal, Sadie and Shazza, and she could still feel his hand on hers. They all spent the rest of the evening talking and laughing, telling stories, filling each other in on who they were, what they wanted out of life, where they wanted to go, all the wisdom they had accrued so far... the usual wonderful intensities that only being young and a little inebriated can foster.

Finally, it felt as though they would have to surface and go home. Outside the bar, the five of them stood, swaying slightly, the sound of the music from The Grace O'Malley, the noise of the voices, the unreal feeling of being in the world but away from it, still lingering.

Fergal and Sadie hugged them goodbye. 'We're getting a taxi,' said Sadie. 'But come out with us another time?'

Shazza was nodding. 'I only sail on *Pansy-Pearl*,' she slurred. 'Nothing else will do. It's *Pansy-Pearl* for me!'

Shazza, Kitty and Tom walked back to Sandycove, talking as though they'd been friends forever.

'Don't tell Tara we were drinking,' said Shazza, as they stood outside her house. 'She'll go mad and blame our next loss on the alcohol...'

Tom laughed. 'Oh, I don't think our next loss can be blamed on alcohol…'

Kitty hugged Shazza goodbye.

'I totally and completely love you,' said Shazza. 'You know you deserve so much better than that eejit Dave… he's like… he's like…' She flailed around, her arms stretched out, and stumbled a little. 'He's like the biggest IDIOT IN THE VILLAGE!' Her voice echoed around the street. 'Did you hear me, SANDYCOVE?' She shouted again into the blackout world, lit only by stars and a sliver of a moon. 'DAVE IS THE BIGGEST IDIOT IN THIS AND EVERY VILLAGE IN THE WORLD!' She then toppled to the floor laughing. 'Oh my God,' she said, 'how I love my life… my lovely life with my best friend and how we have fun. Her too little, me too much and now just right!'

Curtains began to twitch, and a bedroom light in the house next door had been switched on. Kitty pulled her up with both hands.

'I'd better go to bed,' said Shazza, in a still too-loud voice. 'If I am to have a little less fun, then it's time for bed, is it not? Isn't that sensible and grown-up of me? Don't you think so, Tom? Amn't I sensible?'

'Very,' he said. 'Come on, where's your key?'

She handed it to him and he went through her small front garden, opened the front door, turned on the hall light, and stood to one side.

'Thank you, kind, sweet man,' said Shazza, hugging him. 'Kind Sweetman!' And she began to laugh. 'I love you two,' she said, standing at the door. 'You look very nice together, standing in the light of the moon. So long! Farewell! *Auf wiedersehen*!' She began blowing kisses.

When her door was closed, Kitty and Tom stood for a

moment looking at each other. Kitty knew she was smiling, her whole body fizzing with energy. Whatever they had drunk in the secret bar was sensational.

'You don't have to walk me home,' she said. 'I don't live too far.'

He was looking at her with the same kind of smile as she knew she had.

'But how will I know if you got home safely?' he said. 'I'd be worried.'

And she suddenly laughed at the sweetness of him, thinking how nice it was that someone cared and she didn't allow herself to think about Dave and how he'd never cared how or if she got home. There was a giddiness between her and Tom as though they were in the middle of some great adventure and it felt so natural to slip her arm through his as they made their way along Harbour Road towards Kitty's house.

'So... good day?' asked Tom.

'You have no idea,' said Kitty. 'I didn't even know it was possible to have days like this. It was...' She couldn't think of exactly the right word to sum it all up. 'It was magical.'

He laughed. 'It was,' he said. 'And on days like this, I remember to think how lucky I am to be alive, you know?'

Kitty was nodding. 'Absolutely. It's as though everything in the world is right... ordered, perfect and there is nothing you need to do to make it better. It just is.' They had arrived on Sea Road and her little house on the corner. 'Here's me...'

They stood for a second, looking at each other.

She assumed he was going to hug her, just as he had with Shazza, but he didn't. Instead, he gently kissed her cheek. 'I'll see you tomorrow, for Sunday lunch?'

She nodded. 'Thanks again, Tom...'

And he stood, lit by the street light, as she fumbled for her key and let herself into her door, realising that she'd had the best day of her life.

24

ANNIE

Hola! From Ibiza! Having a muy bien tiempo! Just in the airport, waiting for flight home! Ciao!

CATHERINE

Wonderful! Glad to hear it all went well!

ANNIE

Just having a cheeky Prosecco now… don't want to come home!

CATHERINE

I've just been in your house and put fresh milk in your fridge! See you soon xx

Shazza was already in the kitchen of Roz's house the following day when Kitty arrived for Sunday lunch, armed with a bottle of champagne and a box of posh chocolates. Shazza held a large glass of red wine in her hand and was sitting by the Stanley range. 'So, I said to him, Roz...' she was saying, just as Kitty entered the kitchen, as though she and Roz were best friends rather than only meeting that day, 'that no one was going to treat me like that ever again and it was about time I found my pride...'

'Quite right too,' said Roz.

'And so I have entered a virtual nunnery...' Shazza looked up and smiled when she saw Kitty. 'Roz and I are just getting acquainted.'

Roz moved towards Kitty, her arms wide. 'Hello,' she said. 'How lovely to see you again...' She kissed Kitty and then took the champagne and chocolates. 'This is too much,' she said, shaking her head. 'It's too gorgeous of you!'

Shazza stood up and hugged Kitty. 'How are you feeling?' she asked before turning to Roz. 'Your son is a bad influence... led us astray last night...'

Roz smiled. 'Now, if it was Rory, I might believe you, but Tom isn't the type...' There was a sound of someone coming through the back door. 'Ah, here he is now.'

Tom ducked his head under the low lintel and smiled when he saw Kitty. 'Sleep okay?'

She nodded. 'You?'

'Very well,' he said. 'Which I don't normally...' He glanced at his mother and she gave him a quick smile in return, as though sleep and the pursuit of sleep was a topic of conversation which they had regularly.

It was a large Victorian house, on the end of a terrace on Harbour Road, and it had a relaxed, lived-in feel, the edges softened by Virginia creeper outside, the paint on the door a little scuffed, the carpets worn, but it was warm and comfortable, the mantelpiece above the Aga had a collection of jugs and bowls and a photograph of three smiling boys, all sitting in a tree. There was Rory, the smallest, on the lowest branch. The biggest, with a huge smile on his freckled face, was Tom, and then in the middle, a tall teenager, handsome and blessed with youth, his whole life ahead of him, was Paddy.

'Well, isn't this nice,' Roz said, 'it's lovely to have young people around. When my boys were growing up there were always kids running in and out, playing football, asking for juice or snacks, or when they were teenagers, all in the den watching some film... do you remember, Tom?'

He nodded and then turned to Shazza and Kitty. 'Mum loves children...'

'And adults,' she said. 'Nice children always turn into nice adults...'

Rory and Tara arrived next and Tara shook Roz's hand. 'So kind of you to invite me,' she said, pleased. 'I don't normally get invited anywhere on a Sunday.'

'It's a pleasure,' said Roz. 'Lovely to meet Rory and Tom's new friends.'

'Is there anything I can do?' Tara went on. 'Peeling, chopping, table laying?'

Roz beamed at her. 'Nothing. Sit down and tell us all about football and how everything is going. My oldest son, Paddy, I'm sure the boys have told you, well, he was a great footballer. Always practising. Wanted to play for Manchester United...'

'City,' said Rory.

'Same thing,' said Roz.

'Paddy would be appalled,' said Rory. 'Thank goodness he's not here to hear it.'

Roz laughed, as Rory stood behind her and put his arms around her shoulders.

'He wouldn't be impressed at all.'

She shook her head. 'I know,' she said, as Rory released her and sat on the edge of one of the old wooden kitchen chairs. 'Paddy took football very seriously.'

'As these lads don't,' said Tara. 'I think they think they are there to have fun. They are leading the two girls astray... or maybe it's the other way round?' She turned to Kitty and Shazza. 'Isn't that right?'

'It's them leading us astray, definitely,' said Shazza. 'All we want to do is play football, isn't that right, Kitty?'

Kitty laughed. 'Absolutely.'

'And I have no idea why I have a raging hangover, or nausea or incredible tiredness. And a bruised arse. What happened? It's like I fell over or something! But this wine, Roz, is helping magnificently.'

'Good to know, Shazza,' said Roz. 'You help yourself to more and, Tom, make sure Tara has a glass as well.'

'Have you started without me?' said a voice and Kitty turned to see Edith coming through the back door. 'Hope you have opened the Côtes du Rhône I gave you last time?' She stood for a moment, taking everyone in. 'Ah! It's the five-a-siders! How lovely... Oh, Tara... she's Sally-Anne's god-daughter, did you know, Rosamund? She's always running or kicking something... and Shazza, from the Newsletter, and Kitty, who was volunteered rather than volunteering... and how was the bread from yesterday? Good, yes?' She held Kitty's hand, beaming at her. 'It makes marvellous sandwiches...' went on Edith. 'My favourite is a ham and Dijon, with some cornichons, and my secret ingredient, Cashel Blue. Divine.'

They all sat around the table, Kitty in between Rory and Edith. There was roast chicken and roast potatoes, stuffing, carrots, gravy, apple crumble and ice cream for dessert.

There was a tap of a wine glass as Roz stood up. 'Just a quick toast to absent loved ones... if anyone here has lost anyone, then now is our chance to remember them... they are here in spirit at least... to loved ones!'

'To loved ones...' everyone echoed.

'Your father was a footballer, was he not?' said Edith, turning to Kitty.

'I think so,' said Kitty, eating her apple crumble which was still warm and spiced with cinnamon.

'A very talented player, I hear,' said Edith.

'Was he?'

'Yes,' Edith went on. 'I was talking to the chairperson of the Sandycove Seafarers and she was saying that she remembers him scoring a winning goal. It was the last time our club made it into the Dublin final thingamajigs. Or whatever they were called. Anyway, it was a big moment. And then, sadly, he was injured.'

'I don't know much about it...' admitted Kitty.

'Don't you? Perhaps he doesn't like to talk about it?'

'Perhaps,' said Kitty, but she was thinking she hadn't let him talk about it and perhaps she should have listened more, and been more forgiving about his faults. She had enough of her own.

* * *

After they'd eaten, Kitty was drying the dishes, handing them to Tom, who was then putting them back into the cupboard.

'My mother is a little obsessed with trying to create a happy home,' he said. 'I hope you don't mind being forced to hang out with us.'

'I loved it,' she said. 'Your mother is lovely.'

'She's always been used to cooking vast quantities,' said Tom. 'Three boys, we all ate a lot... and I think it's nice for her to have people around. So thank you.'

'Any time...'

'Is that a promise?'

Perhaps it was the way he looked at her for a moment, but Kitty felt herself blushing for some reason.

'I've been meaning to say that your dad was Paddy's coach,' went on Tom. 'Paddy loved football... that's why Rory and I joined the five-a-side, trying to carry on something for him. We're not good at it, not like Paddy was. He was brilliant. He spent his whole childhood with a ball in his hand. At dinner, it would be on the chair beside him, he would sleep with it. He wouldn't walk to school, but he would dribble a ball the whole way.' He rolled his eyes. 'We'd all get so annoyed with him. Would you ever put that ball down? But what I'd give to hear him kicking it against the back wall, over and over...' He gave a small laugh. 'Sorry to go on... but it was just that I wanted to tell you how good your dad was to Paddy. We lost our dad when we were really young and football was always a real solace to Paddy and later, when he was struggling with his mental health, as long as he was down here, on the pitch, he was okay... football kept him going longer than if he hadn't had it.'

Kitty nodded. 'That's good to know...' She felt something akin to pride, thinking of her dad. She'd never been proud of him before, she realised, and it was nice to know that he'd been a source of good in someone's life.

'And your dad was always so nice to Paddy, even when he was finding it hard to play. A couple of times when he couldn't get out of bed, your dad came and talked to him... I think he'd been through a few dark days himself...' He was looking at Kitty, his head slightly on one side. He pressed his lips together. 'Anyway, enough about all that, I just wanted to say he was so good to Paddy.'

Kitty nodded, a little overwhelmed to speak for a moment. It was so wonderful to know how instrumental Billy had been in someone's life, to have cared for Paddy, to have been good to him made her feel proud of Billy, a pride she had never allowed herself to feel before.

'I'm so glad,' she managed. 'I'm so pleased...' She felt a lump in her throat. Life, she thought, only had meaning if you were surrounded by the right people and she was sure, for the first time in her life, that she had exactly that.

Later, Kitty and Shazza said their goodbyes and walked back to the village together. The days were becoming longer, there was warmth in the air, the trees a shimmer of green leaves. There was a lightness and freshness to the world. Fun was something you had to make yourself, Kitty thought. You didn't just wait for it to happen to you, you actively had to hunt it down or seek it out or magic it up. And when you realised that, fun and adventure and all those wonderful things that you find in the cracks and crevasses of life, in all the spaces beside the building blocks of just staying alive and sane, there was fun to be had. Kitty could almost feel herself lifting skyward, as though being tied to a bunch of helium balloons.

25

In the office, on Monday morning, Hughie was at his desk, reeking of his aftershave, working away.

'Hello, early bird,' said Kitty, slipping off her jacket. 'You smell good. Hugo Boss again?'

'It's a Paco Rabanne kind of day,' he said. 'Musk, sandalwood and a soupçon of ennui. Only joking,' he said, as Kitty giggled. 'Couldn't be better. I've finished the nut bar campaign, and done some mock-ups for the posters for Welcome Ireland. I've used your copy, I have photographs of some of the great sights of Ireland. I've put the camper van on top of Mount Brandon, it's doing a wheelie around the Giant's Causeway, and there it is again parking up at the Barack Obama Plaza to go and buy a burger and chips.'

Kitty laughed. 'I think the last one can be left out... but...' She came and stood behind him, looking over his shoulder at his two computer screens.

They both gazed at the screens, neither saying a word, trying to take it in and imagine it as double-page spreads in magazines or on billboards in Boston.

'What do you think? Happy?'

They looked good. Great colours, nice design, lovely idea of the little camper van heading around the country. 'Follow me!' it said, and there was a QR code which would take you to a map of the van's journey.

'It's cute,' said Kitty.

'Isn't it?'

'Sweet,' she said.

'It really is.' Hughie nodded.

'Fun,' she said.

'Yes, very fun...'

'I like it...'

'So do I.'

'But I don't love it.'

He shook his head. 'No... neither do I... there's someth—'

'Don't say it.'

'Okay then.' He clamped his lips shut.

'But you're right,' said Kitty.

Hughie, with his lips tightly shut, made some unintelligible noises.

'You can speak,' she said.

'Something is missing,' he said.

'I know.'

They looked again at the screens, taking it all in. Kitty wished there wasn't something missing, but there was. But they'd made it fun. Wasn't that enough? But the something missing was a vacuum, this big hole of nothingness which gaped emptily at them. But to fill it with what? But before Kitty could come dwell on it for long, her phone vibrated with a text from Billy.

DAD

Fancy a kickaround?

Kitty stared at the phone for a moment. He'd always been slightly mysterious to her and Catherine, as though he worked on an entirely different clock and to very different principles. She had sometimes wondered how on earth she shared the same DNA... but perhaps it was time to learn something about him. And also ask him about the effect his injury had on him. And the glow of pride she'd felt the previous day lingered.

KITTY

Why not? 7pm? At the Ground?

DAD

Great. See you then.

Kitty spent the rest of the day starting to develop their Welcome Ireland ideas. She began by writing a story, which was how she always began. Get the people in place, their backgrounds, what they want and need, and then find out what to do with them. She had something, but over the next week, she was confident she would have more. And with Hughie and Alex working on their elements, they could have a pretty good campaign.

She looked up from her desk.

'I know that smile,' said Hughie, grinning at her. 'It's the look of someone who has got a good idea.'

'Really?' said Kitty. 'You can tell that from my face?'

He nodded. 'Well, either that or Dave came home. Something is making you look brighter.'

He was right, she did feel brighter and lighter. 'It's not Dave,' she said. 'He's still at his mam's.'

'Well, then? What or who is it?'

Alex and Mary Rose were both looking across at her.

'If I have anything to tell, Hughie,' she said, 'you'll be the first to know. But I was sailing on Saturday and got windburned.'

'It suits you,' said Alex. 'You look like you are glowing from the inside.'

Kitty felt as though she was glowing from the inside, she could feel it, as though the soft embers were beginning to catch fire again. Her desk was messy, pens everywhere, two half-drunk coffee cups, her orchid looking a little droopy, there were crumbs from her lunchtime sandwich. Before, this sight would have been horrifying, but for some reason, it didn't disturb her. She gave the orchid a quick drink from her water bottle and brushed some of the crumbs off, but it was a desk, it didn't matter. And she couldn't remember the last time she had cleaned out the inside of her handbag, or dropped anything off at the charity shop, or even brushed Romeo's fur in a futile bid to keep the house hair-free. She'd been obsessed with order, she realised. And now it didn't really matter.

* * *

Later, after work, Kitty walked down to the Seafarers' ground, where Billy was waiting for her. Even that was a surprise. He was never on time, but he was obviously making an effort and she even found herself feeling slightly nervous. It was easy to dismiss someone and refuse to let them in, but to open up took more bravery than she had thought.

'Hi, Dad...'

He looked up, his face smiling. 'Kitty!'

They observed each other for a moment. He was dressed in an old blue tracksuit, one she'd seen him wear a hundred times. His hair was grey and long on the top and slightly receding at the temple. He had a thin face and a long nose and when he smiled, his whole face lit up, his eyes crinkling. He would have been quite charismatic back in the day, she thought. But there was something about him that she hadn't noticed before, a quiet sadness, a reserve.

He held open his arms. 'Come and give me a hug,' he said. 'How are you? Work okay? Your mother doing well? How is that Dave of yours?'

'All fine,' she said, allowing him to briefly envelop her and kiss the top of her head.

Behind Billy was a net of footballs. He picked one up. 'Shall we begin? Well, what's this?'

'A football...'

He shook his head. 'No... well, yes, obviously it's a football... but it's more than that... so much more... it's energy... it's a representation of the earth's energy, that's what it is. When you are playing a game of football, do you think you are just kicking a ball around?'

Kitty nodded. 'I thought that's exactly what it is...'

He shook his head. 'That's what it isn't. What is the aim of a game of football?'

Kitty was sure she knew the answer. 'To score goals. To win?'

He shook his head again. 'It's to find the flow, to find the flow of energy that exists between you and your band of brothers or sisters, to work together, to harness all the energy in the air, to pass it between you, to be so in the flow that you hardly remember you are playing. You have to submit entirely to the game, to the team, to your other players, to be so focused on the ball and the fact that you are a speck in the universe, to know your place, to be humbled, to be fortunate enough to exist on this beautiful planet... and you honour it.'

Kitty was deeply sceptical. 'Are you sure it's not just to kick the ball into the net?'

'The goals will follow,' he assured her, spinning a ball on his right index finger and then catching it again. 'Just find your flow.'

'How do I do that?'

'Catch the ball...' he said. 'And see it for what it is... energy.' He tossed it to Kitty and miraculously she caught it. 'When I threw it, I drew on reserves of energy, it created even more as it flew, and then you accepted all that energy when you caught it and created even more... and on it goes. Stay in the moment, focus on the ball, on the blades of grass, on the sounds of your boots in the turf, your breathing... stay low, remain small... you're a speck in the universe, remember. Be humble.'

He's more eccentric than I could have imagined, Kitty thought. But she nodded, as though she understood. But, also, he seemed more in control of things than she'd ever witnessed. It was as though, here on this pitch, on this field of green, he belonged, and it was the rest of the world, with its clocks and times and rules, that couldn't conform. He was all about flow.

She dropped the ball to the ground.

'Look at it,' he said, 'focus. See where it is and what it represents... what does it represent?'

'Energy...' she said.

'Molecules, atoms... things we don't understand. Life force. Now, see it, feel it and pass it to me...'

Kitty went to pick it up.

'No, with your foot... see its path through the world before you make contact. And then kick it... gently...'

He had moved to around thirty yards away, and Kitty imagined what she wanted it to do and then pulled her right leg back and swung it towards the ball. It spun, like the earth in motion, whizzing around, and she could have sworn she saw the kinetic energy she had helped create. It lifted in a smooth parabola and then landed just in front of the right foot of her father.

He was smiling. 'Not bad,' he said. 'Not bad at all. You just might have inherited some of your old dad's ball skills.'

Kitty couldn't help smiling back.

They spent the next hour kicking the ball to each other, and Billy showed her how to create even more energy by tapping it and giving it a sharp spin at the same time. Kitty watched, delighted, as the ball curved away from her and then back in towards Billy.

It was dark by the time they finished, and with no floodlights the pitch was black and the stands were emptily eerie.

'Time to call it a night?' said Billy.

She nodded, wondering what would happen next. Would they just say goodbye or would he want to spend more time with her? She hoped it was the latter, but she hated feeling so vulnerable. What if he just wanted to get away from her? All her life, she'd tried to protect herself from needing him, and she thought she'd succeeded.

'What about a hot chocolate?' he said. 'I'll bring you to a little late-night café on the other side of Sandycove.'

Kitty found herself nodding, not ready to say goodnight to him. 'I'd love to,' she said.

26

The old café hadn't changed since the last time they'd been there, more than twenty years ago now. It was a small, slightly run-down place, far removed from the trendier village cafés, with Formica tables and chairs which scraped across the floor. Now, at this time of the night, there was Ella Fitzgerald on the speakers, candles on each table. A couple were playing an intense-looking game of Connect 4 in the corner, there was a woman on her own, reading a novel and eating a bowl of ice cream, and on the wall were old Sandyfest posters.

'It's been a while since we were here,' Billy said.

'I used to love it.'

'Well, now we've renewed our acquaintanceship, we should keep up the visits. What do you think?'

Kitty nodded. 'That would be nice.' And for a moment they book looked at each other as if thinking about all the time they'd missed. *It was both our faults*, thought Kitty. *We were both to blame.*

They talked of her work, and she told him about the Welcome Ireland campaign, and how it wasn't quite there yet, but she was waiting for inspiration. And he talked about his job as the caretaker at the local national school and how he had bought some monkfish the other day. 'I was amazed how good it tasted,' he said, and then, 'so tell me about this fella of yours. Dave. What's he playing at?'

And she told him about Dave needing a break, about how much pressure he'd been under and how we all needed some time away from everyday life. Billy listened, taking it all in.

'You deserve better,' he said, when Kitty eventually stopped for breath. 'Far better. You need to value yourself more. Think what you want... I always like to think that life is a game of football. Surround yourself by the right team, people are working with you, who are *literally* on your side...' He smiled. 'And then play for your life. And it's not actually about winning... because that's nice... but it's not what life is all about. Life is about having a goal and if you miss... that's okay because you've learned something. And you try again next time... there's always another goal. But most importantly, build the right team. You live or die by your team.' He smiled again at Kitty.

'I think I'm getting better at that,' she said.

The looked at each for a moment. 'I could have been a better father,' he said. 'I didn't understand the importance of teams... *off* the pitch. I was too busy playing my own game and I'm sorry.'

'That's okay,' said Kitty. And it was. It didn't matter. We were all trying our best, thought Kitty. All of us tried hard and made our own way and attempted to learn those constant lessons that life keeps teaching you. 'Why did you stop playing football?'

For a moment, he said nothing, and then, 'I was injured which is all part of the deal. You play every match knowing it could be over in an instant. And there was nothing special about me, it was going to be me as much as it could have been another lad.' He played with his teaspoon, running it around the rim of his mug. 'Took me a few years to get that philosophical, I can tell you.'

Kitty nodded, hoping he'd say more.

'Football was all I was ever good at,' he continued. 'It was like a language I was born speaking. Fluent I was. Talking with my feet and a ball, I could create poetry, I really could. And for all my life, from the age of three or four, people would stop to look at me when I had a ball in front of me. They would watch as I ran past them, the ball wherever I wanted it to be, like a trained dog or something, you know? It was years later that I realised about all the flow and the energy. You're lucky. You took the shortcut. I told you all my secrets.'

Kitty smiled at him as she was filled with a warm glow of the intimacy and closeness she had craved.

'Couldn't do school, couldn't spell or write and think... everything jumbled up all the time... but what I could do was play. And that got me respect. Loads of it. Even my teachers, the ones tearing their hair out at me in the classroom, would nod and say "Good game" or "You played well out there today". I remember being at Mass one day with my mam – your grandmother – and the priest, the old dope, was going on and on about gifts from God and how we all have a talent, we are blessed. And there was me going, this is it, this is a blessing from God. Other people can spell or do mathematics and all that craic, but I can play football, you know? And I tell you something, I used to think how lucky I was, that out of all the blessings in the world, I got football!' He shook his head, smiling, remembering. 'The best blessing in the world. All the boys envied me. The girls loved me. And I was going places. Sandycove Seafarers, Dundalk United, Shamrock Rovers, and then, when I was twenty, I was sent over for a trial with Liverpool.' He smiled again. 'I mean, would you ever believe it? Liverpool! And off I trotted. On the ferry, bag over my shoulder and played my heart out, was in the flow, all that... I was a week there and they were making all the right noises about the lad from Dublin, and on the last day, the Friday, I was tackled by this fella from Newcastle. Huge he was. He slid into my calves, but I heard a crack, it echoed around Anfield. I swear, you would have heard it back in Dublin. My ankle. A lateral ligament injury, to be exact. And I stayed there, in the mud. The pitches were muddy in those days. Not like the green carpets they have now. And I sat there and I knew that was it. I was blessed no more...' He stopped and gave a little shrug. 'Long time ago, long, long time ago... but it still hurts, you know? I realise that we never leave who we are behind, you take every part of you along to the next stage, you just keep on gathering memories, experiences and... well, tragedies along the way.'

'I'm so sorry,' said Kitty, finally getting an understanding of her father that had been missing her whole life.

He shrugged again. 'For years, I thought that the injury stopped me from playing premier division,' he went on, 'that it stopped an international career in its tracks. I was angry and resentful. Foolish. Immature, I know now. But I blamed the world. But I probably wouldn't have made it. I was good. But not that good. And if Liverpool were thinking of taking me, it wasn't for the first team, it would have been just a sub's sub, a reserve's reserve... probably wouldn't have seen a match ever, just there to assist with training matches. But I think it took a long time for me to pull myself together, you know? I wasn't a good husband to your mam, or a good dad to you... and I'm sorry.'

'It's okay...' Kitty placed her hand on top of his, wishing it was easy to tell him that she loved him. Because she did love him, she always had. It was just complicated. Love wasn't easy.

Billy patted her hand back and gave her a nod. 'All right, love?'

She nodded back. 'Shall we make a move?'

They began walking home.

'When's your next match?' he said.

'Friday...'

'What about another training session next week?'

'I'd love to,' she said, smiling. 'And I'll buy the hot chocolates.'

At Kitty's house, he put out his arms and she allowed him to wrap them around her again, breathing in his smell of washing powder and soap, an aroma that would be forever him.

'Whatever you do,' he said, 'do it with your heart and soul until you can't do it any longer... that's what makes me feel proud. Knowing you gave it everything. If you do something with heart and soul, it doesn't matter if you don't have it forever, you have had it enough. No point having something forever that you don't believe in. See you next week?'

27

The following morning, Mary Rose brought in treats for their brainstorming meeting. 'Flapjacks,' she said. 'They're the only thing I can make because I made them once in Girl Guides as a baking badge and I've never evolved any further.'

Even Alex stood up to take one, nibbling at the edge of it, like a hamster. 'Not bad,' she said, 'although I shouldn't. Flapjacks are deceptive. They lure you in with their innocently healthy demeanour and then deliver enough calories to keep you going through a particularly cold winter.'

'Calorie-free,' said Hughie, who was already on his third. 'That's what I like about working in offices, all the free food. I have to keep my strength up,' he went on, 'or I'll fade away.'

'When Sylvester and Sandra first told me that they were running off together, I couldn't eat anything but flapjacks. They are most soothing.'

'Next time you meet someone,' said Hughie. 'Make sure he deserves you.' He paused. 'And he's not called Sylvester. I knew a Tarquin once.' He shuddered. 'Lived up to his name.' Hughie turned to Kitty. 'You too, Kitty. This Dave sounds like a right tool.

God... why do the best women give the time of day to the worst men? What about you, Alex? I hope you have someone who deserves you?'

Alex shook her head. 'I don't... but I'm not one of the best of women...'

'Ah, will you stop,' said Mary Rose. 'We're all great. Hughie's right. We all deserve better than Sylvester. And Dave and John-Paul... we all deserve so much better. Maybe one day, we'll start to realise it.'

'I'll believe it when I see it,' said Hughie.

'Now, where are we at with the Welcome Ireland campaign?' asked Mary Rose, looking hopeful. 'Kitty, Alex? Updates?'

'I have finished my copy for the camper-van story,' said Kitty. 'It's okay. Needs some work. I can't help thinking that it feels a little cliché...'

She looked over at Alex, waiting for her to speak.

Alex held up her hands in a kind of surrender. 'Don't look at me,' she said. 'I know I am chief whatever copywriter thing. I just... I just...' She faltered and stopped. 'To be honest, I have feck all. It's like my brain is empty. Nothing is coming...' She looked almost tearful. 'I don't know what's wrong with me. It's like I have some kind of creative block. It's horrible. Ideas used to come to me so easily. And now there's nothing in there.' Her voice cracked, but she kept her body tightly packed, her arms crossed at her chest, her shoulders clenched, as though protecting herself from attack, and then she picked up her another flapjack and crammed it into her mouth.

'You need a retreat,' said Hughie. 'Worked for my pal Anthony. He's a writer. Got the old block. Went to this camping retreat in Connemara, slept under the stars, and woke up with a sheep's behind in his face, his sleeping bag drenched from what was hopefully merely rain... but, crucially, he had an idea for a short story about a man who runs away from the rat race and then gets savaged by some terrifying scraggly ruminant. He won the Hennessy the following year.'

'Thanks for the suggestion, Hughie,' said Alex. 'But I'm allergic to the outdoors.'

'Just a suggestion,' said Hughie, laughing. 'Trying to be useful, that's all. Some people don't like to be helped. They are allergic to that as well.'

'Burnout,' said Mary Rose. 'It happens to us all. Usually after a period of overwork or trauma. I've been through it myself. But Hughie isn't wrong. His cure might not suit everyone or indeed anyone, but time off or time away is always a good idea...'

Alex had begun to cry. 'Don't be nice to me,' she said. 'You wouldn't be nice to me if you knew what was going on. Just don't...'

But Mary Rose had her arm around her, shushing and hushing.

'I'm going to lose us the Welcome Ireland pitch,' Alex sobbed. 'Which will probably mean you won't get your probation and you'll have to leave Mulligan O'Leary. And anyway, I am going to have to leave... but I can't think of a thing...'

'You need to go home and rest,' said Mary Rose. 'Take a break. Nice bath. Watch some inconsequential telly. That daytime show with Cat Jones... she's lovely. Fashion, food and all that.' She smiled at Alex. 'And don't worry about my probation. Life, I've discovered, is rarely what you plan. I expect the unexpected these days. You just mind yourself. Okay?'

Alex shook her head. 'No, I'm fine,' she said firmly. 'I'll be grand. I'll just go and get some fresh air and I'll be right back.'

Mary Rose, Kitty and Hughie all looked at each other in surprise. Since when did Alex become so emotional? What on earth was triggering it all?

28

That evening, as she stood at the side of the pitch for their Tuesday evening training session with the Sandycove Seafarers, Kitty tried to explain the concept of flow and energy to a distinctly unimpressed Shazza.

'I think you are unnecessarily complicating what is a simple interaction between foot and ball,' Shazza said. 'Hence the name. The game isn't called kinetic-flow-spin or whatever you said, is it?'

'No... but...'

'But something tells me that you're beginning to enjoy yourself, am I wrong?' teased Shazza. 'The woman who never went out, now never stays in.'

Kitty didn't like to admit it, but life seemed so much bigger than it used to be. Time stretched away from her, enticingly. Minutes and hours that before were to be endured now were full of possibility. You never knew what was around the corner and it was the very possibility of life which was exciting. Kitty was beginning to enjoy these time-filling activities, and yes, if Dave did come home, she might even keep one or two of them going. She liked her new life... and new friends.

'There are the lads,' said Shazza, giving Rory and Tom a wave. 'How's it going?'

'Grand,' said Rory, giving Shazza's hair a pull, making her twist away and flicking him back.

Tom gave Kitty one of his handsome smiles. Getting to know Rory and Tom was possibly the nicest part of this new life she was leading. They were both so nice and it was as though they'd all known each other for years. She smiled back at him. If nothing else, she thought, she'd made an amazing new friend, and when Dave came back, perhaps they would all be friends. Maybe Dave would be sociable again, and they could all continue going to The Island or perhaps on *Pansy-Pearl*. Except Dave once felt seasick while they were watching a documentary about killer sharks.

'I hope Tara is in a good mood tonight...' Tom was saying.

'And not her angry, sadistic one,' said Rory. 'I'm exhausted and not in the zone for star jumps or running around too much... I've been working too hard.'

'Rory,' said Shazza, 'you serve food from the comfort of a van... it's hardly working too hard. Try nursing or coal mining. Or... journalism!'

Rory laughed. 'You try peeling potatoes for 500 drunken festival-goers who are in desperate need of soakage...'

But Rory's premonition about Tara came true and she turned up in a bad mood, her killer instinct back with a vengeance, and made them run the length of the pitch over and over until Shazza and Kitty collapsed on the sidelines.

'I think...' gasped Shazza, lifting her head, '...I am having a heart attack... quick...' She fell back to the ground, 'send...' She mumbled something inaudible.

'What was that, Shazza?' asked Rory.

'Send the alcohol,' managed Shazza. 'Send the St Bernard dog with the brandy.'

Rory laughed so hard, he too collapsed to the ground, and lay on his back, kicking his feet, while Tara stood over them, stony-faced.

'Right, you lot,' she said, 'twenty push-ups, and then we will practise our passing and then on to shooting...'

Kitty tried to remember everything she had learned the previous evening. Focusing on the blades of grass, thinking of the ball as being part of her, giving the ball spin with a flick of her toes. 'Here!' Shazza kicked the ball towards her and Kitty stared as it came to a standstill at her foot, and then she had an idea that she needed to send it across to Rory, and after a glance at his position, she thwacked the ball with the side of her foot, watching as the ball swooped towards him.

'Nice one!' he called over.

Had she just kicked a ball successfully? Was she playing football? For a few brief moments, she had been concentrating so hard that she had forgotten where she was, almost as though she had glimpsed that usually elusive 'flow'.

* * *

Finally, practice over, they all made their way back to the changing rooms.

'So, what do you think, Tara?' asked Shazza eagerly. 'Are we improving?'

Tara contemplated them. 'The bad news is I'm resigned to you never actually improving very much,' she said.

Shazza looked crushed. 'What's the good news?'

'The good news is that you didn't get any worse.' Tara smiled.

'It's an improvement,' she said. 'Of sorts. Miniscule. Tiny. Infinitesimally small. But an improvement nonetheless, especially you, Kitty. What have you been doing? Taking a magic pill?'

'Something like that,' said Kitty, smiling back.

29

Kitty and Alex spent the whole of Wednesday afternoon going through ideas for Welcome Ireland and throwing most of them out again.

'Why is it all we can think up are clichés?' Alex asked. 'What is wrong with us? I think that man cursed us. It's like we'll never be able to come up with anything original again.'

Kitty tried to stay calmer. 'It'll be grand,' she soothed. 'We'll come up with something.'

But Alex looked at her as though she'd been microdosing. 'How can you be so sure? We can't pitch to Welcome Ireland, in front of those other companies, and deliver only clichés?'

But they might have to, thought Kitty. Either that or pull out.

And then, beside her, there was a sound like a sob.

It was Alex. Tears were rolling down her face, as she leaned down to her bag, digging around for a tissue.

'Alex?' Kitty whispered so no one else would hear, although Hughie still had his headphones on, and Mary Rose was yet to return from her meeting. Alex looked up, her eyes red. 'What's wrong?'

Alex nodded. 'Nothing...' She tried to smile. 'Just... tired.'

Kitty wheeled over to Alex's desk. She had never seen Alex show this kind of emotion before. 'Are you still upset about that man saying something was missing?'

'Of course not! Jesus! That eejit. No!' For a moment, there was a flash of the usual Alex, as indignation pushed through the tears.

'So why are you crying?'

'I'm not crying,' insisted Alex. 'Well...' she relented, 'I am crying, but it's just personal... it's because... I've been stupid, that's what. Really stupid and I hate myself.' She smiled tightly. 'Have you ever done anything that you can't forgive yourself for? It feels excruciating... I don't know what to do... I can't make it better.' She dabbed her tissue at the edges of her eyes. 'I just...' she began just as Mary Rose came back into the office.

'I've just been at a meeting with Mr Mulligan and Ben O'Leary,' said Mary Rose, who seemed preoccupied and didn't notice Alex quickly giving herself a small shake, widening her eyes and trying to look normal. 'They were asking how we were going with the Welcome Ireland pitch, and I said I wasn't sure...' She looked at Alex and Kitty.

Hughie had pulled off his headphones and shrugged in response.

'We have something,' said Kitty, glancing at Alex. 'And we like it...'

'But you don't love it?' Mary Rose paused. 'Because I think that if we don't love it, then we'll pull out...'

'But that means you won't get your probation,' said Kitty.

There was a knock on the office door and Ben O'Leary poked his head around. 'Hello, ladies,' he said, flashing a big smile. He looked around the room, blankly, as though trying to remember everyone's names. 'Hello... people.' He hesitated for a moment. 'Mary Rose, the invoices? Remember to send them to me?' His gaze alighted on Alex, as though spotting her for the first time. 'Ah, Alex... could I see you for a moment? Won't take long.'

But Alex didn't move.

'Alex?' He tried again. 'Just a quick chat... about the thing we talked about the other day? Your contract? Yes, your contract...'

Alex clicked her mouse, swirling her cursor around the screen.

'Alex?' He tried again, but then Mary Rose stood up.

'I think that Alex is too busy for a chat at the moment.' She smiled at him. 'If you don't mind. And we're all in the middle of our pitch for Welcome Ireland, so very, very busy...'

He blinked at her, his mouth opening and closing, and for the first time, Kitty saw beyond the expensive suit and the silk tie and the big hair... he was actually quite ordinary, just someone with buckets of confidence and an amazing orthodontist.

'Yes, yes, of course,' he said. 'I just wanted to sort something out...' He looked pointedly again at Alex, who still didn't move a muscle. 'But it can wait... of course, it can wait.' Finally, Ben O'Leary retreated.

No one spoke. Hughie's eyes were like saucers as he and Kitty looked at each other.

Alex cleared her throat. 'I am sure you've all guessed what has been going on...'

'You don't need to tell us anything,' Mary Rose said, moving towards her. 'Just as long as you're okay...'

But Alex started crying again. 'Don't be nice to me,' she said. 'Whatever you do, don't be nice to me... I don't deserve it, so it's best if you don't start now...'

Mary Rose had an arm around her. 'I'm not going to stop,' she said, as Hughie and Kitty hovered at Alex's desk.

Alex looked up at Mary Rose. 'Did you know?'

Mary Rose nodded. 'I guessed. And there were rumours.'

'Did you know?' mouthed Hughie to Kitty.

She shrugged, but it was falling into place that Alex had been having some kind of fling with Ben O'Leary... who was married and had just had a baby.

'It's been terrible,' said Alex. 'I didn't think it through... I was selfish and thought only of myself... and then his wife confronted me. I was just coming home and there she was, sitting on the step outside my house... looking furious... not that I blame her. And she had her baby with her. In a sling. I could just see his head, in a little hat. And seeing her... and the baby... I felt the worst I could possibly feel, I regretted everything. Everything. How had I allowed it to happen? I walked towards her, knowing I had to face my own failure, my stupidity, my vanity...' Alex was still crying, the tears rolling down her face.

'I think you should go home,' said Mary Rose. 'Take some time off and return when you have recovered... I'll square it with HR, don't worry.'

They helped Alex gather up her things and walked her down the emergency stairs, just in case Ben O'Leary intercepted her on the way out, before waving her off and watching as she made her way down Merrion Street.

'And the moral is,' said Mary Rose, as they walked back to the office, 'never, ever rely on someone else for your self-esteem.'

Hughie was nodding. 'Mine is rock-bottom at the moment, but I refuse to be involved with someone until I gather my own strength again.'

'Kitty?' said Mary Rose. 'You may have to do the pitch on your own? Think you can manage?'

Kitty thought of her mother, and how courageous she was. She would call in to see her on her way home. 'Of course,' Kitty said, sounding braver than she felt. 'It will all be fine.' *But don't expect us to win*, she thought.

30

'How've you been?' Kitty said after Catherine had hugged her.

'Grand, fine...' Catherine tried to smile, but Kitty could see she looked disappointed. They walked to the kitchen together. 'Have you heard from Himself, yet? You haven't? What is he playing at?'

'I don't know,' said Kitty, and then she realised wondering about other people's motives was exhausting. You just had to take them at their word and stop trying to second-guess them. Dave had left. What else was there to say? It was almost as though he didn't matter any more, there were too many other things that were gathering at the front of her mind which were dislodging him, everything from work to football to Billy... to the one memory which kept replaying itself like a film – the night in The Grace O'Malley and then the walk home with Tom.

'How is the Welcome Ireland project going?'

'Not great,' said Kitty, frowning a little. 'We have something, it's good enough... but it's missing something crucial and I can't work out what it is... I keep looking at the storyboards, reading the copy and it's still not quite right.'

'You'll find it,' said Catherine. 'I know you will.'

Kitty felt slightly panicky about it, but she didn't want to think about work. 'Any news on your promotion?'

'Well...' Catherine cleared her voice and shifted in the chair. 'Life, as you may have realised, is far too short, and so I've resigned. Handed in my notice today. I've decided that I'm worth more than all this and so I'm withdrawing my labour. It's time I stood up for myself... and got myself out of what has become a desultory place to work. I want to be happy,' continued Catherine, 'and there's more to life than hoping that my worth will finally be recognised. I just got there before them.'

'Aren't you scared?' asked Kitty.

Catherine shook her head. 'Not at all. It would be scarier to stay,' she said. 'That would destroy me, hanging on somewhere I wasn't wanted.'

Catherine was always a superwoman, but this was on another epic scale of impressiveness. Kitty felt almost envious that Catherine had taken charge of her life so easily. The ability to say no, to leave somewhere where she wasn't wanted or appreciated and to take a risk into the unknown was awe-inspiring. But still, Catherine looked a little in shock. Kitty wished she could make everything better for her.

'What are you going to do?'

'I have two weeks left as notice and then... who knows?' Catherine shrugged. 'Now, let's have some more tea?' she went on. 'I want to hear more of your news.'

Catherine obviously didn't want to talk about her work situation any further, but Kitty burned in indignation for her mother. Catherine deserved so much more.

'How is the football coming along?' Catherine was saying. 'I was wondering if you had inherited any of your father's skills?'

Kitty shook her head. 'I don't think so, but he's given me a few tips. It's all about flow, apparently.'

'Isn't everything?' said Catherine. 'And how is he? Is he still coaching?'

Catherine and Billy rarely saw each other these days, as though they had never been together.

'Not as much as he used to,' said Kitty.

'He was always meant to be a very good coach,' said Catherine. 'He wouldn't have gone to America if he wasn't.' She sighed. 'Pity he was injured. I think not being able to play, being stopped from the one thing he loved, was so hard for him. He never recovered, really. I didn't know him as a player. When I met him, it was as though he was trying out different identities, finding out who he was.' She sighed. 'It was a lot for him to deal with... and I don't think he ever really dealt with it properly. However much I tried, I couldn't get us to work. But then, I was too bossy, too controlling... we were both to blame.'

The doorbell rang.

'Ah, there's Annie. She borrowed my Yves Saint Laurent jacket for a new date. He's an estate agent and she wanted to impress him,' said Catherine, jumping up and heading out into the hall. Kitty heard her mother's voice as she opened the door. 'Well, you look lovely... it suits you more than it suits me... come into the kitchen, Kitty's here...'

Annie barged in and flung herself onto the leather sofa along the side wall of the kitchen; the jacket crumpled as she reclined and there was red wine on the lapel. 'Remind me never, ever, ever to go out with an estate agent ever again. All they do is talk about houses. And if it's not houses, then it's property. And if it's not property, it's buildings. Sweet holy Mary of the divine Jesus and all his disciples, I have never been so bored to complete distraction in my entire life.' She slid lower on the sofa, the jacket now straining the buttons at the front. 'He was no craic at all, just droned on and on and on.'

Catherine laughed and didn't seem to mind that her hugely expensive jacket was being mistreated and reached for an extra cup. Kitty had to restrain herself from smoothing out the jacket or insisting Annie removed it.

'Where did you go?' Kitty spoke through gritted teeth. She loved Annie but she also took advantage of Catherine. She always had. And it just wasn't fair. There was Catherine who had bravely handed in her notice while Annie just skated along in life.

'Just that fish place on the seafront,' said Annie, switching position so the jacket rode up, the seams at the arm straining. 'The Sea Shack. He had the burger – the cheapest thing on the menu. We shared a portion of chips and one glass of wine, and then split the bill. At that stage, I couldn't hear about another property deal or about his ex-wife, who he says is crazy… and I was thinking to myself, if I was married to him, I'd go crazy.' She lay her head down on the end of the sofa. 'Cath, may I stay here tonight? Sleep in the spare room? I don't want to go home and you can make me breakfast in the morning, you know how much I love your breakfasts. Those scones. The proper coffee.'

'Of course you can, Annie,' said Catherine. 'Stay as long as you like.'

Annie basked in the glow of her older sister's ministrations. 'How lucky am I?' she said to Kitty. 'Best sister in the world.'

But all Kitty could think about was wishing their relationship went both ways and, from time to time, that Annie made Catherine breakfast or minded her. But Annie had never had to look after anyone but herself. A bit of growing up was a good thing, even Shazza would have to agree.

* * *

Kitty walked home and as she turned the corner onto her road, she could hear a car idling outside her house, and someone was leaning down and talking through the car window. As she got closer, she realised it was Dave's mother's car, and there she was, in the front seat, while Dave was leaning on the open passenger window.

'I can't just let myself in...' Kitty heard him say.

'Of course you can,' said Maureen, in her nasal foghorn. 'It's your house.'

'It's technically Kitty's,' said Dave. 'She owns it and pays the mortgage...'

'Under common law, it's yours as well,' replied Maureen. 'You have squatters' rights and it's half yours. Now, just go in and take your things...'

Kitty cleared her throat, making Dave jump and turn around. She wanted to correct Maureen that her son did not have squatters' rights and that this was her home that she paid the mortgage on, not Dave.

'Kitty!' he said in a high-pitched squeak, as though caught stealing or going through her handbag. 'You're back... I tried the door, but you weren't in... I was just...'

He was looking pastier than normal, thought Kitty, even paler than his usual Daz-white skin. He also looked dead behind the eyes. Did he always look so vacant?

There was a buzzing sound as the passenger window of the car was lowered even further as Maureen obviously couldn't hear their conversation as well as she wanted to.

'How have you been?' Dave asked.

'All right,' she said, as he nodded, the blank look in his eyes giving the impression that he neither cared one way or the other. 'How have you been?'

Would he say he wanted to come back and that he missed

her? But Dave was looking shifty as he glanced at the car. 'It's been nice, actually,' he confessed. 'Like a holiday.' He looked up at the sky. 'Let me see... what have I been doing?'

'Watching *Countdown*,' came Maureen's voice from the car. 'We never miss an episode, do we, David?'

'No,' said Dave, 'we don't. Gets the old brain going, that conundrum thing. I got it in... what did I get it in, Mam?'

'Three seconds,' came the voice.

'Three seconds,' he repeated.

'That's excellent,' said Kitty, trying to smile, hoping she conveyed the impression that she was ready for him to come home and however much fun she'd been having, she still cared about him and was sorry for everything she had put him through and the pressure she'd put him under. And also, the sooner he got away from his mother, the sooner he might look less vacant. 'Dave...?' She began, but there was a slight roar from the engine, as though Maureen had put her foot on the accelerator.

He glanced at the car. 'I'd better go,' he said.

'Did you not come for any of your things?'

He nodded. 'Dad's old cardigan,' he said. 'I was worried... or rather Mam was worried...' Another engine roar. 'Well, we thought, well, you might have given it away to charity, you know how you like a good clear-out.'

'It's still there,' Kitty said. 'On the hooks behind the door.'

Dave nipped through the gate and opened the front door with his key.

Kitty leaned in through the open car window. 'How are you, Maureen?'

'Very well, Kitty,' said Maureen, her lips pursed. 'Very well indeed.'

'Good to hear you've been enjoying *Countdown*... I never see it because I'm at work. But I know it's very popular.'

'It is, Kitty,' said Maureen, formally. 'It's very popular with those of us who aren't constrained by office hours.' Maureen fixed Kitty with a look. 'David needs a great deal of rest. He's ragged, like a dishcloth that's come to the end of its life and it either needs to be thrown away or it needs...' Maureen paused, flummoxed as to how to finish her simile. Describing her son as an old dishcloth was her first mistake.

Kitty tried to help her out. 'He needs to be put in the washing machine and he'll come out like new?'

'Yes,' said Maureen, not at all grateful to have been saved. 'He'll be all clean again in no time.'

'Got it...' Dave was behind them, wearing his dad's cardigan over his shoulders like a cape. 'Right...' He paused in front of Kitty. 'Thanks for that,' he said. 'I'll be in touch.'

The engine revved and, before Kitty could answer, Dave was back in the car and there was a squeal of the tyres as the car sped off as though it was in the middle of a heist.

'No rush,' said Kitty to the receding, speeding car. 'Take your time.' Instead of feeling bereft or upset, Kitty was surprised to realise how calm she felt, even relieved to see the back of the speeding car. Dave wasn't on her team, she realised. Her life team, as Billy would have said. She still wanted him, of course... didn't she? But she couldn't think about that now, not here on the street. Maybe he would decide to come back but, until then, she just had to get on with her life.

31

It was Friday evening and Kitty, Shazza, Rory, Tom and Tara stood in a huddle, under the floodlights, trying to focus on their match.

'Right,' said Tara, hands on her hips. 'We're playing the Sallynoggin Soldiers, right? Not known to play a beautiful game but famous for their ability to declare football war...'

Kitty felt even more nervous, trying to remember everything Billy had told her. Focus. Breathe. Be in the moment. Think about nothing but the ball. Feel the game.

'Concentrate on the tactics we've discussed,' instructed Tara. 'Rory, I'm going to be passing the ball to you to score goals, okay? Tom, your job is to get balls back into possession and, Shazza, you're in defence when Rory's got the ball. If he loses possession, you need to get it back to him.' She fixed Shazza with a glare of such intensity that there was a collective bristling to attention. 'You hear me? You get the ball back to Rory so he can score.' She turned to Kitty. 'And you're to... you're to... support the guys, pass the ball to any of us and we will try to score.'

They all nodded, clear with Tara's instructions. Apart from Kitty, who looked over to the stands, where Billy was sitting in the front row. He'd made it, she thought, surprised and pleased, as she smiled over at him. He gave her a thumbs up and then tapped his head, urging her to focus. She tapped her head in return. Billy then flapped his arms and sucked in his mouth and crossed his eyes.

'What?' she called over.

'Float like a butterfly,' he shouted back. 'Be a butterfly!'

Kitty laughed and, weirdly, for the first time, her nerves were completely gone. She was smiling as they walked onto the centre of the pitch.

'Good luck,' said Tom.

'You too,' she said.

The referee, who was short with rumpled socks and massive spectacles which dominated his face, blew the whistle, and Tara led the action, booting the ball down the pitch to Rory, who deftly caught it with his foot, and Kitty saw him trying to look for a way through the Sallynoggin Soldiers' defence. They were all huge players, three men and two women, all built like the Galtee Mountains and faces as though they'd been moulded out of clay, all lumpy with tiny, hidden-away eyes. One of them crashed into Rory, taking the legs from under him, and Rory crashed to the ground but was up again immediately, and somehow still had the ball. He darted around the Soldier and then swung his leg back to kick, but just before he made an impact, he kicked it in an entirely different direction, towards Tom, who then kicked the ball up the pitch, straight towards the goal, and then there was Rory again, who shot it straight into the net.

The Sandycove Seafarers began jumping up and down, cheering. Kitty finally understood why proper footballers celebrated their goals with dances and handstands and kissing and hugging. It was the best feeling in the world. Even Tara was smiling and Shazza was performing a kind of *Saturday Night*

Fever routine, and Rory joined in, the two of them disco-dancing in the middle of the pitch, much to the disgust of the Soldiers.

Now, it seemed, it was war, and for the rest of the first half, the Soldiers found their groove. Kitty never managed to gain possession of the ball and was tripped up by one of the opposition. It was their turn to celebrate a goal, running at each other, bouncing off each other's chests and making grunting sounds. And then, just before the referee blew his whistle for half-time, the Sallynoggin Soldiers scored another goal – 2-1.

Tara still looked determined, as the five-a-siders gathered. 'We're not going to let those big feckers beat us,' she said. 'I went to school with two of them, and they had as much sporting prowess as a bag of turf.' Her face was set, her jaw clenched, her eyes steely. 'We have to win. One of those bags of turf, Lorraine Houlihan, once stole my lunch from me. It was ham made by my mam… God, I've never forgotten it. And I was starving that day.'

'I suggest we use their size against them,' said Rory. 'We just keep running around them, be so quick that they can't see us or the ball.'

Tara looked at him. 'That's your plan?'

'I think it's quite a good one,' said Shazza, smiling at Rory.

'Thanks, Shazza,' he said, smiling back.

'I think we focus on the ball,' suggested Kitty. 'Don't think about the other team, stay in the game, the moment, just think about the ball being like energy being passed around…'

Tara thought for a moment and then nodded. 'Go on,' she said.

'Well,' said Kitty, 'I think we just need to breathe and take a moment to hear the sounds, to notice the mud on our boots and to stay in the now…'

'Now is all we've got,' said Tara. 'Right, COME ON!'

The second half began and that's exactly what they did. Kitty focused on her breathing and when one of the Soldiers came towards her, she heard his big, snuffly, nostrilly breaths, like an out-of-condition man-mountain, all size and no actual skills, and away she went, ducking around him, seeing the clods of earth which had been dug up by their studs, the blades of grass glittering under the floodlights, feeling her heart beating in her chest, the breeze on her skin as she ran towards Tom. Then, just as the man-mountain bore down on her, she passed the ball, giving it the slightest bit of topspin, and watched as it flicked over to Tom, who caught it, turned around, and kicked it to Rory, who then tapped it straight into the back of the net.

This time, they didn't celebrate, the Sandycove Seafarers were back in the game immediately, focused on the ball, their faces serious as Buddhist monks during daily prayers. One of the mountains tackled Tara as she had run out from the goal to kick a ball. For a moment, she was tossed to the ground and a shout of 'Lorraine! Jesus!' echoed around the stand, but the referee missed it all as he had been fiddling with his socks. But then Tara was up, and running with the ball, the wind in her hair, an expression on her face which Kitty knew was when she was in her special place, when she was winning. She passed the ball to Shazza, who manoeuvred it to Rory, who ducked around one of the Soldiers, then another, and was just about to be tackled again, when he tapped it to Kitty.

Blade of grass, she told herself. *Breathe breaths, keep on breathing breaths*. And she did, as she tapped the ball forward and watched as it circumnavigated around the woman mountain who was bearing down on her, but Kitty was too quick, and she had the ball again, and there was the goal, looming ahead of her, another Soldier glaring at her, his arms outstretched, and Kitty had no choice but to kick it again. Her heart was beating in her ears, the far-off sound of people shouting her name, and this time, just as her foot made contact, she remembered to give it that little flick and suddenly time stood still, the world stopped turning, it was like the volume of the universe had been silenced as the ball lifted into the air in a perfect arc and looked for one moment to be going over the goal, but it kept its trajectory and neatly, perfectly, like Cupid's arrow or a bolt of electricity, slipped straight under the bar, and flew into the net.

The referee blew the whistle and it was all over. The Sandycove Seafarers had won 3-2. And now the disco-dancing began again. On the sideline, the five of them began throwing some moves, Shazza was singing, 'Feel the beat of our tamboreeeeen!' And they were laughing and dancing and clapping their hands and shaking their bodies. It was, Kitty reflected later, the least cool celebration ever recorded, but none of them minded.

'You were magic out there,' Billy said to Kitty. 'Like a little rocket. Chip off the old block.'

'I hope so,' she said, allowing him to pull her into his arms. She'd spent her life being adamant that she was nothing like him, and now, here she was being pleased and delighted that they shared so much. Tara grabbed her and ruffled her hair roughly, making Kitty laugh.

'Jesus, this little one is a powerhouse... you're not leaving the team, right?' she said. 'You and Shazza are here to stay.'

Rory and Shazza were still dancing and had by now a choreographed routine. 'Then we turn, clap, wiggle... over to the right... shimmy down...' Shazza was saying, and then it was showers and all off to The Island for more celebrations.

In the village, Billy said, 'I'll leave you young ones here. You were marvellous out there, the lot of you. Monday? More training?'

Kitty nodded and waved, before turning to her team, who

were already heading into the pub. 'See you, Dad!' she called back. 'See you soon!'

Her heart felt full, and she realised that it was the first time in her life she'd felt totally and utterly content, nothing was wrong with anything and, if it was, she didn't care or it didn't matter. Because the now was wonderful.

32

The five-a-siders couldn't get a seat outside in the courtyard of The Island but managed to find a small, private snug, with two long benches on either side of the table.

Tom bought a round, returning from the bar with a pint of Guinness in both hands, a gin balanced between them, the tonic in his top pocket, and two packets of crisps between his teeth. 'One minute,' he said, heading back to the bar to collect two margaritas for Shazza and Kitty.

Being on a team bonded you instantly, thought Kitty. The winning, the losing, it didn't matter, you'd done it together and whether you were commiserating or celebrating, you all felt the same.

The Sandycove Seafarers shared stories and confidences as though they'd known each other forever. Even Tara was relaxed, telling them about being a carer for her nan and how sport was the only thing that was just for her. 'My nan would ask me how I'd got on that day, and if I'd won the hockey or the athletics or the Gaelic football, and when I'd say yes, she'd have the biggest smile on her face. When she died, she was buried with my GAA jersey on, Dublin colours... everyone else was like, sure, wouldn't she want to be in her best dress, but I knew she wanted to be playing sport like me.' She raised her gin and tonic. 'To Nan! I love you, Nan!'

'We love you, Nan,' everyone echoed.

Rory told them about going to college to do accountancy but hating it so much, he used to hide in the toilets of University College Dublin, so he didn't have to go into the lectures. 'It didn't strike me until later that I just needn't go at all. I could stay in bed. Only then did my anxiety improve.' He turned to Tom. 'Don't look at me like that. Anyway, it's all turned out for the best.'

Tom shook his head. 'What a waste of a year,' he said. 'All that lying you did. Mum was so worried about you. And then you announce you're going on the Ballymaloe cooking course and off you go...'

'And now look at me, food entrepreneur. You've got to follow your passion, have you not?'

Shazza was nodding. 'My passion was always journalism. My dream was to write for the *Times* or the *Independent*. I'd grown up reading them, hoping one day I would have a byline. And the thrill... every time I saw my name, I kept staring at it... and then... I don't know... after everything that happened with Mr Unmensh, handing in my notice and getting the job on the Sandycove Newsletter, I've realised what is important. And it's not bylines or politics, it's being here, having fun... it's like my ambitions have changed. I just want to be happy, you know?'

They all knew. Nodding and raising their glasses, they agreed that happiness was the best ambition to have.

'Since Paddy left us,' said Tom, 'that's all I want too. I want to have a life he'd be happy to see me have. Which is why I made the move back to animal care. Academia has its plus points, but I missed meeting the animals and I missed chatting to their owners and just being part of a community again. Paddy wouldn't want me working long hours or trying to make as much money as possible...'

'Lucky that,' said Rory, making Shazza laugh. He grinned at her. 'I like to drink Guinness and sit in pubs because I know Paddy would like to see me being happy.'

Tom shook his head, but he was trying not to smile. 'I'm just glad that we had Paddy for as long as we did. He was a brilliant brother.'

Rory had stopped laughing and was looking serious. 'We were lucky to know him,' he said.

'We've still got each other, though,' said Tom, looking straight at him.

Rory nodded. 'I'm lucky to have had two brilliant big brothers...'

Shazza wiped away a tear and then laid her head on Rory's shoulder. 'I love you two,' she said. 'If I had a brother, then I would like him to be the two of you. Pity all I have is Shona, who's been my nemesis since the day I was born. She hated me on sight, and the hatred has only increased with age. God knows how much she will hate me when we're old. I'm going to have to stay out of her way before she beats me up with her Zimmer frame.'

Tom was laughing, looking at Rory. 'He doesn't look too happy,' he teased.

Rory was looking suddenly all innocent.

'What's wrong?' asked Kitty, quietly to Tom.

'I think it was the fact Shazza said she wanted him to be her brother...' He laughed again. 'He's been brother-zoned... not quite what he wanted.'

'Pity Shazza is off men,' said Kitty. 'Rory is the exact opposite of the usual ones she goes for. She likes the horrible ones, the emotionally stunted, the unavailable, the ones with addiction issues or commitment problems.'

Tom laughed. 'I've decided that you have to be careful with who you fall in love with,' he said. 'You need to mind yourself, not shut yourself off, but mind yourself, because life is too short and you don't want to get stuck for too long down some kind of rabbit hole. We tend to find someone and cling on for dear life rather than addressing or asking if this person is right for us, but you're only wasting precious time. You know that quote, tell me what is it you plan to do with your one wild and precious life?'

Kitty nodded.

'I thought about that a lot when Paddy died. Life is precious. I don't want to waste it.'

'So what are you doing with your wild and precious life?'

'Spending it wisely,' he said. 'With the right people. People who make the world a better place and who I can learn from...'

Kitty pulled a face. 'All the time?' she said. 'I mean, even now?' She laughed, self-deprecatingly. 'I think you should go and find someone else to talk to.'

He raised an eyebrow. 'You think I am not exactly where I want to be, talking to the person I want to talk to?'

A strange and wonderful feeling rippled through Kitty's body, and she found herself smiling at him again. 'Me too,' she said.

'You have to appreciate the moment because each moment is precious.' Tom looked at her. 'So, what are your ambitions...?'

'Her only ambition is to get Dave to come home,' said Shazza, butting in. 'She's only wasting time until the prodigal idiot returns.'

Perhaps it was the drink or the adrenaline from the win, but Kitty realised she didn't care if Dave never returned. She liked this new freedom to meet new people. She liked drinking in pubs and playing football and having fun. Worse, she had a suspicion that when he came back, she'd have to give it all up. 'I don't care if he does come back,' she announced. 'I'm sort of thinking I hope he doesn't... I quite like living in a house where I don't have to pick up someone's underpants or hear them slurp their tea.'

'Hooray!' said Shazza. 'You are officially emancipated. Welcome back from the dark side.'

Kitty glanced at Tom, who was smiling at her, a look on his face which seemed affectionate and friendly, as though he was pleased for her and that picking up Dave's underpants was in her past.

* * *

Later, they all walked home, dropping Tara first as she lived closest to the village. Shazza and Rory walked on ahead, Shazza's arm through Rory's.

'Is that a brotherly link or a romantic link?' asked Tom.

'Romantic,' said Kitty, pleased that Shazza had decided a life of a nun wasn't for her. Her celibacy had lasted for an impressively long time, thought Kitty.

'Maybe she's on men again?' said Tom as Rory and Shazza started snogging.

'I think you might be right,' said Kitty. 'She's off off men... didn't take long.'

'Come on,' said Tom, 'let's leave them to it and I'll walk you home...'

It seemed so right to slip her arm through his, as they wove their way along the streets of Sandycove, talking and laughing.

At her door, they stood outside, and Kitty found herself staring up at his handsome face, he was staring right back at her, both of them grinning. He brushed her hair from her forehead, his fingers feeling soft and warm, and just as she was thinking how much she wanted his fingers to touch her again, they were kissing each other... and it wasn't remotely like kissing Dave, with his hard, puckery lips and downy face, the thing he did with his tongue and all that saliva as though he was playing some repulsive party game. She hadn't realised that kissing could be so nice. She'd put up with crap kissing while this, with Tom, was an entirely better experience.

'I'm so glad you said what you said...' he said, eventually.

Kitty looked at him. 'About what?'

'About not caring if Dave came back. I was getting worried...'

'Why?'

'Because I thought you were waiting for him and you'd never give me a chance...'

She was suddenly suffused with joy and happiness. 'I like everything that has happened since he left.' She looked straight up at Tom, and that fizzing feeling of happiness spread through her.

'I've liked you since I first met you at the meeting in the community centre,' he said. 'I was thinking who is this gorgeous woman? Why haven't I seen her around before...?'

'I've been under house arrest with Dave,' she joked.

'You don't mind if I release you then?'

'No, I don't mind at all...' She pulled him inside and that was that. A good night turned into a fabulous night. And playing football just got very interesting indeed.

33

Kitty woke up and for a moment she thought it was Dave curled around her. But something was different... the smell for one thing. Dave's slightly sulphurous odour – which she wondered if it emanated from the lack of vegetables in his diet – wasn't there. Instead, the person next to her was bigger, his skin softer and he wasn't making those yogic breathing sounds from the back of his throat which Dave made because of his sinus issues.

Tom.

She smiled and snuggled in closer and deeper. Memories of the previous evening filtered through. The match. The final goal. The drinks in The Island. The walking home... and then the kissing on the doorstep.

'Morning...'

Tom was awake.

'Morning...' Kitty rolled onto her back, Tom's face close to hers, his left arm around her shoulders, his right hand resting lightly on her stomach.

'Sleep well...?'

'Yes, you?'

He was smiling. 'Pretty good... nice bed, good company...'

But Dave. She hadn't meant any of this to happen. This wasn't the deal. She had told him she would wait, while he got his head sorted, and she'd gone off and slept with someone else.

'Look, Tom... I'm sorry about last night... I know we've both had a bit to drink...'

He frowned slightly. 'Are you saying you're regretting it?'

'A bit,' she said. 'I mean... I'm not technically single...'

There was a rustle at the end of the bed, as Romeo hopped up, and made his way over the duvet towards them, purring loudly.

'True,' Tom said, absent-mindedly stroking Romeo, who curled around his hand. 'I think I may have conveniently forgotten that fact last night, so overcome by your beauty...' He nibbled at her ear, making her laugh. 'So overcome by the look in your eye, the way you score goals, the way you lick the salt off your margarita... your loyalty to Shazza. And...' His mouth was now kissing her neck. 'I like the way you taste... like honey... doughnuts... sherbert... lemon drops... Jelly Tots...' He came up for air. 'You taste exactly as I imagined you would... like a sweet shop.'

Kitty laughed, but his mouth was now moving over her body, small kisses that were like nothing she had ever experienced. 'Maybe I could conveniently forget that I am technically in a relationship again?' she suggested before she found herself unable to speak coherently for a while.

* * *

Later, they sat up in bed, drinking tea and talking, Romeo curled at the end of the bed.

'He's not normally this friendly to strange men,' said Kitty. 'He didn't even like Dave very much.'

'Well, I like animals,' said Tom. 'And the feeling seems to be mutual. Thankfully. It would be awkward in my work if it wasn't.' He reached across and gave Romeo a few more long and languid strokes. 'He's a gorgeous cat. I love cats when they get to be old... they become even more regal. Like an ancient king or queen.'

'He's had a few run-ins with this tabby called Timmy. I had to bring him to your practice recently. Mr Kelly stitched him up.'

'He's healed well...' Tom examined the ear. 'I hope Timmy lays off him. He likes going out at night, does he?'

'Loves it,' said Kitty. 'Wouldn't miss searching for mice or whatever else he gets up to. And I think he's learned to stay away from Timmy. He's not going to make that mistake again.'

'So...' He took her hand now. 'You're not technically single. And I am...'

'Yes...'

'How can we rectify this mismatch?'

'I'm not sure,' said Kitty. 'How long have you been single?'

'Long enough...' he said. 'I was seeing someone when Paddy was becoming increasingly unwell and I just couldn't focus on anything but him at the time. So, I ended that, tried to keep my studies going and the rest of the time I used to go and bug Paddy. I'd make him go for long walks with me and... God...' He leaned his head back on the pillow and stared at the ceiling for a moment. Tom turned back to Kitty. 'What was going on in his head, I couldn't have done anything about... the fact he thought the world was a better place without him still confounds me... I mean, really? Do you think that? Because you are so wrong, so incredibly wrong. The world is a worse place without someone with your beautiful soul in it, without your lovely heart...'

'Poor Paddy,' said Kitty, putting her hand over Tom's.

He nodded. 'So many families go through it, we're not unique to lose someone to suicide. But I loved him, will always love him and it's made me want to live the best life I can... for him. He couldn't. But I can.'

Kitty stood up, pulling on her dressing gown. 'Hungry?'

He nodded, smiling at her.

'For food!' Kitty laughed. 'Tea and toast? A nice coffee?'

'Sounds good to me.'

They ate breakfast sitting in a patch of sun in the courtyard, surrounded by Kitty's geraniums, Romeo stretched out in the sun.

'So what have you learned since you've been filling in your time?' Tom's knee touched Kitty's briefly.

'Life has just seemed more interesting somehow... being out and about more, meeting people... and I've just felt more open, somehow... and the football team, meeting you and Rory...'

He smiled at her. 'Well, I'm pretty happy about that.'

'We're presenting a big new pitch next week for Welcome Ireland. At our last big pitch, one of the clients said something was missing.'

Tom was looking puzzled. 'And what's the problem?'

'Well, this man didn't like it...'

'Right...'

'And...' Kitty was running out of ways to explain why it had felt like a failure. 'Normally, we receive better feedback,' she said.

'You can't fear failure,' Tom said. 'Paddy used to say that. Get used to it, be comfortable in it... and don't fear it. And he was right. If you take away the one thing that stops you from doing things... then life just opens up. You're immediately happier.'

Kitty was nodding. These last couple of weeks, she hadn't cared about failing. Instead, she'd just been living. From football to sailing to feeling emotionally and physically connected to someone new, it was as though her world was so much bigger.

Except for work. Failure in work was still something to be feared. Maybe it was because you were paid to be there or you had to be in charge and vulnerability and lack of success made everyone around you nervous.

Tom was smiling at her.

'What?'

'Just that... I think you're a good person...' He took her hand. 'You want to make the world a better place than the way you found it... am I right?'

'Doesn't everyone?'

He shook his head. 'No, no they don't. But you give the very strong impression that you worry about people, about making everyone happy... and that's a really lovely thing. I just really like being around you.'

She smiled at him, liking the idea of who he thought she was. It was something to live up to, she thought. Being with Tom was so different to Dave – here was a man who listened, who liked Romeo and who Romeo liked in return and smelled nice. She couldn't help but feel a glow inside, her insides warm, her body feeling light, as though filled with an air of excitement. But she wasn't quite free... not yet. She was waiting for Dave to release her or to reclaim her. Either way, she was in limbo.

* * *

In the afternoon, Tom had to go back to the Sandycove Vets for an emergency weekend cover. 'I'll be back later,' he promised, kissing her goodbye. 'And I'll bring dinner.'

At 5 p.m., there was a knock on the door and Kitty, a little flustered, butterflies in her stomach, answered the door. But instead of Tom, standing there, it was Dave.

'Howya,' he said.

'Dave…' Her mouth opened and closed as she tried to form more words.

'Aren't you going to let me in? I thought I lived here too?' He sounded wheedling, almost petulant.

She stood to one side, wondering why he had come.

'You look nice,' he said, glancing at her. 'New dress?'

'No… old…'

He peered at her face. 'You look different…'

She shook her head again. 'I don't think so…' There was that old sulphurous whiff. Yes, Dave was back. She followed him into the living room, where he stood turning around, as though taking it all in again.

'You know, I've missed this old house,' he said.

'My old house,' she said, quietly.

'Mam's is pretty cluttered. So many knick-knacks. Jugs, little china people, her panda collection… her crystal animals… and she can't throw anything away – magazines, crappy books, yoghurt cartons, parish newsletters, jam jars…'

'How is your mam?' It was the only sensible thing that Kitty could trust herself to say. She had been waiting for this moment for the last couple of weeks and now it was happening and real, she was blindsided.

'She's good…'

'And you?'

'Never better.' He smiled at her and she thought how little he smiled, really, and when he did, it looked more like a grimace. Dave was one of those people who looked better when they were either angry or unhappy. 'Anyway,' he said, 'I'll get to the point. I want to say that the time away did me the power of good. I did a lot of thinking and I thought about you, and you and me, and about me…'

Mostly you, Kitty said to herself.

'And I want to say how much I missed you and that I am sorry for being such a misery guts and I don't think you were putting pressure on me to get married. It's your right to want to know where the relationship is going. And we've been through so much together... and I love living with you...' He dropped to his knee and for a moment Kitty thought that perhaps he'd had a stroke or a heart attack. But he grabbed on to her hand, looking up at her. 'Kitty, you were right, I was wrong... we can't throw everything we have away. We're a great team. I want to spend the rest of my life with you. Will you... will you marry me?'

Kitty still couldn't find the words.

'You are the only person who would put up with me,' he went on, still grimacing. 'Without you I am miserable, without you I have no life.' Still clutching at her with one hand, he reached around to his back pocket and took out something wrapped in a square of toilet paper. 'It's my grandmother's ring,' he said, his voice going wobbly, his eyes tearing up. 'And it would do me the profound honour if you would wear it. Will you?'

Kitty hesitated.

'Please?' He slipped the ring on to Kitty's hand. 'It's a bit loose,' he said. 'But it's nice, isn't it? The emeralds. Mam says those are diamantés. Are they a thing? She says they are much better than diamonds because if you lose one, you can get it replaced. The same with the emeralds.'

'It's... it's...' Kitty couldn't get the words out, and she'd started to cry.

'Don't get upset, sweetheart,' Dave was saying as he stood up. 'Any bride is bound to get emotional when she's getting married. I know what you women are like. Always crying. I mean, I just wish my old dad was here. He'd like you, I know he would. Well, most of you. Not the hyper-cleaning part of you.' Dave chuckled to himself. 'Or the way you fold your T-shirts as though they are origami. And…' For a moment, Kitty thought Dave was going to list all the ways his father wouldn't like her and she had to remind herself to close her mouth which had been hanging open with shock. 'Anyway…' Dave seemed to collect himself. 'I've got a bottle of champagne on the doorstep. Well, it's not exactly champagne, it's sparkling wine. Only €5.99 in SuperValu. Isn't that good?'

Kitty still hadn't managed to get a full sentence out and, before she knew it, she was standing with a warm glass of fizzy vinegar.

'Delicious, isn't it?' said Dave, still smiling. He looked so happy now and it seemed as though he wanted to get his life back together and perhaps the old Dave would re-emerge. And maybe he would eat vegetables and he would smell less sulphurous. Maybe everything would be okay. And as for Tom, Kitty barely knew him, and it was Dave who she was obliged to be with because of their long history.

The doorbell rang again.

'I'll get it!' Kitty ran to the door and flung it open. Tom was standing there, a takeaway from the local Afghan restaurant in his hand. Kitty shook her head at him. 'I can't,' she said. 'Dave's here…' She held up her ring. 'He asked me to marry him.'

Tom frowned again. 'What?'

'You have to go… You have to go.' She shut the door and, for a moment, she leaned against it and closed her eyes, trying to keep her breathing steady. This was the right thing, she told herself. She had an obligation to Dave, she couldn't just abandon him when she had spent so many years working for and building some kind of future. It was like walking off a job or stopping a building halfway through. She had to see this through. She had everything she wanted, so why were tears rolling down her face?

34

KITTY

I'm really sorry. I don't know what else to say.

TOM

...

KITTY

It just happened so quickly.

TOM

Okay then. Well, good luck with everything.

KITTY

Thank you. You too.

You too? God. How pathetic she was. What a tangled web she'd woven and it was all her fault. She'd said she'd wait for Dave, but she hadn't. What must Tom think of her? And it had only been two weeks since he'd gone. How could everything have changed so much in such a little time?

It was Saturday morning, and Dave had just finished talking to his mother on the phone. 'Mam says your mam should invite her round,' he announced. 'Now our families will be one big family.'

'I didn't think she liked me,' said Kitty. 'Surely, she's not celebrating?'

'Mam's resigned to my choice,' he said, a little gloomily, as though his mother had finally accepted he was dropping out of medical school or his inadvisable tattoo was here to stay. 'When I told her I was going to ask you to marry me, she started to cry. And they weren't happy tears, more tears of disappointment. But I knew Mam would come round and then she was grand with it. She wouldn't have given me the ring otherwise.'

Kitty looked at it on her finger – slightly too big and possibly the ugliest ring she'd ever seen in her life. But it was the very least of her problems because even more glaring was the fact that Kitty had very much changed her mind about marrying Dave. It was agony to realise that she was now utterly repulsed by something she had desperately wanted only two weeks earlier. Hopefully, she would find the old Kitty again, and remember the reasons why she had wanted to marry Dave.

Except, she liked the new Kitty much more. And there was Tom who she liked more than she liked Dave. Much more. Except, how could she leave Dave? Her world was far more chaotic and crazy than it had been only weeks earlier, everything she had wanted and relied upon had been turned upside down, and it was her fault, not Dave's. All he had done was leave for a couple of weeks, which wasn't a long time, and yet she had gone off and created a whole new world. She should have just stayed where she was. She wasn't one of those people who deserved love and passion, not like Shazza. What did she say about the two of them? Shazza was too much and Kitty was too little. For a while, she had kidded herself that she could change and she deserved a bit more than too little.

Perhaps marrying Dave could be a good idea? Or rather it would be once she transitioned into the old Kitty again. Better the Dave you know. And they had been together for five years, a history that shouldn't be thrown away, not after a break of a fortnight, and not when he now wanted what she had wanted. Once. And yes, this was her one wild and precious life, but you couldn't just do whatever you wanted, whenever you wanted to... could you? Companionship, familiarity, knowing someone's tics and habits better than you knew your own was preferable to having to start all over again, only to discover your new lover chewed with his mouth full, air-guitared to Pink Floyd and never shared his KitKat.

Except... Tom.

She liked everything about him. *Everything*. From the first time she had met him in the community centre, to the day on *Pansy-Pearl*... to the walk home and the night they'd spent together. It was as though she'd walked through a magical door and the world was suddenly in gleaming technicolour, like putting on a new pair of glasses after a lifetime of squinting.

With a pang, she thought of the look on Tom's face when she'd closed the door.

'Would tomorrow suit your mam?'

She hadn't been listening to Dave. 'For what?' said Kitty.

For a moment, a look of irritation flickered over his face, but he quickly managed to change to a more passive expression. 'For our engagement gathering,' he said, patiently.

'I'll ask her.' There was no sense in putting off the inevitable. This was what she had wanted, wasn't it? Kitty picked up her phone but there was a message from Tom.

TOM

Just wanted to say that I hope we will be friends. I've really enjoyed meeting you and Shazza.

'It's better in your mam's as my mam has just bought a new carpet and doesn't want people walking on it. So will you ask your mam? 3 p.m.?'

Kitty was barely listening and instead was trying to take in Tom's message. Could they be friends? Would they? That old gnawing feeling was back.

She called Catherine from the kitchen, away from Dave. 'Mum,' she said. 'A bit of news. Dave has proposed...'

There was silence.

'And it's what I wanted...'

Still silence, except for slightly strange sounds as though her mother was trying to find the words but nothing was coming out.

'Aren't you going to say anything?'

'Of course, of course...' But Catherine still sounded as though she'd forgotten how to speak in proper sentences.

'Well...?'

Finally, Catherine found her voice. 'Well, if you're happy, then I'm happy...' She hesitated. 'Are you happy?'

'Of course I am,' said Kitty. 'Who accepts a marriage proposal without being happy?'

There was silence on the other end of the line.

'Mum? I thought we could come over at 3 p.m. tomorrow and celebrate. Dave and me, you and Maureen. Dad. Shazza? What do you think?'

'Darling, it's wonderful news,' said Catherine, sounding a little more normal. 'And, of course, Dave and his mother should come here for a celebration tomorrow. I'll do champagne and cake. And I'll phone Annie, to see if she wants to come.'

'I'll text Dad,' said Kitty. 'Is that all right with you?'

'Of course...'

Kitty texted Billy.

KITTY

Dave and I have just got engaged. Mum is having drinks and cake at her house, tomorrow at 3 p.m. Please come! And remember practice on Monday night? You said you'd go through a few things with me xxx

She looked at the text and thought it was almost a normal interaction with her father, making plans and being loving and friendly. For a moment, she felt a glow of happiness. She was having an actual relationship with her dad and it felt really good.

Shazza was next and it was the call Kitty was dreading the most.

'I hope you're joking,' said Shazza. 'I mean, you are joking... you're having me on? Nice one!' She began to laugh. 'You nearly had me there! Kitty! You're terrible, you are! And what happened with you and Tom? Spill the beans, tell me everything...'

'Shazza, I'm not joking...' Kitty made sure the kitchen door was closed behind her and she spoke in barely whispered tones. 'I'm serious. He came back yesterday evening...'

'But...'

'And he proposed...'

There was a deathly silence, which chilled Kitty to the very bones. Shazza was never silent. It was all very well for Shazza to have grand plans for the two of them, but it wasn't real life.

'Will you come to Mum's at 3 p.m. tomorrow to have some champagne?'

'Champagne? Don't you have that when you are celebrating?'

'We are celebrating,' said Kitty, firmly. 'You know this is what I wanted. I love Dave, and he loves me, and that's that. We had fun over the last two weeks, but it's time to accept reality and get back to the way things were.'

'But what about Tom? I thought you liked him? Rory said how much he liked *you*...'

'That was nothing...'

'*That?* So something *did* happen! I was wondering when I saw the two of you wander off together...'

'You were snogging Rory!'

'Doesn't mean I still can't keep half an eye on my best friend and I saw you and Tom walking away into the sunset together...'

'It was pitch dark...' Kitty felt empty inside as she remembered that wonderful, golden evening.

'I thought to myself, there's a man who will look after my best friend, there's a man who deserves her! Not like—'

'Don't say it...'

'But—!'

'Shazza, have I ever passed judgement on any of the ludicrous men you've attached yourself to? Have I ever told you what to do? Have I ever criticised your choices? And some of those choices you have made have been woeful...'

'No...'

'So, go with this for me. Pretend Tom never happened. Pretend Dave and I weren't on a break and everything is hunky-bloody-dory and we're just going to meet at my mother's house tomorrow for a glass of champagne and be happy about it! Okay?'

'Okay.' Shazza sounded anything but happy for Kitty. She sounded resigned, which was exactly how Kitty felt too.

35

Dave had been tired after all the emotion of the proposal, he explained, and had gone to bed early, much to Kitty's relief.

'And there's nothing on telly,' he'd said. 'Mam's got all the channels. We should get them too.'

Kitty had nodded, miserably, not sure quite what she was agreeing to, but too confused to ask questions or to draw any attention to herself. She was trying to think clearly, to sort out the chaos which was muddling her brain. She even tried to organise the cutlery drawer but gave up when she realised that decluttering and tidying no longer gave her the comfort it once did. It was as though nothing she relied on before worked any longer, as though she had changed as a person in just a fortnight. It couldn't be true, she told herself. She just had to remain calm and wait for herself to return to normal.

On Sunday afternoon, Kitty was pleased to see Shazza had made a sartorial effort and had on her leopard-skin dress, which she only wore on special occasions. It made Kitty feel that Shazza was more supportive than she had seemed.

Kitty hugged her on the doorstep of Catherine's house. 'You're the first to arrive,' she said. 'Mum and Dave are in the living room.'

The atmosphere had been a little stilted but that was only because Dave wasn't the best at making small talk and Catherine was still a little taken aback by the shock news. But there was cake and sandwiches and sausage rolls, and Catherine's crystal flutes on the table, with the best Irish linen napkins and matching embroidered tablecloth.

'Kitty was saying you are hoping to find a new job,' Catherine was saying, as Shazza and Kitty walked back into the front room where Dave was.

'That's right,' Dave said. 'I was thinking something at executive level. Information technologists are highly sought after and someone of my level of experience...' He looked up at Shazza. 'Ah, Sharon,' he said, holding out his hand. 'It's you... again.'

'Dave!' Shazza had her best smile on. 'Congratulations, it's such wonderful news...' She shook Dave's hand heartily. 'Now, you look after this precious girl of ours, right?' She turned to Catherine, who stood up to hug her hello, and Shazza and Catherine clung to each other for a bit too long. 'Now, isn't this lovely?' Shazza went on, when she and Catherine finally released each other, her eyes glazed.

'I'll just go and get the sandwiches,' said Catherine, standing up and leaving the room.

'I'll help you!' shouted Shazza, breaking into a run and almost skidding as she disappeared around the door.

Dave and Kitty were left alone, and for a dreadful moment, Kitty thought they had nothing to say to each other. Perhaps she and Dave were just a little overcome by everything and therefore it was difficult to talk about normal things. They had a wedding to organise and so many big conversations to have, so perhaps small talk was impossible.

He'd slicked down his hair with a jar of Brylcreem which he'd found in his parents' wardrobe and had belonged to his dead dad. 'No point in wasting it,' he'd said. 'This stuff doesn't go off.' He looked like a ventriloquist's dummy with his combed-down hair and weird suit. She had a very strong suspicion that this brown three-piece number belonged to his dead dad too but couldn't bear to be told the truth so didn't ask.

'I think...' she began.

'Shall we...?' He stopped. 'You go...'

'No, you.' Maybe he would say something loving towards her, how he appreciated her and how he wanted no one else on his team but her... something which would ease her panic.

'Okay.' He grimaced again. 'Shall we order cable television? There are good deals on packages at the moment or should we stick with Irish terrestrial TV? I mean, now we are to be married, it might be a good idea to invest in a decent entertainment system, all the sports channels and everything else.'

'I don't know, Dave,' she said, weakly. 'You're the information technologist after all.'

He puffed up his chest a bit. 'Yes, I am. Well, it will be the first decision I make as a newly betrothed man.'

The doorbell rang again and Kitty almost ran to open it.

'Good afternoon, Kitty...' It was Dave's mother, dressed in a white dress, white jacket and white high heels, with a white bag which was the kind of drawstring bag that was usually reserved for flower girls. She looked as though she was dressed for her own wedding rather than mother-of-the-groom.

'Hello, Maureen,' said Kitty, knowing, with horror, that there would always be three of them in her marriage.

'Show me the ring,' demanded Maureen, her fingers like tentacles reaching for Kitty's hand. Maureen pored over it. 'It's not every woman who can carry off a ring like that... it takes a certain kind of elegance to do it justice...' She looked straight at Kitty. 'But never mind... just don't lose it, will you?' And she dropped her voice to a hissed whisper of barely suppressed menace. 'And if the two of you divorce at any point, bring the ring straight back to me? Don't you go selling it, you hear me? It's my ring and you'll return it.'

'Of course, Maureen.' Kitty forced a smile. 'Would you like to come in?'

'Is David overheating? He's wearing his father's suit and I was worried all day. Those old suits don't have any of those modern moisture-wicking qualities and the poor boy might be sweating buckets.'

'He's just in the front room,' said Kitty.

Kitty left Maureen to it and walked quickly to the kitchen, where she noticed Shazza and Catherine stopped talking, looking startled when she walked in.

'Yes, Catherine,' said Shazza, in a loud voice, 'I prefer window boxes to hanging baskets as well. Horizontal planting is easier on the eye. Oh, hi, Kitty...'

'Dave's mother has arrived,' Kitty said, looking at the kitchen clock. 3.10 p.m. Billy should be here soon. 'You have to come and say hello.'

They sat in the front room, drinking tea.

'David,' said Maureen, 'tell everyone about the washing line you installed for me. You see, David is very good with his hands. Very talented, always was. He was very good at the old Lego when he was young. I remember he built a car once, with wheels, wasn't it, David?'

'That's right, Mam,' said Dave, looking delighted with himself. 'Go on about the washing line because it was not an easy installation job but the kind of thing that wouldn't be worth the time of your common or garden local handyjobman. So, Mam was stuck, weren't you, Mam?'

'That's right,' she said. '"Don't worry, Mam," says David. "I'm here. I wouldn't let you down or leave you in the lurch with nothing to dry your smalls on." So, off he goes, hammer, screws... what else did you have, David?'

'Posidrive,' he said proudly. 'It's a type of screwdriver.'

'Posidrive,' repeated Maureen. 'I'll have to write that down. That'll come up in *University Challenge*, will it not? Everything does at some point. We love that programme, don't we, David? The youngsters are so clever, aren't they?'

'Not that clever, Mam,' said Dave with a hint of irritation. 'I mean, it's not that impressive... Anyway, so there's I with my tools...'

'All belonging to David's late father, David senior...' said Maureen. 'And I have to go to the little girl's room. I find sausage rolls a little too greasy. They go straight through.'

'Should we open the champagne now?' asked Catherine.

'Just wait for Dad,' said Kitty. She slid her phone out of her pocket to glance at the time and to see if Billy had texted. Nothing. 3.30 p.m. now.

The doorbell rang. Thank God.

'I'll get it,' Kitty said, jumping up and rushing out into the hall. She pulled open the door, a big smile on her face...

But it was Annie. 'Sorry I'm late... lost my keys and couldn't find my purse and had to ask someone for a lift, but I'm here now... let's get the party started!'

36

The champagne unopened, the sandwiches only half-touched, the guests not quite ready to begin without the bride-to-be's father's presence, Kitty couldn't quite look at Catherine, not wanting to see an I-told-you-so expression. Not that Catherine was that kind of person, but Kitty didn't want to risk any kind of acknowledgement that she had been hasty in her rush to forgive and forget. Billy wasn't a bad person, just perennially unreliable – something which Kitty had thought could only hurt her as a child. But as she sat there, one ear out for footsteps on the drive-way, one eye on the clock on the mantelpiece, she tried not to show how hurt she was. Kitty felt five years old again, abandoned, forgotten about. She'd let him in and opened her heart. She'd been so willing to start all over again.

Annie kept the conversation going, talking and talking about Ibiza, about everyone she had met there, the cocktails and the clubs, the beaches and the bars. Maureen kept trying to insert herself into the conversation, but for once, she was unable. Annie's Ibizan zeal was too strong.

Eventually, Kitty stood up. 'Right, champagne, everyone?' She went to the kitchen to retrieve the champagne and, returning to the front room, began pouring it into glasses in a slightly angry, perfunctory and distinctly non-celebratory fashion.

'I'm going to give a speech,' said Shazza, standing up, her glass in her hand. 'I just want to say thank you to my best friend in the whole wide world, who I love like a sister, who I love more than my sister! Kitty, you're the best. I love the way you put everyone's needs ahead of your own, and how you would prefer to be unhappy just to make others happy. We've had such a laugh together over the years, but especially recently... I love you, Kitty.'

Catherine was next. 'To my wonderful daughter Kitty. You deserve to be happy, loved and appreciated. I don't know what we'd all do without you. You are so wonderfully dependable.'

Annie insisted on standing up next. 'I just want to say that I am so proud of my gorgeous niece Kitty... I hope you and Keith are very happy together.'

'David,' said Maureen. 'His name's David!' She glared at Annie, who laughed.

'Sorry! I'm terrible with names,' said Annie. 'Barely remember my own most of the time. Apologies, Mary...'

'Maureen!' shouted Dave.

'Catherine, any more of that delicious champagne? I like the real stuff. Prosecco and all the others give me a headache. Could drink this all day long.' She looked over at Catherine. 'By the way,' Annie said. 'You know that jacket of yours... the posh one...'

'The Yves Saint Laurent one?' said Kitty.

'Whatever it's called,' said Annie. 'Anyway, I left it somewhere... I can't find it. I've searched all over...' She paused. 'It needed a clean anyway. Save you the price of the dry cleaning.'

Kitty's blood began to boil and she clutched her champagne glass so hard, it was in danger of shattering. She knew she shouldn't take anything out on Annie, but why was she in this situation, pathetically waiting for Billy and being forced to marry Dave?

Kitty tried to collect herself. She was being ridiculous. Anyone would think he'd held a gun to her head and made her say yes when it had been her idea all the while. But it wasn't fair. There was Annie who just turned up and drank and behaved irresponsibly, and even Shazza had nothing weighing her down. It was so easy for her to come up with plans for her and Kitty to change their lives. She could snog Rory and just have fun, whereas Kitty was being dragged backwards, as though caught in a riptide. She thought of Tom and wondered how he was and what he thought about her being engaged to Dave.

He would just find someone else to go sailing, or walk home… or sleep with.

* * *

Later, when Dave had gone to take his mother home and the rest of them were clearing up, Kitty turned to Shazza. 'So what,' she asked, feeling a strange and unsettling edge in her voice, as though it didn't quite belong to her, as though nothing belonged to her, 'happened with you and Rory?'

'Oh, I'm not going to see him again,' Shazza said, airily. 'I told you, I was going to change. I need to be more sensible, remember? My self-imposed virtual nunnery was going so well…' She broke off to explain to Catherine and Annie what she meant. 'I'm still off men,' she said, 'for my mental health. And I've got to say it works a treat. I was back on the wagon briefly, but I reined myself in and got back into man-rehab ASAP.' She turned back to Kitty. 'One of us has to stick to our side of the bargain…'

'What do you mean?' Kitty felt suddenly furious. 'All this is easy for you, Shazza, flitting about, in and out of man-rehab and virtual nunneries when you feel like it. You're not getting married like I am and I'm not going to be flitting about, in fact, I am doing the grown-up thing. You are always so incredibly critical of me, just because I operate on an entirely different moral compass. It just isn't fair.'

'Moral compass?' repeated Shazza. 'What on earth do you mean by that?'

'I mean, that I do the right thing, always have done. I am a loyal friend to you, a loyal partner to Dave, and guess what? You just see me as a pushover, you're always making me the butt of a punchline, showing me up, but I don't complain...'

'Kitty...' Catherine began, but Kitty held up her hand.

'And I don't go on about myself and tell people about where I'm at and if I'm on or off men... the number of people who you have told about Mr Unmentionable! God, he's the most mentioned unmentionable in the world, ever! Anyone would think you were the only person to be heartbroken!' She was crying now.

'Kitty,' began Annie, 'look, Shazza is just...'

Kitty flung around. 'Don't you start,' she said, 'treating my mother like a bank machine and taxi driver and chef... and she lent you her beautiful jacket and you go and lose it! It's so typical of how little you value her! You don't deserve Mum.'

Annie stared at her, her eyes wide, hurt, confused.

'Kitty, what is wrong with you?' asked Catherine.

'Why are you being so horrible?' said Shazza.

'I think I should go,' said Annie, gathering up her things. 'Thank you for a lovely afternoon, Catherine. Bye, Kitty. See you all soon.'

'I'll come with you,' said Shazza, close behind her. 'Kitty, call me when you feel like talking.' She gave Catherine a meaningful look. 'Catherine, thank you for everything...'

When it was just Catherine and Kitty left, Kitty felt utterly dreadful. Why had she turned on the people she loved the most? Why was she being so horrible? She couldn't sort out any of the emotions which were whirring around in her head. They were moving so fast.

'I'm going to go home,' said Kitty, stiffly, wishing she could unburden herself, but she didn't know what she wanted to say. She couldn't remember ever being so unhappy. She had work in the morning and she had to somehow be her better self again, except she didn't know where she had gone and if she'd ever come back.

37

It was Monday morning in the office and before she turned on her computer, Kitty looked at the ring on her hand. It was gaudy and horrible and made her hand look as though it belonged to someone else. She felt she was living a life which no longer belonged to her. Why had she thought marriage was the answer to her problems? She sat at her desk and then realised that there was a light sprinkling of dust on her computer screen. She hadn't wiped anything down for a week or so now, and everything was okay. She could see the screen and she hadn't died from bacteria or germs. In fact, the orchid on her desk looked even perkier and was coming into bud again. All those routines and rituals that she had staked her entire existence to were just a waste of time. Where had all that control and order and neatness got her? Precisely nowhere.

Kitty picked up her phone, typing first a message to Shazza and then one to Annie.

KITTY

I'm sorry. Will you forgive me?

KITTY

I am so sorry for all the things I said. Will you forgive me?

Her phone remained still, the messages not read, making Kitty feel totally alone. How could she make everything better? Or perhaps it was too late for all of that. Kitty's self-loathing settled into her bones like a rainy Sunday. She deserved everything she got, she'd brought this on herself.

ANNIE

You were absolutely right to speak the truth. I love u. Nothing changes anything!!!! Let's just forget about it!!!!

ANNIE

Will pay you both back!!!!!

Kitty felt even worse. Annie was just such a sweet person. It was like kicking a dog or a cat. How horrible Kitty was. She put her head in her hands for a moment, the ring on her finger pressing into her forehead. How could she have treated Annie so badly? And Shazza? This was dreadful. She would have to talk to them both. A text just wasn't enough.

'Is that an engagement ring?' She looked up to see Mary Rose staring at her hand.

Hughie's eyes were also on the ring. 'What,' he said. 'The. Flying. Jesus. Is. *That*?' His expression was one of revulsion combined with complete and utter bewilderment.

Mary Rose was also looking slightly confused. 'I think,' she said, 'it's diamanté and faux-meralds.'

'Faux-meralds?' said Hughie. 'Do you mean what I think you mean?'

Mary Rose nodded. 'My family owned the jewellers in

Fairview for thirty years, I know my way around gemstones and their pretenders. Not,' she said quickly, 'that there is anything wrong with faux-meralds and diamantés... I'm quite partial to a saphfaux myself... it's just that the settings are unique... the way the stones are so randomly placed. It's either art or it's...'

'A mess,' said Hughie. 'I thought you had taste, Kitty. You work in an advertising company. Bling is not king, here. Tat is not all that.'

'It's the ugliest ring I've ever seen,' agreed Kitty. 'But what can I do?'

'Not wear it?' suggested Hughie. 'But why are you wearing such a thing?'

'I think it has a certain folksy charm,' said Mary Rose. 'As though it's an anti-ring, so wrong it's right. But am I right in thinking that it is an engagement ring? And if so, then it doesn't matter what we think, if you love it...'

'I don't,' said Kitty. 'But what can I do?'

'Wait,' said Hughie. 'So Dave asked you to marry him?'

Kitty nodded.

'And you said yes?'

Kitty nodded again.

'But...' began Hughie, looking bewildered and perplexed as though Kitty had suggested she was moving to the moon or giving up chocolate for Lent. It did not compute.

But Kitty was thinking of Tom, wondering where he was, and what was he doing. She hadn't answered his text because she didn't know what to say. If she allowed some time to pass and not go to practice, then they might be able to move on and beyond what had happened. They just needed a little bit of distance and with the benefit of the passing of time and – if she avoided leaving the house and remained a hermit – perhaps they could be friends.

Except... she didn't want to be *friends* with him. She wouldn't be able to sit there across from him in The Island and not want to reach over and touch him. At the end of the night, she would hate having to say goodbye, knowing that Dave was at home waiting for her.

'Change it for another ring,' Hughie was saying. 'Honestly, it's worse than one you might get in a cracker.'

'I can't... it's his mother's...'

'Well, give it back,' said Hughie. 'Tell her the ring is shite and you will not disrespect your hand for one moment longer...'

'It's not that easy,' said Kitty.

Even Alex was looking at the ring with a slightly horrified look on her face.

'Kitty,' said Mary Rose, 'one day you will realise that you don't have to please people and that you can say no.'

'That day,' said Hughie, 'is obviously yet to arrive. And BTW are you sure you want to actually *marry* Dave? As in betrove yourself, be bound by him in those gridirons of patriarchy, stay with him through sick and thin. Of all the men in all the world, he is the only one for you? There is not a single other man who does it for you? No one sexier, handsomer, more intelligent... kinder... because leaving you to go to his mam's isn't what I would call a kind thing to do...'

Kitty thought of Tom again, her heart crumpling like an old drinks can. 'No one,' she said, her voice breaking slightly. She cleared her throat. 'No one else.' She really had to move on and forget about him. That was a dalliance, a diversion in the road of life. Nothing more to say, except to get on with her life.

But Hughie was peering at her. 'Oh my God,' he said. 'There is! There is someone else. I have watched enough *Judge Judy* in my life to know when someone is lying, and you are lying! Am I right?'

Kitty tried to shake her head, but somehow it turned into a nod. 'But there's nothing I can do,' she said, desperately. 'Someone once said that you have to be careful about ending up down a rabbit hole with the wrong person and that's exactly what's happened to me. I can't get out. How can I hurt Dave after everything?'

Hughie was looking incredulous. 'You just do,' he said. 'Like ripping off a plaster. Done. Gone. *Sayonara. Adios. Slán go foill.*'

Kitty shook her head, miserably. How had being proposed to made her feel totally out of control? Where was that woman who had been drinking in The Grace O'Malley only a week ago, swimming off the islands of Dublin Bay, and scoring goals and... well, scoring Tom? She had thought she and Shazza were changing their lives for the better, but it was only Shazza who had the real strength to do it. She was stuck and couldn't see a way out so all she could do was crack on and make the most of it.

But Hughie and Mary Rose were both looking concerned.

'Everything's fine,' Kitty insisted, trying to smile, but knowing she looked deranged. 'I mean, I'm getting married! It's all I've ever wanted!'

38

Kitty arrived home, hoping to see signs of functional activity, such as CV writing, the house tidied or even a clean and showered Dave. But there were only signs of dysfunctional activity as Dave still had sleep in his eyes and he was wearing his old, saggy-kneed jogging bottoms and, despite it being a warm evening, he had on his dad's ancient argyle jumper.

'Nice day?' Kitty said, hoping she didn't sound sarcastic. If she was to make the best of this, then she would have to crack on.

'Very nice day,' he said, happily. 'I've rested. Watched *Countdown*. And *A Place In The Sun*. Such a relaxing programme. And it got me thinking.'

'Oh yes?' Kitty noticed the amount of crumbs that had been scattered after Dave's various snacks throughout the day. You could make a whole new loaf if you stuck them all together. She resisted the temptation of getting out the tiny vacuum and giving it a blast. What was the point, anyway? Everything just became messy again.

'Well... I was thinking I don't want to be an information technologist, but perhaps we could buy a little place in Spain or Portugal and drink wine and eat olives...'

'Dave, you don't like olives,' said Kitty. 'You don't even like wine particularly.'

'No, but that shouldn't stop us. And I was thinking it would be good for Mam. She loves Spain. She was saying she would love to come with us...'

Kitty had to hold on to the door to stop herself from falling over. Nothing had changed, she thought. Nothing was different. She was right back where she'd always been. Square one. She looked at the clock. Nearly 7 p.m. She was meant to be meeting Billy down at the ground in half an hour but she couldn't decide just to stay away. What if he stood her up again? How many chances was she going to give him? But what if he turned up and she wasn't there? She couldn't bear to think of him waiting for her, and for some reason, it was easier to be stood up herself, rather than doing the standing up.

She quickly changed upstairs and then boiled a kettle, poured the water over some instant noodles, stuck in a fork, and handed it to Dave.

'Dinner,' she said, with a smile. 'I'm going to football practice with my dad.'

He took the bowl but looked perplexed. 'Football?' he said. 'Since when do you *play* football? You don't even know what *football* is.'

'I just started recently,' she said. 'Shazza...'

'Oh, Shazza! I might have known!'

Kitty left the room and had her hand on the front door, ready to go, but Dave had followed her.

'But Mam's calling in,' he said. 'She wants to start planning the wedding. What time will you be back? Although I still can't believe you're going to football...'

'About 8.30.'

'She'll still be here,' he said. 'Pick up some full-fat milk on your way home. You know she hates the kind you usually buy. And biscuits. She likes a lemon puff.'

On the walk to the ground, Kitty tried not to think about Dave. There was still room and time for him to change, but perhaps she had to change. Wasn't that it? You couldn't change other people, you could just change your responses to them. Surely that was all she had to do, not worry so much, be more zen, be chilled, let everything wash over her. And maybe that was her problem, she let things fester, wanted everything to be perfect and tried to control everything and everyone.

She thought of Billy. What would she say to him about Sunday? Should she mention it? And why was she giving him a second chance? He'd blown it yesterday and yet here she was again, handing him another opportunity to let her down. But surely he wouldn't let her down again, would he? Surely he'd learned his lessons by now? She hadn't texted him to make sure he remembered. If he turned up, then she knew he cared. If he didn't, then that was the end. No more Billy. Ever. But she remained hopeful. He would be there. He would. He loved her and she loved him, in their own way.

But Billy wasn't at the Sandycove Seafarers' ground when Kitty arrived and so, ever hopeful, she sat on the sideline for a bit before finding a football and practising dribbling, and then she did some of the stretches she'd seen proper footballers do, the ankle grab, the heel-to-bum one, the wild arm-swinging one and the hip openers where you dislocate your joint and open and close your legs as though they were a door.

Tomorrow, she thought, she would see Tom again at five-a-side training. Would he try to talk to her? What would she say?

How could she explain it? Perhaps she should probably give up the football and make it less awkward for everyone.

It was getting on for 8 p.m. now. The light was beginning to fade and in another half an hour, they wouldn't be able to play. Had she and Billy definitely arranged to meet here? Kitty tried to remember what he had said exactly. Maybe he had said to meet at the café for a hot chocolate? Or maybe he was ill? Why else would he miss the engagement gathering yesterday?

She began walking quickly, out of the grounds and down the road towards the village. Billy lived in a small, one-bedroom cottage behind the main street. As Kitty turned up towards it, she saw him, chatting with someone, looking as though he hadn't a care in the world.

'Dad!'

He looked over and froze for a moment as the man he was talking to shuffled off and then it was just Kitty and her father looking at each other.

'I thought we were meant to be meeting to play football?' she said.

'Were we? Sorry, love, I was late...'

'And yesterday, you were meant to come to Mum's to celebrate me getting engaged...'

'Sorry... I've a head like a sieve...'

Kitty couldn't understand how you could forget that you were meeting your one and only daughter, the person with whom you had spent such a lovely evening only a week ago. The person who should mean most to you in the world but so obviously didn't? So he wasn't ill. He'd just forgotten. As he had all the other times he'd forgotten or been late or hadn't bothered. He would spend his whole life letting her down, she knew it. She had been so willing to love him and he'd thrown it all away.

She turned and began walking away.

'Kitty!'

She turned briefly. 'I'm tired, Dad... really, really tired.' She kept walking, feeling done with everyone and everything.

* * *

Back home, Kitty sat on the arm of the armchair, her head full of everything else in her life and wishing she didn't have to talk to Dave or Maureen.

'Another lemon puff, Maureen?'

Dave glanced up. 'Kitty bought them specially, Mam,' he said. 'She knows you like them.'

Maureen put one whole into her mouth and another on her saucer. 'I can resist most things except temptation and lemon puffs,' she said, with a cackle. 'Who said that? Some writer...'

'Oscar Wilde,' said Dave, who was sitting on the sofa, his eyes fixed on the blaring TV.

'Oh, you are clever, David,' said Maureen. 'Isn't he clever, Kitty?'

'Yes, very...' Kitty felt like crying, her mind full of Billy, Shazza, Annie and Tom. A few days ago, she had been so happy, her life full of these wonderful people. And now everything looked so much smaller and shallower.

Maureen's shoes were off and her feet were on the coffee table, clad in a pair of giant pink velvet slippers.

'I thought I'd leave these slippers in your house,' she said to Kitty. 'One pair in mine and a pair in yours.'

Kitty wondered if the charity shop would accept something so hideous.

'Let's have a chat in the kitchen,' said Maureen, rising to her be-slippered feet and groaning with the effort. Her eyes fell on

Kitty's hand and she grabbed her wrist, twisting the horrible ring so the stones were facing upwards.

'It's a little big on me,' explained Kitty.

'It needs to be *seen*,' said Maureen. 'What is the point of having such a glorious treasure if it is going to be twisted around and not on display? You want the world to know you are engaged to a man who thinks so much of you he has given you this special ring.'

'Mam,' said Dave, his eyes still on the screen, 'will you put the kettle on?'

Maureen nodded. 'Yes, David, just after Kitty and I have a little chat. Come, Kitty, while I make us all a fresh pot of tea.'

In the kitchen, Maureen gestured to one of the stools for Kitty to sit on, while she stood looming in front of the fridge.

Maureen closed the door. 'Now,' she said, 'I thought we'd have a little heart-to-heart about the needs and wants of my David. As you know, he spent a little time with me in the family home...'

'I'm aware of that...'

'Indeed. Now, David has been run-down... he's been finding it hard to fulfil all the obligations that life...' – at this, Maureen focused her laser eyes on Kitty – 'forces upon him. And I know my David, and I know his heart is in the right place and he wants to do the best for all of us, but we, I mean, he...' – she gave a little laugh – 'decided to ask you to marry him because he is such an obliging young man and he wanted to be kind. Which is how I've brought him up. "David," I said, "are you definitely 100 per cent fully and completely sure?" And he said yes. And I said, "Well, in that case you can have my ring." A ring which should be admired by all and Sunday.'

'It's sundry,' said Kitty, who was already plotting her escape. Back door and over the side wall? Dash the door and straight through the living room to the front door? Or just feign illness and collapse in the middle of the kitchen floor?

'Anyway, so I thought I would give a little feedback about what I know about my David. Well, number one, he doesn't like being told what to do. I know no man likes being told what to do, but David will do the opposite. So if you say make sure you shower today, he'll make sure he doesn't. It's a funny little quirk of his but easily worked around. And we all know how high your standards are. Some might say that you were a little too clean and tidy, and as your mother-in-law-to-be, I should not be complaining. Who wants their future grandchildren living in a pigsty? Some of the homes of the daughters-in-law I hear about would make your skin crawl. But, Kitty, lower your standards and you might be much happier because, to be frank, you don't seem that happy and our family is a happy one. Always with a funny story and buckets of Irish charm. No one wants to live with someone with a face like a drain. And you'd be quite pretty if you smile from time to time.'

Kitty didn't smile now.

'And,' went on Maureen, 'what's all this about football training? I am not sure if football is entirely appropriate for women. What if you get injured? And think of your unborn children? You might get kicked in the stomach. I think you shouldn't go any longer. Hmm? Now, shall we go back into the living room and join David? And we can start to plan the wedding. Although, he's just ordered himself a Sky box. You know men, doesn't take much to keep them happy. Now, David, will you give me a hand with something?'

Maureen went outside, Dave behind her, and there was a rustle and a bustle as the door opened and a huge shape entered the room, much like if a giant bin bag took on a life of its own, but this turned out to be a dress carrier, with Maureen behind.

'I had to buy it,' she was saying. 'You know what they say: see it, pounce on it, hand over the old credit card! Or is that cakes? I don't know!' She laughed, delighted with herself, while Dave laughed along. 'Anyway, I thought I would wear this to the wedding. As mother-of-the-groom, it's my day too, isn't it?'

'Mam, you do know it's not your wedding, don't you!' Dave teased, turning to Kitty, still laughing at his mother's unbridled bridal joy. 'She thinks she's the one getting married!' He gazed at his mother with such affection.

'I just thought I had to show the two of you,' she said. 'The big unveiling... talking of which, there was a matching veil... Now, it's not remotely like your veil would be, just a little bit of lace... more of a hair accessory than anything.'

'Mam, we're in suspense,' said Dave. 'Show us all of it!'

Maureen and Dave wrestled with the long zipper on the bag and, like a giant, frilly monster, something began to creep out, until eventually officially the world's worst dress was revealed. Layered, ruched, puffy... it was everything a dress shouldn't be. Kitty's main feeling was one of overwhelm, as though she was drowning in a tsunami of tulle, a lake of lace, an avalanche of snow-white. This was a nuptial nightmare on an epic scale.

'Now, it's not white,' Maureen was saying. 'It's actually a cream... very, very pale...'

'It looks white,' said Kitty.

'Mam, I think it's lovely,' said Dave. 'I know nothing about dresses or anything like that, but as a layman, I would say it's very nice. Wouldn't you, Kitty?'

'I'm slightly stunned,' said Kitty. 'It's an unbelievable dress...' It was literally unbelievable. These kind of schemes and stunts would be her life... forever. Maureen would be pulling these kind of tricks for years to come.

'Isn't it?' Maureen held the dress against her as she gave them a twirl. 'And now for the veil – I mean the hair accessory...' From the bag, she pulled out a veil – an *actual* wedding veil – and put it on the top of her head. 'It's lovely, isn't it? Reminds me of my own day. Now, obviously, that was much longer, this is more like a Spanish mantilla, except white...'

This was all madness, Kitty thought, needing to get out. Her first thought was of Annie, she had to see how she was.

She stood up. 'I have to go out,' she said. 'I have to go and see my auntie Annie.'

Maureen wrinkled her nose. 'That one? The one who goes on about her holidays? I thought she'd never stop droning on, as though no one else had ever left the country ever.'

'You've never left the country, Mam,' said Dave.

'That's not the point.' Maureen silenced him with an icy glare. 'But just to say that your auntie Annie is a bit of a bore. No one cares, I wanted to say. I mean, the event in your mother's was to celebrate your engagement to my son, not a travelogue to wherever she had been...'

'Ibiza,' said Kitty quietly.

'Wherever that is. Probably full of people with tattoos and smoking those vape things and speaking in loud voices to each other.' She gave Kitty a nod. 'Your auntie Annie would fit right in.'

'Actually, she's probably the nicest person I've ever met,' said Kitty. 'She's always cheerful, never gossips about people, never has a bad thing to say about anyone. She doesn't sit and judge, she just goes and lives her life...'

Maureen opened her mouth to speak but Kitty held up her hand.

'I have to go and see her,' she said. 'I won't be long. I'll leave you both to your programme.'

'You do that,' said Maureen. 'We're all right here, aren't we, David?'

'We are,' he said.

'Close the door on your way out,' said Maureen. 'There's a little bit of a breeze on my neck.'

* * *

'Who is it?'

'It's me, Annie. Kitty.'

Annie answered the door, her eyes red. 'Is everything all right? Is your mother okay?'

'We're fine,' said Kitty, her heart breaking to see Annie's tear-streaked face. So Annie hadn't been all right. 'How are you?'

'I couldn't be better,' said Annie, trying to smile. She was wearing a tatty black satin dressing gown, the faux fur around the edge a little moth-eaten. 'But what brings you here?'

'I wanted to apologise again,' said Kitty. 'In person. I wanted to say that I love you and I'm really sorry...'

Annie began to cry again. 'I'm so sorry,' she said through her sobs. 'I don't know what's wrong with me. You don't need to say sorry to me... you were right to say everything you did. I suppose the truth hurts.'

'But it wasn't the truth,' said Kitty, desperately. 'I was in a bad mood and blamed everyone but myself. It's the mess I'm in... and it's nothing to do with you or Shazza.'

'Poor Shazza,' said Annie. 'How is she?'

'She hasn't forgiven me,' said Kitty. 'Not yet.'

'You'd better come in,' said Annie. 'Before the neighbours see me. They already think I'm one of those flibbertigibbets... I don't want them seeing me crying. You know what I always say? Laugh and the world laughs with you, cry and no one cares...'

'I care,' said Kitty. 'I really care.'

'I know you do,' said Annie, sadly. 'I've let you down. I've taken advantage of you and Catherine.'

'You haven't...' Kitty stepped inside and Annie closed the door behind them, wiping her eyes with the corner of her dressing gown.

'What's wrong?'

'I haven't stopped crying since Sunday,' admitted Annie, looking so small and vulnerable. 'It's just a few home truths came as a bit of a shock. I mean, of course you were right to say them...'

'I wasn't...'

'And I've been reflecting on everything.' Annie managed a small smile, looking up at Kitty. 'You and Catherine are my world. My world. My everything. As Barry White used to say. Once, twice, three times my world. Anyway. Something like that. But you're my everything and to think that I have done anything to make you feel as though I'm not your everything... and of course I'm not. You have so much more. You have Keith...'

'Dave...'

'Exactly. And I have just you and your mother.'

'Annie,' said Kitty. 'You are my world. You are my lovely, precious aunt. You are my family. You are my everything! I love you.'

Annie was smiling. 'I love you too.'

'I really am sorry.'

'So am I.' They clung to each other for a while, both crying and patting backs, trying to soothe the other.

'Let's just forget about it. And you go back to Keith...'

'Dave...'

'And give him my very best love from his auntie-to-be.'

They hugged again and after reassuring each other of their love, Kitty left, feeling slightly better but determined never, ever to hurt anyone ever again.

39

On Tuesday morning, Mary Rose returned from a meeting, looking a little pale, as she cleared her throat. 'Right... may I have your attention, please?'

Kitty and Hughie looked up.

'I've been told by Mr Mulligan that if we don't win the Welcome Ireland pitch, then the team is going to be dispersed and absorbed into others in the company.'

'Dispersed?' Hughie stood up. 'I will not be dispersed. No one gets to disperse me!'

Mary Rose smiled wanly and Kitty noticed her hands were shaking a little. 'Look,' said Mary Rose, 'career disappointment is a normal part of life. You two will be fine, you'll be on another team soon and all will be well.'

'But I like this team,' said Hughie. 'It's like you hate your family but you don't want another one. We're all dysfunctional together and we know each other's foibles... I mean, who else knows my coffee order? Who else knows that Kitty only eats tuna and mayonnaise sandwiches? And where is Alex going to go when she recovers from whatever it is she is recovering from?'

'Alex won't be coming back,' said Mary Rose. 'Not while Ben O'Leary is still head of the company. But look, all is not lost. I will get another job... and I'm going to sell my house. Buy a new one, smaller, perhaps further out from the city... Dundalk, I was thinking...'

Kitty looked at Hughie, and he shrugged and opened and closed his mouth, as though he'd run out of words. So had Kitty. For a copywriter to run out of words showed just how desperate their situation was.

* * *

At lunchtime, Kitty wandered over to the National Library, half-hoping that Tom and Roz might be there and... God, she didn't know what she was doing or why, when she was the one who told him to go away. She had behaved terribly, allowing herself and Tom to get close and then abandoning him as soon as Dave returned.

She walked through the library reading room. There was the old man again, asleep on the chair, and another couple of toddlers being read to by their grandmother, and there were the students, diligently working away. Kitty sat down on one of the low couches and wondered if it was possible to stay here forever and never leave. Would anyone notice if she just fell asleep like the old man? Perhaps they wouldn't like to disturb her and on she would slumber. As long as she kept her eyes closed, they would leave her alone. She edged down a little and shut her eyes.

* * *

When Kitty arrived home, she was determined to make the best of her life. After all, she did care for Dave and was certain that things would improve... if she learned to be less selfish and a nicer person. She shuddered when she thought of how awful she had been to Shazza and Annie.

'Shall we watch *World's Greatest Manhunts*?' Dave was flicking through all of their 300+ channels from the Sky box, which had been installed that day.

'No thanks...' said Kitty.

'What about *Machetes and Maracas*... you have to stand blindfolded and they throw things at you and it could be either a...'

'*Machete or a maraca*? No thanks.' Kitty was going to have to agree to something soon or they'd be like this all night. She had to just accept that this was her life, that they watched terrible TV together. The thought of her other life, the one spent on the pitch of the Sandycove Seafarers, or in The Island, or even on board *Pansy-Pearl*, seemed now to be a figment of her imagination. Had any of it really happened?

'Or *Survival In the Desert*... these celebrities have to...'

'Survive in the desert? Maybe...'

'Or *Celebrity Bear Wrestling*?'

'Go on then...'

It was worse than Kitty could have imagined, but Dave seemed happy, his arm around her shoulders, allowing small burps to escape from the side of his mouth. 'Apologies,' he said when a bigger than usual one was released. 'Must be the lasagne.'

She'd added lots of hidden vegetables into the lasagne, hoping they would aid his sulphurous smell, but it seemed that the influx of veg had created a new problem.

'Mam is really looking forward to the wedding,' said Dave. 'Which surprises me as I never thought she would agree to me getting married.'

'Maybe you should have proposed to her,' said Kitty.

Thankfully Dave laughed. 'Maybe... but, seriously, she's still looking for outfits for herself... she says she needs an evening dress... one to change into for the speeches and the dancing. By the way,' he went on, 'I saw your friend Shazza earlier. She was in a van with two men... two men! Can you believe it?'

'Easily,' said Kitty, with another pang of pain. 'It was probably Tom and Rory...'

'One had a beard is all I know,' said Dave, 'and my dad used to say only serial killers and filthy articles have beards, so I don't know who Shazza is hanging about with, serial killer or filthy article?'

'Perhaps he's both,' said Kitty. 'Maybe we should save her before she's indoctrinated in their cult...'

'Oh, you can save her,' said Dave. 'I couldn't be bothered. She's always getting herself into trouble, that girl. She's not like you, thankfully. Always off doing mad things, whereas you are not. You like to stay home with your financier' – he meant fiancé – 'and watch TV...' He smiled at her with his slightly yellow teeth which had some of those hidden vegetables stuck in them. Not so hidden now, Kitty thought.

She checked her phone. Nothing from Shazza. She realised that a text from Shazza was the only thing which would make her happy. The thought of a Shazza-less existence was unbearable.

And nothing from Tom, but that was understandable, and probably for the best. She would see him later at training and they wouldn't have to talk. And she could give up the football if it was too awkward. It was a terrifyingly claustrophobic feeling. And there was work to think of, the Welcome Ireland pitch dominating everything. She was inching closer to a finished idea, but there was still something missing. What on earth could it be? She'd gone through everything with Hughie and Mary Rose earlier and they too liked it but didn't love it.

40

That evening, Shazza was already in the changing room when Kitty entered. 'Hi...' she said, but Shazza was examining the laces on her football boots and didn't look up.

Kitty sat across from her and began removing her kit from her bag.

'I didn't think you'd be coming,' said Shazza, still focused on her laces.

'Why?'

Shazza looked up at her. 'Well, not after you treated practically half of the team badly.'

'I'm sorry,' said Kitty. 'I don't know why I said those things...'

'What's the point of saying sorry?' said Shazza. 'It's what you think, isn't it? I can't be friends with someone who I will always be thinking that they hate me...'

'I don't hate you,' said Kitty, near tears again. But Shazza was right. If the roles were reversed, she wouldn't be able to forgive her either. 'How do you know I treated Tom badly?'

'Rory told me everything,' said Shazza. 'Tom was really

upset... said he turned up, all happy and everything and basically you told him to get lost...'

'But it wasn't my fault...'

'Of course it wasn't. Those words didn't come out of your mouth. Someone ventriloquised you.'

'I'm so sorry, Shazza,' said Kitty. 'I wasn't myself...'

'You looked like you.'

'I know... I'm sorry.' Kitty felt more miserable than ever. 'Do you think I should just leave now?'

'What? And abandon yet another commitment?'

'What other commitment have I abandoned?'

Shazza looked up, her eyes shining with tears. 'Your commitment to me and our pact to have fun and be there for each other! Our commitment to be friends. Our commitment to be good people and not shout and put the other down...'

'I'm sorry... I really am.'

'Well...' Shazza shrugged. 'It's done now. And you've hurt Tom. Why don't you just kick him with your football boot, right in his testicles? You may as well finish off your hatchet job on the poor man.'

'Shazza...' she began.

'It's Sharon to you from now on,' said Shazza, haughtily. 'Shazza is only for my inner circle, of which you are no longer a member.' She walked outside, leaving Kitty trailing behind her.

Tara had already got Rory and Tom started on their warm-ups and she was taking them through their jumping jacks. 'Another twenty,' she said. 'And then push-ups.' She smiled when she saw Shazza and Kitty walking out along the lumpy grass. 'Here they are,' she said. 'The terrible twosome... how's it going, girls? Any news? Recovered from Friday?'

Kitty could barely remember last Friday night, it seemed so long ago, but she managed to smile and joined in with the jumping jacks, standing beside Shazza. She spent the rest of the training running around, trying to show that she wasn't miserable.

Tom had given her a polite wave and Rory had given her his usual 'howsitgoing' but she was feeling separate. Tom would be all right, she knew that. He'd move on and barely give her a thought. And that Robyn looked more than keen. But it still left Kitty alone with the horror of having ruined something lovely, this little group of five, this little band of brothers and sisters.

Rory kicked the ball in her direction, and she chased after it, not able to think of any of the tips Billy had filled her head with. She'd tell Tara at the end of the practice that this was her last session and that she would have to find someone else.

But, afterwards, Tara had to race off to pick her mother up from the train station after a week in Alicante. 'See you all Friday,' she said. 'Big match against the Glenageary Goers.'

'Yeah, see you, Tara,' said Shazza/Sharon as she picked up her bag. 'See you, Kitty. I'm getting a lift with the boys,' she said, and she too was gone.

Kitty blinked back the tears, turned around and walked towards home. How did you get someone to forgive you, if they weren't ready to forgive? What if Shazza/Sharon never forgave her? Shazza was the very person who made life fun, otherwise, it was just work and Dave... and work was definitely the more pleasurable of the two. But the worst of all, she didn't love Dave. The affection and the regard she once had for him was pretty much all gone. She couldn't pretend any longer.

* * *

A summer storm was gathering, and the rain began to fall as Kitty walked home that evening. Great puddles were forming around the gutters, the world waterlogged and sodden, the ground drenched. She sheltered under an awning for the new wine bar on Sandycove's main street. There was a rattling roar of an engine and she looked up to see a van, Rory behind the wheel, and beside him was Shazza, both singing along to a song, totally oblivious to Kitty, who was standing on the pavement. The van beeped its horn and Rory waved... but not at Kitty, at a woman who was also sheltering from the rain. It was Roz, Tom and Rory's mother.

'What a dreadful evening,' said Roz, coming over to her, holding her hood up over her head. 'I'm meeting Edith for a drink in the wine bar. Would you like to join us? Or at least for one?'

But for some reason, Kitty began to cry.

'What's wrong?' asked Roz, the same look of concern in her eye that Kitty remembered seeing in Tom's. 'Everything all right?' She caught a flash of the ugly ring. 'You're engaged... and you're not... well... is it not what you want?'

All Kitty could do was shrug and shake her head and then nod. 'I am perfectly all right,' she managed finally, 'couldn't be happier, I really couldn't...'

But Roz had her hand through Kitty's arm and was manoeuvring her through the door. 'Two glasses of the house red,' called Roz to the waiter. 'And some of those lovely Spanish almonds.' Kitty found herself being seated on a chair at the head of a long oak table, Roz beside her. 'Now, you tell me what's going on,' she said.

'My problems aren't as bad as some people's,' Kitty said. 'I mean, other people have it so much worse. You lost Paddy...'

'But he's still with us,' said Roz. 'I still talk to him and he's in my mind and my heart.' She glanced up at the waiter as she tasted the wine he had just placed in front of them. 'Thank you,

Lorenzo,' she said. 'Delicious.' She turned back to Kitty. 'Yes, of course, we miss his hugs and seeing his face and the shock of that empty chair around the dinner table is...' She stopped for a moment. '...It's awful. It really is. But on we go. My greatest blessing is my three boys. That doesn't change. I have Paddy's heart and soul wrapped around me. Forever. No one can take that away from me.' She smiled at Kitty. 'And remember, heart and soul are the only things that matter. When they align with someone else's, you have all you need.' She took Kitty's right hand in both of hers, and it felt so warm and comfortable, as though the human touch was what was needed to feel someone's heart and soul. 'Now, promise me, you'll come for lunch on Sunday? You and Shazza? Promise?'

And Kitty found herself promising even though she knew she couldn't be there.

'I've been trying to have fun,' she said, through her tears. 'Shazza told me I wasn't having fun and that it would solve everything and I did have fun and it was working for a while and then it made it all worse.'

'But fun isn't the point,' said Roz. 'Fun is something that happens when you have heart and soul. Fun isn't something you can set out to have, it just happens, like all the other wonderful things in life. Love, happiness, success... they are all on the same paradigm. But you can't force any of them...' She patted Kitty's hand again. 'Just think about the last time you had a lot of fun, when you laughed, when you were happy, when you felt as though you were in love with life.'

Kitty immediately thought of diving off *Pansy-Pearl*, into the cold depths of the Irish Sea and resurfacing with a feeling of complete and utter freedom. And happiness. And Tom.

'Well,' continued Roz, 'I bet your heart and your soul were at play that day, and without them, you don't get fun, or love or happiness. Without them, nothing is worth it. And when they are, everything just flows.'

Flow. To be in flow with life, to glide through it, to stop struggling. It was a lesson Billy had tried to teach her. And what Edith had said about the cracks being where the light was to be found. You couldn't tidy up life, you had to embrace the chaos because only then did you have a chance of your heart being open, your soul being free.

Kitty began to smile. That was it... that was the something missing from the pitch to the Department of Health, from her life with Dave, and the Welcome Ireland campaign.

Heart and soul. Without them, you were doomed to struggle, without them, there was no flow, no ease. Without them, you were lost. And Kitty was most certainly lost. A life without heart and soul stretched ahead of her, a life without love, a world without purpose. Without fun. Without Shazza. Without Annie. And without Tom.

41

The following morning, on her way to work, walking along Westland Row, Kitty saw Tom walking in her direction. Tom was dressed smartly, in a pair of navy jeans, a round-neck navy jumper and a bright yellow rucksack on his back. He was accompanied by a woman, who was laughing along to something he had said. Her hair was short, blonde and chic, and she had the kind of self-confidence which you only saw on influencer posts on social media.

Kitty looked around for somewhere to hide and was about to run into a coffee shop when Tom looked across and saw her, his face clouding for a moment, and then he smiled. 'Kitty! Good morning!'

He hates me, Kitty thought, as she gave a small wave, trying to smile.

'On your way to work?' he said.

Kitty nodded. 'I wish I wasn't,' she said, wanting to talk to him about everything. He might have advice, he might tell her how she could save everything... Shazza, Annie, Billy. And even herself. Right now, it felt as though she was drowning. She smiled at the woman. 'It's just work... you know how it is.'

'Absolutely,' said the woman. 'It's called work for a reason.'

'This is Robyn,' Tom said. 'Robyn, this is Kitty... Robyn is one of my fellow tutors at Trinity and Kitty... Kitty is a friend from Sandycove.' He smiled at Kitty.

I've been friend-zoned, thought Kitty. But it was better than nothing.

Robyn shook Kitty's hand. 'Good to meet you,' she said, smiling. 'Now, I'm trying to persuade Tom here to come to staff drinks tonight...' She rolled her eyes flirtatiously at him. 'But he's playing hard to get... Don't you like drinking? Or maybe it's the pub. Is there one you like to go to?'

Tom shrugged. 'I like a couple...' he said. 'But I am fussy... I know what I like when I see it.' He didn't look at either Robyn or Kitty.

'Where do you like going?' Robyn asked Kitty. 'Any recommendations? I'm American so I like everywhere...'

'There's a nice place in Dún Laoghaire...' began Kitty, thinking of the magical Grace O'Malley. She glanced back at Tom and she thought she detected a look of concern – or something indecipherable. Perhaps Shazza had told him she'd gone mad and was a horrible person.

'Where? You mean out of town?' Robyn laughed. 'I'm not commuting for a pint! That would be ridiculous.'

There was an awkward silence for a moment and then Kitty turned to go. 'Better get things going,' she said. 'Work waits for no man. Or woman.' She gave a kind of jazz-hands wave at them and walked away, feeling her face burning up. Why had she said such a ridiculous thing? She wished she could just talk to him again, go back in time and do everything differently. If only she could just start all over again, make better decisions, and perhaps then she might look forward to her future. But all, it seemed, was lost. Was it possible to go from wanting to marry someone to falling for someone else entirely in a matter of weeks? How could she be have been so certain of one thing, only to rethink her entire feelings a matter of days later? But it was true. She didn't want to marry Dave... and she was falling for Tom. Except it was all too late.

* * *

'Would anyone fancy a drink?' asked Mary Rose, tentatively.

It was 5.34 p.m. and Kitty was dreading going home to Dave. And to Maureen's slippers, which she knew would be stacked beside the sofa. How could slippers, the most inoffensive of items, be almost menacing?

'Just a quick one,' Mary Rose went on. 'Nothing mad, you know. Just a quick little team-building drink.'

'It's Wednesday night,' said Hughie.

'I know,' said Mary Rose, apologetically. 'I mean...'

'It's a brilliant idea,' beamed Hughie. 'Wednesday night is the worst night of the week, too far from either weekend...'

'Hump day,' said Mary Rose. 'So you're on?' She was smiling.

'Consider my arm well and truly twisted,' replied Hughie. 'Which is how I expect to be once I start drinking.' He looked over at Kitty, who had spent the whole day trying to work out how the powers of heart and soul could be applied to the Welcome Ireland pitch. Without Alex to bounce ideas off, she still felt lost.

'I could be persuaded,' she said, as the smile on Mary Rose's face broadened.

'Good,' she said, 'because I need a drink. Everyone ready? Grab your things, no hanging about. We are leaving now.'

* * *

Three and a half hours later, they stumbled into a karaoke bar off Wexford Street. Somehow, between O'Donoghues and the karaoke bar, they had linked arms, Hughie in the middle, and were clutching and clinging to each other. If they didn't, thought Kitty, they'd probably fall over. But she didn't care. She didn't want to be at home with Dave and his crap television or Maureen and her slippers.

'This used to be my spiritual home,' said Hughie, as they entered the neon portal of the karaoke bar. 'It's where I used to worship every weekend. Me, Jägermeister and a microphone. Heaven.'

'My friend Ailish used to bring me here,' said Mary Rose. 'She was a karaoke queen. Mariah Carey and Celine Dion were her favourites.'

'What shall we sing?' Kitty asked.

'"Baby Love",' said Hughie, immediately. 'I'm Diana Ross, you're the other two.'

'Florence and Mary,' said Mary Rose. 'My grandmother ran The Supremes Irish fan club. My mother is called Diana, my aunts are Florence and Mary. I know the words to every song.'

Hughie was shaking his head at her, mouth open, impressed. 'Oh. My. God. Why didn't you tell me? We could have formed our own supergroup three months ago.'

They waited their turn and then stood in front of the crowd of office workers and karaoke professionals, the type who turned up just for the chance to sing in public, and then they began, Hughie transforming into Diana, with Mary Rose and Kitty as The Supremes.

Later... much later, they sat in a booth in the back of the room, three large fruit-adorned pina coladas in front of them.

'Can't believe you haven't lost that ring yet,' said Hughie. 'I would have thought you would accidentally on purpose lose that thing down the toilet or in the Liffey.'

Kitty looked at the ring on her finger. 'I can't,' she said. 'Dave's mother would kill me and I've decided I like being alive too much.' And then she thought of Tom and realised that he was the reason why she liked being alive. Kitty began to cry. She shouldn't have had that fourth pina colada.

Hughie patted her on the shoulder. 'It's the ugliest ring in the world,' he said. 'But there's no point crying about it.'

'It's horrible,' said Mary Rose, 'but Hughie's right. No point wasting good tears on bad jewellery.'

'It's not the ring,' said Kitty. 'Well, it is the ring...' Her head was spinning, her speech slurred, and she tried to focus on what she wanted to say. 'It is the ring... it's totally the ring... because I don't want to marry Dave and it's too late now. I wanted to, he didn't, and now he does, and I can't say no. What kind of horrible person does that?'

'You can't marry him,' said Mary Rose, her eyes wide.

'No you definitely can't,' agreed Hughie. 'I'd prefer to wear that ring for the rest of my life than marry someone I didn't want to.'

'But I have to,' said Kitty, miserably. 'But what's worse is...'

'His mother?'

'She's awful,' agreed Kitty. 'But worse still is the fact that I've met someone else... and I like him. And I've messed that up because I sent him away...'

'Where?' It was Hughie's turn to look horrified. 'Where did you send him?'

'Just away. Back home... anyway, it doesn't matter. It's all my fault... and what's worse than all that?'

'There's worse?' said Mary Rose.

'You've murdered someone?' asked Hughie.

'Nearly,' said Kitty, really crying now. 'I was horrible to my best friend Shazza and my aunt Annie and I said awful things...'

'You're just under pressure,' said Mary Rose. 'You made a mistake. They'll understand. They'll forgive you.'

'But I can't forgive myself,' said Kitty. 'I'm a horrible person.'

Hughie shook his head. 'You're a great person,' he said. 'And I'm a good judge of character. I can sort the good from the to be avoided blindfolded.' He put his arm around Kitty and kissed her head. 'Now, you know what you need?' he went on. 'What we all need?'

'No, what?'

'Another pina colada!' he said, waving for one of the waitresses. 'It's the only way. If you're not going to be married to Dave, you need to develop a better coping mechanism and pina coladas could be the best coping mechanism ever invented.'

Mary Rose was sucking on her straw, making sure she vacuumed up the last of her pina colada before the next one arrived.

'Promise you won't say anything to anyone about me and Dave,' said Kitty. 'Or the other man...'

'Who would we tell?' said Mary Rose.

'On my pet parrot's life,' said Hughie.

'But you don't have a parrot,' said Kitty.

'But I've always wanted one,' sighed Hughie. 'The words I would teach it. The songs we would sing together. My pledge is based on my future parrot. So consider my word my bond. Now we need another round of these things to seal the deal!'

42

Kitty arrived home just after 11 p.m., a little on the inebriated end of the sobriety spectrum. The train journey, which rattled its way along the coast, had brought her a little to her senses.

She put her key in the door, quietly, so as not to wake Dave, but as soon as she stepped into the hall, there he was, his mother's slippers over his socks, looking discombobulated.

He's leaving me again, she thought, with a surge of adrenaline. This time, she'd do it all properly. This time, she wouldn't let him back.

'Everything all right?'

'Well...'

There was something wrong. For the last decade, Romeo had welcomed her home without fail. He'd weave in and out of her ankles in a figure of eight and he was nowhere to be seen. Perhaps he was out hunting or had found a new gang to hang with and was having fun. Except she knew something was wrong. He wasn't having fun.

'Where's Romeo?' she asked.

'On the sofa...'

'Thank God...'

'He's been attacked again.'

Romeo was curled up, sound asleep, when Kitty bent down over him, her hand on his soft body. His eyes didn't open, his breathing was laboured, and when she moved her hand down slightly to his stomach, it was wet. Blood. Tears filled her eyes. Not again. Poor Romeo. She remembered when he had first arrived as a tiny kitten and she'd fallen in love with him and his little pointy ears and pink nose and, for the first few weeks, he drank saucers of goat's milk and slept inside one of her sheepskin slippers.

'Oh Romeo,' she said, leaning close to him, tears falling onto his fur.

'Is he dead?' asked Dave. 'Because if he is, Mam knows what to do... there's a fella who will collect dead pets for €20...'

Kitty looked up, aghast. 'He's not dead,' she said, firmly.

'It's just that it's expensive to cremate animals. And Romeo is ancient. If he's not dead now, he soon will be.'

'He's only thirteen,' said Kitty. 'That's young for a cat. Well, not young exactly but not old either. I know someone who had a cat until they were nineteen.'

Dave was shaking his head sceptically, and at that moment Kitty would have done anything to vaporise him, sci-fi-style, just have him gone, so she could concentrate on Romeo's trembling little body.

'Have you any idea how much they charge?' persisted Dave. 'This man just does a job lot at the same time... it's either that or bury it in the back garden, but I am no hole digger... and you're even worse.'

'Stop it, Dave,' she said, wanting to block Romeo's ears. 'Just stop it. You're digging your own kind of hole.'

'But Mam...!' began Dave.

She held up her hand to shut him up, trying to think what to do. Tom would be the obvious person to call. But she couldn't phone him. Shazza would have some ideas, she thought, before remembering that Shazza wanted nothing to do with her. Mum and Annie were no help, both of them equally wary of Kitty at the moment. It was as though she had gelignited every relationship she loved. She'd almost had a new life, she was almost having fun… and she had destroyed all of it. And now Romeo was ill. But he'd survived Timmy the tabby before and once she got him to the vet, he'd be all right. Hopefully.

Dave looked furious. 'Honestly, what I put up with from you. Your moodiness around my mother, your working late, your awful friend, the clutter in this house…'

'Clutter?'

'Yes, clutter. All your things… stuff everywhere. Your bits… like this!' He picked up a paper fan which she had bought in Seville the previous summer with Shazza. 'Or this!' He held up a little cat figurine which she had bought in Greece, again with Shazza. 'And this!' He picked up a framed photo of her and Shazza taken in a photo booth in Berlin, years ago, the two of them laughing…

She missed Shazza so much it hurt. What if they finally forgave her and Kitty did it again, or did it to someone else, and did it repeatedly for the rest of her life until she was known as the mad cat-less lady who snarled and fumed and was generally crazy? All her life, she had tried to be a good person, to be nice, to be helpful and kind, and she was left feeling angry and upset. It didn't make sense.

Dave was still talking, picking up things and crashing them down, but Kitty watched him dispassionately. She had held on to an idea of him for such a long time, but that funny, clever man she had thought he was hadn't been very apparent for a long,

long time... years and years, to be honest. But it wasn't a phase, it was his personality. While he'd been at his mother's, she'd glimpsed a life which could have been hers, but through some terrible glitch in her matrix, she had to ruin it all and say yes to Dave's proposal.

And what about Tom? She'd loved that night and morning they had spent together... And the sailing and the secret bar. And even the football. She had loved everything.

The doorbell rang and Dave went out into the hall. 'Mam!' she heard him say as Kitty's heart sank even further. 'No, the cat's still alive... come on in.'

Maureen entered the room. 'I know a fella...' she began, and then she spotted poor Romeo and before Kitty could stop her, she picked him up. 'He needs to be finished off...' she said. 'Once cats get a shock like that, it's the end of them...'

Before she knew what she was doing, Kitty was trying to wrestle Romeo off Maureen, but Maureen, being a foot taller, held little Romeo up in the air, like Simba. 'David, keep her down!' shouted Maureen. 'I know what I'm doing. We had thousands of cats when I was young.'

Dave had his arms around Kitty, pulling her away from poor Romeo.

'Maureen, please! Dave, no!' Kitty wriggled out of his hands, crying. 'Please, just give him back... just give him back and let me look after him.'

'But the vets are extortionate and you and David need to mind your pennies for the wedding.'

'It's fine... it's fine...' Kitty knew there would be no wedding, but now she had Romeo in her arms again, her only plan was to get Maureen and Dave away from her. They were whispering together in the hall.

'Sorry, Romeo,' said Kitty. 'Sorry for that undignified

moment.' She began to cry again and her foot brushed over what she thought was a rat and she nearly shrieked, but it was Maureen's horrible slipper which had fallen off Dave's foot.

There was another knock at her door, and she heard Maureen answer it. 'Yes?' Kitty heard her say. 'No, Kitty is not at home... Or rather,' continued Maureen, imperiously, 'she is indisposed. Whom may I say has called?'

Kitty went into the hall. It was Billy.

'It's your auntie Annie,' he said. 'She's in hospital and it's... well, it's not good. Your mother couldn't contact you and she asked me to call in. I can bring you in if you like?'

43

Billy drove Kitty to the hospital in his old Renault van. Kitty had Romeo wrapped in a blanket on her lap. There was no way she was leaving Romeo with Dave or Maureen, who seemed hell-bent on finishing him off. But Romeo was looking a little better, his trembling had ceased, and his breathing was more regular, and the bleeding had stopped.

'Look, sorry again about the other night...' Billy said.

Kitty, now completely sober, was in no mood for small talk. The thought of Annie being in the hospital was too dreadful. 'So what happened to Annie?'

'Not sure of the details, but she collapsed earlier... I don't know anything more than that.'

Kitty held Romeo close to her chest. It was all her fault because she shouldn't have allowed him outside.

Billy pulled up to the front of the hospital. 'Do you want me to park and come in with you?'

She couldn't take Romeo into A & E. She hadn't thought clearly and had just wanted to keep him away from those cat-snatchers.

'Look, Dad,' she began. 'I need you to do something for me. Something really important...'

'I know I've let you down,' he began. 'I just forget things...'

'I don't care about me,' she said. 'It's Romeo. I need you to mind him for tonight and I'll take him to the vets in the morning. Can you do that for me?'

'Your cat?' Billy looked startled at this turn of events.

She placed Romeo in his arms. 'Just mind him, okay? Don't let me down. I can't take him in. Make sure he's warm and comfortable. Just look after him, promise?'

Kitty had no choice but to trust Billy yet again but she couldn't leave Romeo on his own. He had to be with someone and that someone turned out to be Billy. But he nodded. 'I promise,' he said. 'Stay in touch, okay?'

In A & E, Kitty spotted her mum, sitting in the corner.

She looked up and smiled. 'Ah, Kitty... your father found you... I just thought you'd want to know. I was so worried.'

'How is she?'

Catherine shook her head. 'Not good... not good at all... she's not been feeling well... tired, so exhausted, she says she doesn't even want to get out of bed. She thought the holiday might do her the world of good, but it made her worse, she was saying...'

'What was it?'

'Pain. Everywhere. Kept getting tests. All clear. MRIs. Clear. Lungs clear. But it's her heart, I think... she says it's been beating so hard out of her chest. This is my little sister. The life and soul, the heart and soul of every gathering. But when she collapsed...' Catherine closed her eyes for a moment.

'I can't believe I said what I said to her,' Kitty sighed. 'What if she doesn't make it?'

'We all say things we don't mean,' said Catherine. 'She knows you love her.'

'I hope so.' Life was short, she knew. She hadn't treasured the things which made life worth living, like best friends or best aunts, or sailing on a warm Saturday. Or drinking cocktails or playing five-a-side football. Or laughing so much at something Shazza had said her stomach hurt. What if she actively pursued happiness, found joy in the small things and stopped waiting around for the big things? What if there was gold to be found in the cracks?

Except... Kitty was stuck with Dave and Maureen, which made her become so angry, she had attacked Shazza and Annie. She had unceremoniously dumped Tom. And Dave was marrying a woman who couldn't stand him.

She gasped. Was that really how she felt? Yes, yes it was. Lack-lustre as Dave was, he deserved better. But she was going to take a leaf out of Annie's book and bring heart and soul to everything she did. It was time for a new approach. It was time to start taking the lead role in her own life.

She thought of Annie and Kitty's eyes filled with tears. And of course Shazza... the thought of not seeing her, or being together. They were meant to be growing old together, they'd made the pact. They were going to buy a retirement home and live there forever and ever. Kitty had to change and do everything differently. Starting with Dave. It was time to move on, for both of their sakes. And work, she would have to find a way of saving the pitch and keeping them all together. And Billy... she had to make peace with him and find a way of loving him with no judgement.

'Look,' said Catherine. 'I wanted to say something about Annie. She's my little sister and I have taken care of her all my life and I will always take care of her. And does she take advantage of me? Absolutely! Does she take me for granted? Of course. Will she ever change? Never. Do I mind about any of it? Not at all. Because taking care of Annie was what kept me steady when we were growing up, having to be home from school to make sure she was okay... Mam wasn't well, at all... now it would be diagnosed, but we didn't know why she was in bed all the time or what was wrong with her and why she couldn't be like all the other mams on the road. But Annie was there and she was my little family. She was enough. And so I've brought her with me into adult life... and she doesn't understand what it's like to be the carer, but she lost out on her mam...'

'I was trying to protect you,' Kitty explained, but feeling something shift in her mind as her mother spoke.

'I know you were, and thank you.' Catherine looked over at her. 'You're my heart, my soul, my life... I'm so lucky to have you. But I like taking care of Annie,' said Catherine. 'It made me feel capable and grown-up, it gave me a sense that I was able to bring order to the world, that amid chaos, I could control some of it and make our lives better.' She reached over and took Kitty's hand. 'I think you may have inherited some of my genes...'

'I think so too...' Kitty smiled at her.

'But I also think you've inherited some of your father's too. All his good ones...'

'I'm not as bad at football as I thought,' admitted Kitty. 'But hopefully not as unreliable.'

'No, you're definitely not that.' Catherine smiled at her again.

When a doctor came over to them, Catherine looked up.

'How is she?'

She and Kitty clutched hands.

'She's completely fine,' he said. 'I think it's just a case of burning the candle at both ends. Overdoing-it-itis. Has she been gallivanting?'

Catherine nodded.

'She needs a rest,' he said. 'A few days of peace. No rushing about. And a break from gallivanting. She can go home immediately.'

Catherine slipped her arm through Kitty's. 'You're my heart and soul,' she said. 'From the moment I laid eyes on you, thirty-two years ago, in a dingy room in Holles Street Hospital, I thought to myself, this baby has my heart and soul in the palm of her hand. And it's true.'

Catherine smiled at her, but Kitty was staring back at her. 'I have heart and soul already? I don't need to find it. No, I have it already. It's always been there. I have it!' She began laughing again, as Catherine shook her head, puzzled.

'Of course you have it, you've always had it.'

'It's everywhere,' said Kitty. 'Don't you see? It's everywhere, it's all around. We all have it. We just have to know it to feel it...'

Catherine was smiling. 'I suppose...'

'So, I can just harness it... like an energy...' She grabbed Catherine's arm. 'I have an idea,' she said. 'I have an idea for the Welcome Ireland pitch. I have an idea and I think it has everything...'

44

At 7 a.m., after a few hours of sleep, Kitty took out her phone, knowing Billy was one of life's early risers.

'Dad? How's Romeo?'

'He's asleep,' he said. 'Very sweet, he is. And breathing, so don't you worry. What do you want me to do with him? I can take him to the vets if you need to work?'

'I do need to work,' she said. 'I've got a lot to do. You're sure Romeo is all right?'

'Look, you don't worry, I'll drop the little fella in. I'll open a tin of sardines for him and take him to the vets when they open, the one in the village, is that right?'

'I'll ring them and tell them you're on your way.'

Tom was more than likely to be in Trinity, she thought. Didn't he say he taught in the morning and then worked in the vets in the afternoon? Probably just as well he wouldn't be there.

Next, she called Mary Rose. 'I'm going to be late today,' Kitty told her. 'I've got an idea for the Welcome Ireland pitch. Just give me a few hours because I have an idea... I am going to work on something here.'

'On your own?'

'No... I'm going to ask some friends...'

Next, she phoned the vet.

'Hello, Sandycove Veterinary Surgery and Day Hospital, your pet is our passion, how may I help you?'

'Is Tom Sweetman on duty today?'

'No, it's Mr Kelly. Prof Sweetman is at Trinity this morning. Would you like to make an appointment with Mr Kelly?'

'Yes, please. My dad is on the way with my cat, Romeo,' said Kitty. 'He's been attacked again and will need stitches. So, he'll drop him in and I'll collect him later. Will you call me when he's ready to come home?'

After making her calls, Kitty's eye was caught by the sight of a little toy mouse belonging to Romeo and she felt her stomach crumple again. Poor Romeo.

'Who've you been talking to?' It was Dave, in his boxer shorts and grey T-shirt, scratching his armpits and yawning, standing at the top of the stairs. 'Because Mam—'

Kitty held up her hand, as though directing traffic. 'I need to go out,' she said.

'I'm hungry,' he said. 'Can't do anything without a bowl of Crunchy Nut Cornflakes.' He patted his belly, like a bear.

'Okay, fine,' said Kitty, turning away.

'Fine? You sound annoyed?'

She turned back to Dave and smiled back up at him. 'Not annoyed,' she said. 'Not annoyed in the slightest.'

'Why are you smiling?'

'I don't know... well, I do know... I'm happy,' she said. 'Really happy. I mean, Dave, I don't want to marry you any more. And I am so sorry, but you're better off with someone else... I made a mistake...'

'What?' He started walking down the stairs. 'What did you say?'

'I said, I'm sorry. I have enjoyed the last five years... okay, that's not entirely true, but I would say that you have enjoyed them as much as I have. I thought I could solve all our problems by getting married and I am sorry for any pressure I put on you.'

He was staggering towards her, still half-asleep, his balance a little off-centre, almost like a zombie.

'Dave, I'm so sorry but I have to go,' she said, 'I have a million things to do! You go back to your mother's. Bye, Dave!'

And she ran out of the house. Just as she was halfway to the village, she realised she still had the ring on her finger. She should have left it behind, she thought. But too late and too much to do, she kept running. Kitty only had the day to win her best friend back, to finish the Welcome Ireland pitch, to save Mary Rose's job, keep her team together and to make sure Romeo stayed alive.

45

'Sharon's working on a story,' said Janet, on the reception of the Sandycove Newsletter, peering through the shop windows of her giant blue-rimmed spectacles. 'She's exceedingly busy.' Janet was a combination of guard dog, special protection officer and Deirdre Barlow, but today Kitty was not to be dismissed so easily.

'It won't take long.'

'I'm only to allow people in if it's a matter of life or death or they come armed with cake.'

Kitty didn't hesitate. 'It's the former, but I can also arrange for the latter...' She had her hand on the handle of the office door. 'Thank you...'

Shazza was sitting at her desk, her feet up on another rolling chair, and she was doodling her name on her notebook. She looked up, startled. 'I am in the middle of a very important story,' she said. Kitty could see she had been doodling flowers and hearts and her name in block letters with some seriously impressive shading and 3-D effects.

'Sorry to interrupt,' said Kitty. 'But this is important...'

She stood in front of Shazza, hands on hips. For a moment,

she felt as though she was in someone else's body, as though she was being dragged around by another far more self-confident woman, like in primary school when you were adopted by the bossy girl in the playground and you discovered the slightly frightening elation of being with someone who barged through life.

'What's wrong?'

'Me,' said Kitty. 'I was wrong. And I need you to forgive me... Because I miss you and because you're my best friend. And no one else in the world has a better best friend. And because I was stupid and I am sorry. I don't want to have another week without my best friend...'

Shazza was still looking at her, and then she smiled... and then she started to cry. 'I've missed you too,' she said, flinging aside her notebook. 'Horribly. Which made it worse. I couldn't understand why you said those things to me...'

Kitty held open her arms. 'I think I was scared and overwhelmed and... angry at myself for not standing up for myself and somehow finding myself engaged to someone I didn't want to marry?'

'Maureen?' said Shazza.

Kitty laughed. 'Exactly.'

'She's monstrous,' said Shazza. 'I don't blame you for being angry with yourself...'

'But I've told Dave I don't want to marry him, Annie's in the hospital, so is Romeo... Dad's taking him to the vets...'

'Are they okay?'

'Annie's going to be fine, just exhausted. And hopefully Romeo will be...' Kitty paused, hoping at this precise moment Romeo was being seen.

'And you dumped Dave?'

Kitty nodded. 'I finally found out what was missing. Heart

and soul. I'm never going to do anything without heart and soul again. And anyway, I just wanted to say how much I admire you. You're so strong and brave and you put yourself out there and you live life...'

'Too much...' Shazza had a wry look on her face.

'I didn't understand what you said about you being too much and me being too little, but I do now... it all makes sense. And you've been getting on with improving yourself and I have gone all squiggly and all over the place, not understanding that I've been hiding all my life...'

'While I've been showing off,' said Shazza, laughing.

'Kind of, yes... but I need to be in charge of my life a lot more. All I've done is enough to get me through... kept everything neat and organised, but that's not living... life is messy...'

'Especially this office...'

Kitty smiled at her. 'So, I'm asking you to forgive me...'

'On one condition...'

Kitty felt nervous suddenly. 'What's that?'

'You forgive me for all my criticisms and one-liners, for always getting at you...'

'You're forgiven.'

'So are you...'

They hugged, smiling at each other.

'It's been horrible without you,' said Shazza. 'I have had no one to talk to, not properly. No one to worry about, no one to nag or to try to make laugh. I've really missed you.'

'Me too.' They grinned at each other. 'Look,' continued Kitty, 'I don't suppose you want to help me today... Janet said you were busy.'

'She always says that,' said Shazza. 'It's her training. She used to work for Alan Sugar back in his Tottenham days and she was trained to always say he was ferociously busy even when he was off watching football, or whatever he did. But I've done my report on the parish council meeting, written up a few planning objections, reviewed St Joseph's national school performance of *Oliver!* and got tips on the perfect cup of coffee from Man The Van at the harbour for our Sandycove Secrets page...' She shrugged. 'So not that busy.'

'Well, I need to come up with a campaign to sell Sandycove for Welcome Ireland,' said Kitty. 'I am going to be giving a presentation tomorrow morning and I need to take photographs, I will write the copy and Hughie can design it all.'

She didn't have to say any more because Shazza was already retrieving her massive handbag from the coat hook. 'We'll go for coffee in Alison's café and discuss everything,' she said, pulling on her denim jacket. 'We're off for the day, Janet,' she said. 'Hold my calls.'

'Of course, Sharon,' said Janet. 'Meetings all day, is it?'

'Absolutely!' Shazza and Kitty laughed.

* * *

In the café, Kitty took out her notebook, trying to clear her head and focus on the vision that she knew was there. The story she had wanted to tell about Sandycove... she hadn't known what she wanted to say, but it was about how she felt about life and what was needed to live a good one, and it was love, heart and soul. She'd been living without really thinking about any of them, but they were essential. Everything she had done over the last few weeks was about connecting the three of those elements. Perhaps she had been scared of fully connecting with the world, seeing how raw and vulnerable you could be when you embraced them, but Shazza was still standing, and smiling. The happiest people she knew were the ones who weren't afraid of loving fully and connecting with their hearts and feeding their souls.

'So, tell me what you are planning on doing...' said Shazza, feeding herself the foam from her cappuccino with a spoon.

'We've been asked to sell the whole of Ireland to visitors and to locals,' explained Kitty, sitting back on her chair. 'It's a microcosm of a campaign that can be widened out to include the whole of the country. We've been working as a team and haven't got far and I couldn't work out what was wrong with it. There was no heart or soul. That was the problem. We forgot about heart and soul... and that's all you need in life, when you have them, everything works. Everything!' Her face was shining.

'Ah...' said Shazza, screwing up her face in concentration. 'So you're going to mention the words heart and soul and bingo! A campaign. Who knew advertising was so easy!'

Kitty laughed. 'About as easy as journalism...'

'Oh, but that's hard...' said Shazza. 'Us, nurses and brain surgeons, hardest jobs around...' She put down her coffee cup.

'Wait right there,' said Kitty, taking out her camera phone. 'Just head in your hands, and look straight down the lens... that's it... smile? Don't smile... eyes bright... lovely...'

She kept the background blurred, but Shazza was crystal-sharp, her face as beautiful as ever. Right over her would be the phrase 'Follow Your Heart'.

Right, to the haberdashery next, to Edith Waters.

But Shazza was already running. 'Come on,' she shouted. 'We don't have a moment to lose! Heart and soul, we're coming for you!'

46

Edith Waters was sitting behind the counter of her haberdashery when Kitty and Shazza walked through the door.

'Good morning, girls,' she said, surprised to see them. 'How are you both today?' She was wearing a bright tomato-red cardigan, a large yellow silk scarf which was knotted around her neck, a pair of emerald-green trousers and orange trainers.

'Edith,' said Kitty, 'I wonder if you would be available to have your photograph taken? I was thinking by the harbour...'

Edith narrowed her eyes. 'What's this for then?'

'A work project, selling Sandycove... it's just for a presentation... no one will see your photograph... unless we win. Welcome Ireland has to choose the best of the best to represent Ireland as a whole. It's just a concept...'

Edith was already nodding. 'I've always wanted to be a concept,' she said. 'And yes, of course, I'm available. I used to help out the boys with their school projects... so lead on. To the harbour!'

The sky was blue with scudding white clouds, and the sun beamed as Shazza positioned Edith on a large granite mooring, smoothed by hundreds of years of rain and storms. Edith looked out to sea, her hair blowing in the breeze. Kitty was thinking of the slogan 'Find your spirit'.

'I feel like a supermodel,' said Edith.

She was a natural, thought Kitty as she clicked away, getting the tones and the light right, and then, within minutes, they were finished.

'I need Rory next,' said Kitty. 'I thought him in his van...'

'I'll call him,' said Edith. She took out her phone. 'Hello, Rory? It's Aunt Edith here! Yes, of course, I'm all right! Yes, grand, all grand... now the reason why I am calling is to see...'

'You don't mind, do you?' Kitty asked Shazza, under her breath.

'Well, I wouldn't mind seeing him. I mean, I was trying too hard to be more like you...'

'While I was trying to be more like you?'

'And maybe I don't need to be quite so nun-like... I mean just because Mr Unmentionable is verboten, it doesn't mean all relations should be...'

Kitty smiled at her, just as they heard Edith say, 'Where are you?' She turned around. 'Oh, there you are!'

Shazza and Kitty turned to see Rory's van turning onto the harbour road, the engine roaring as he came to an abrupt halt beside them.

'Ah, the cavalry has arrived,' said Edith. 'A cavalry on wheels anyway.'

'Hello,' Rory said, stepping out of the van, his long legs first. He kissed Edith, gave Kitty a wave, and then a sheepish, shy smile to Shazza, which she returned.

Kitty quickly explained what the project was. 'I need you poking out of the van hatch,' she said.

Rory was a handsome man with a brilliant smile and it was

no effort to capture him, resting on his forearms, framed by the hatch. 'Feed your soul.'

Kitty nodded with satisfaction. In her head, she was already writing the words, and she could almost guess what colours Hughie would apply.

'Who next?' said Rory, after they had finished. 'I can drop you where you need to go?' He shot another shy look at Shazza, who was pretending not to notice.

'You can drop me back to the shop,' said Edith. 'And then I will leave you young ones to your project.'

Kitty was already calling Tara. 'Hi, Tara,' she said, 'where are you? Would you like to have your photograph taken?'

Rory and Shazza were sitting in the front of the van together. Edith was standing on the steps at the back. 'I've promised to hold on very tightly,' she said. 'I've always wanted to do this.'

The van drove off, with Edith hanging off the back, and Kitty quickly took a few photos before the van stopped for her to catch up.

Rory drove carefully and slowly, back to the village, and they heard Edith's voice. 'Thank you for the lift!' she shouted. 'My new favourite way to travel!'

Rory beeped the horn, and they drove past Edith's flushed and happy face. 'See you Sunday!'

Tara was at the football ground when they pulled in, dressed in the Sandycove colours. 'Right,' she said, 'what will you have me doing?'

'Whatever you want,' said Kitty, ready with her phone, and Tara immediately began keepy-uppies, laughing while she did so. Rory and Shazza were counting along. '...Thirty-nine... forty...' and Kitty snapped away. Right, she was going to be 'Keep up with your life.'

One more, she thought. *I need one more, and then I can email it to Hughie and work on the words and then...* Was she really going to present it all in the morning?

Tara, who had been chatting to Rory and Shazza, said her goodbyes. 'See you tomorrow night for the match,' she said. 'Sandycove Seafarers are going to win!'

Shazza and Rory were kicking a ball between them, laughing, while Kitty called the vets to see how Romeo was.

'Hello, Sandycove Veterinary Surgery and Day Hospital, your pet is our passion, how may I help you?'

'Hello, it's Romeo's owner here,' Kitty said. 'I am just checking to see how he is?'

'Let me just check for you... Right, um... Romeo is a thirteen-year-old tortoiseshell male cat, of a nonchalant, disinterested temperament, is that right?'

'Well, he's only disinterested in other people,' said Kitty, protectively. 'He's interested in me.'

'Right... let me just check for you...'

Kitty waited for the woman to come back to her.

'No, there is no sign of Romeo O'Sullivan yet.'

Oh God. Romeo. He had been cat-snatched by her own father. This was a new low for Billy in a lifetime of lows.

Kitty turned, in a sweat, back to Rory and Shazza. 'Will you drop me home?' She wanted to see if Billy had dropped Romeo there, otherwise this was a case of kitnapping.

They drove as fast as the van would go, skidding on two wheels as they rounded corners and screeched to a halt outside Kitty's house. She took a deep breath, steadying herself before going in there.

'We're coming with you,' said Shazza. 'Aren't we, Rory?'

'Of course we are,' said Rory.

The door was answered before Kitty even put her key in.

'Well, well, well...' It was Maureen. 'If it isn't my son's fiancée, my future daughter-in-law... well, at least, that was the plan...'

'Maureen, I'm so sorry,' said Kitty, standing on her doorstep, Rory and Shazza just behind her. 'It wasn't going to work.'

'No, it wasn't,' agreed Shazza.

'You can keep out of this,' said Maureen.

Behind her, they could see Dave, peering out from behind the living-room door.

'It was a dead horse of a relationship,' echoed Rory, sincerely. 'It wasn't going to work.'

'Who in the holy memory of the late Great Gay Byrne is this eejit?' thundered Maureen, turning on Rory, his hair rippling in the tornado of breath.

'Rory,' he said. 'Brother of Tom and Paddy, son of Rosamund, and owner of that food truck over there. Available for festivals, christenings, communions and weddings...'

'Weddings?' Maureen turned back to Kitty. 'Is this some kind of joke? This morning the wedding was off, is it now on again?'

'It's still off,' said Kitty. 'I'm sorry.'

'We all are,' said Shazza.

'Yes, we are,' said Rory. 'I was actually engaged once...'

'You were?' asked Shazza.

He nodded. 'Decided not to go through with it. Didn't feel right. Realised she didn't make me laugh.' He smiled at Shazza. 'I think she was as relieved as me.'

There was a tap on Kitty's shoulder as Maureen lowered her voice to a barely audible whisper. 'And what,' she said in chilling tones right into Kitty's ear, 'were you considering doing with my RING?'

Shazza and Rory both gripped on to Kitty's arms, as though to hold her up straight or to show that she wasn't alone to have to deal with this lunatic.

Kitty swallowed. 'I was going to give it back,' she said, her voice cracking.

'Were you now?' shouted Maureen. 'In my HOLE, you were! You were going to PAWN the ring, weren't you? That's where you've been all day, touring the city's pawn shops in that old jalopy...' She nodded towards Rory's van.

'Hey...' he began, defensively.

'Trying to see what kind of pretty penny you would have got for my ring... it being priceless...'

'We didn't,' said Kitty, trying to now take it off. It had been loose for days, and now with all the stress and the racing around, she struggled to winch it off. Finally, her finger red and sore, she had it in her hand. 'Here you go,' she said, hand outstretched, and Maureen seized it, grabbing with the speed and agility of a child snatching a sweet, and swiftly popped it down her bra. Then, she pounced on Kitty, shaking her like a Jack Russell with its chew toy. 'You treated my son like a plaything! Something to be discarded, decluttered, dispensed!' Her hands were suddenly raining down on Kitty's head and then her arm was around Kitty's neck in a headlock, and she was aware of Rory and Shazza trying to pull her off, but for a moment, she thought that perhaps this was how her story would end, being pummelled by a woman who was so nearly her mother-in-law.

But somehow Maureen was prised off by Rory and Shazza, and there was a sound of something flying through the air with a *wheeeeee* like a firework. The ring had detached itself from the confines of Maureen's bra – obviously desperate to also get away – and had flung itself for dear life.

'MY RIIIIIINNNNNNNGGGGG!'

They all watched as it landed on the grating of the drain, teetering for a moment before falling through into the dark cavern below.

'MY RING!' shouted Maureen, rushing over. 'David! Call the fire brigade! Call the guards! Call an ambulance!'

Dave rushed out after her. 'Your problem is, Kitty,' he shouted, 'you don't know what you want. Hot and cold. Cold then hot.' He glanced at Maureen, who stood glaring at Kitty. 'Make up your mind. Actually, I'll make up your mind. It's off!'

'Kitty got there first,' said Shazza.

Dave stood in front of Kitty. 'What do you have to say for yourself? You lost the ring.'

'Actually, it was your mother who lost the ring,' said Shazza.

'I shouldn't have asked you to marry me,' said Dave. 'I didn't want to.'

Rory went to the van. In moments he had returned, brandishing a large pair of tongs. 'My sausage turner,' he said, jumping to the ground, and with the light from his phone torch, and one eye closed, he poked the tongs through the drain. They all held their breath. Except for Maureen, who breathed like an asthmatic dragon. But then, like a surgeon, Rory carefully pulled out the tongs. 'Got it!'

And there, clamped in the jaws of his sausage turner was the world's ugliest ring. He held it out to Dave.

'There you go...'

Dave mumbled something which could have been gratitude or could easily have been something much ruder.

'Dave,' said Kitty, 'where's Romeo? Did Dad bring him back here?'

Dave shook his head. 'Haven't the foggiest... I really don't care what happened to that mangey moggy. He can die for all I care.'

And that was the moment that Kitty lost all sympathy for

Dave or Maureen, when she stopped feeling guilty or apologetic for everything she had contributed to this sorry state of affairs. She stood upright.

'I think it's time you and your mother left now,' she said, coolly. 'Go on. Time to go. We've got to find Romeo.'

47

'Can you drop me at the vet's?' Kitty asked Rory. 'I'll call Dad again.'

There was still no answer from Billy, but Rory drove in the same slightly erratic way and, within minutes, they were outside the vet's.

'Thank you so much,' said Kitty, opening the door and about to jump out. 'Thanks for everything.'

'We're all going in,' said Shazza.

'You can't go on your own,' agreed Rory. 'You need people around you.'

Inside the waiting room was a woman with a cat carrier on her lap and a man with a golden Labrador, but there was no sign of Billy. Typical Billy.

'Any sign of Romeo? Romeo O'Sullivan?' Kitty said to the receptionist. 'My cat. He's a tortoiseshell...'

'No... he hasn't arrived,' she said, looking at her notes.

Kitty looked at Shazza. 'He didn't bring him,' she said, incredulously. 'He knew how important Romeo is to me, and he didn't bother to bring him...'

'There's just a Billy here.'

'A Billy?'

'Yes, a Billy. He's a tortoiseshell...'

'It has to be Romeo,' said Shazza. 'Billy just gave his name instead of Romeo's.'

'He came in with PTSD and needing stitches?' said the receptionist.

'Yes!' said Kitty, relieved that Billy hadn't let her down, and happy that Romeo was safe.

'Professor Sweetman has been treating Billy in the emergency room...'

'Romeo,' corrected Shazza, just as Kitty said, 'Professor Sweetman?'

'Oh, it's been all change here,' said the receptionist. 'Mr Kelly was working this morning and then when Professor Sweetman called in to see how everything was going, I told him who we had in... he knows the man who brought in Billy. I mean Romeo. Your cat, anyway,' she said to Kitty. 'He met him coming in this morning and he switched his lectures around. Got someone to fill in for him and came in here. Puts the welfare of animals ahead of everything. Mr Kelly was delighted with the extra pair of hands. He's been on an urgent case of a chihuahua losing the ability to yap. A yapless chihuahua could trigger an identity crisis so it was something of an emergency.'

Kitty could feel her heart soaring. If anyone would take care of Romeo, he would. Oh Romeo, she thought, he was practically the only sentient being she hadn't hurt lately.

'I'll tell Professor Sweetman you are here...'

They sat three abreast in the waiting room, and after only a few moments Tom came out. Their eyes met. She smiled. So did he.

'Kitty?' Tom said, softly. 'Do you want to come in?'

Trailed by Shazza and Rory, she followed Tom into the emergency room, where Romeo was lying on a folded rug on a table. He didn't do any of the normal things he did when he saw her – jumping up, wrapping his slinky body around her ankles, purring like he contained a million bees. Instead, Romeo looked as though life was leaving his body. He was attached to a drip, and his fur had been shaved on his abdomen. He looked half-dead. She hadn't realised he was this ill. If she'd known she would have done something sooner, earlier... there must have been a way to save him.

'Romeo?' Her eyes filled with tears. 'Poor Romeo...' She turned to Tom. 'He's not going to make it, is he?' She couldn't imagine life without him. He held one of his soft little paws, like holding a fairy's velvet slipper. 'Oh Romeo...' She looked back at Tom but he was smiling.

'He's just recovering from his operation,' he said. 'He's going to be absolutely fine. He had trauma-induced peritonitis. Once he's recovered, he'll be back on his feet again. He's a strong little chap. Not one easily underestimated.'

'Oh, thank God.' Kitty kissed Romeo's head. 'Oh, thank God.' She looked at Tom. 'Thank *you*.'

There was a voice from outside. 'How is the little fella?' It was Billy. He entered the room and put his arm around Kitty's shoulders, his eyes on Romeo. 'How is he?'

'He's going to be fine,' said Shazza. 'He has to be on his ninth life by now... he'd better stop having run-ins with that tabby or his luck will run out.' Rory poked her and the two of them began giggling together, as Tom washed his hands at the sink.

'Anyway,' said Billy. 'I was glad you trusted me. Didn't want to let you down. Not again. I'm sorry. I've always been like this. Football was the only thing I could do, the only time I could focus.'

'It's grand,' she said. 'Let's just get on with it, shall we? I'm too much of a perfectionist and it's got me nowhere.'

'No,' he said, 'you're not too much of anything. You're exactly right. You're you.' He paused. 'I was listening to something on the radio the other day. ADHD...'

'What about it?'

'Have you heard of it?'

Kitty nodded. 'Of course...'

'Well...' Billy hesitated again, suddenly awkward, even embarrassed. 'I recognised a lot of myself in it. I looked it up. Did an online quiz...'

'And you diagnosed yourself?'

He nodded. 'Yeah... I mean, I know it's not official. But it's made sense for me. The hyper focus when I play football and the total scatterbrain regarding everything else.'

'And has it made things easier for you?'

'It's explained a few things,' he went on. 'I was always so frustrated with myself. Why couldn't I be like everyone else? Just turn up on time, not always late. Never let anyone down...' He looked at Kitty. 'Maybe it's just an excuse...'

'Or maybe it's a reason...'

'Maybe...' He smiled almost shyly at her.

'Thanks for bringing Romeo here today,' she said, smiling back. 'I appreciate it.'

'I knew how important it was,' he said. 'I couldn't let you down... not again. I wrote notes on my hands, made sure there were reminders on my phone. Post-its on the car dashboard. Bring Romeo to vet at 9 a.m.'

Kitty laughed. 'Well, your system worked. Thank you.'

He kissed the top of her head. 'You're my little Kitty,' he said. 'Always was, always will be. I'll see you for a hot chocolate, okay?

And a bit of football. I think it might be time to learn the great art of dribbling...'

Kitty laughed. 'I can't wait.'

Billy hugged her again and she waved him off, just as Tom came over. 'Romeo will stay here overnight, and he'll be able to come home tomorrow,' he said. 'Five-star treatment, okay?'

She nodded. 'Thank you.'

'You're welcome.' They looked at each other for a moment. Kitty wanted to tell him that she and Dave were over but how would she shoehorn such a thing into the conversation without sounding mad or desperate? And maybe it was of no relevance to him? Maybe he and Robyn had gone to a pub together and he'd moved on to her? And there was the Welcome Ireland pitch to finish.

'We need one more photograph,' she said. 'Could we take one of you? It's for a work project that I have to present tomorrow morning?' She began to explain what it was, but Tom was already nodding.

'What about on the front step? The colour of the door is nice and... I have the perfect prop. I'll meet you outside.'

He came outside holding a tiny tortoiseshell kitten, who looked not unlike Romeo.

Kitty took some photographs of Tom, whose handsomeness, she thought, was only enhanced by the kitten. When she had finished, Kitty held out her hands to hold the little fur baby, clutching it to her face.

'Oh, he's gorgeous,' she said.

'It's a girl...' Tom was smiling. 'And she needs a home, you know.'

Kitty stopped and looked at him.

'Do you need another cat?' Tom went on.

She nodded. 'I do, don't I?' She kissed the kitten. 'Hello, Juliet,' she said. 'You've got yourself a home. I love you. Almost as much as I love Romeo.'

Tom laughed. 'That's the thing with pets. They are so easy to love. She's a beauty, all right.'

Kitty thought she was going to start crying. Just holding lovely Juliet, her tiny fragile body, her beautiful eyes, made her feel emotional. 'I'm going to love you,' she said. 'I'm going to love you forever.'

'Unlike Dave,' said Shazza, coming over. 'Cats are so much easier to love than men, I find. Far less complicated. Although,' she went on, 'I do make exceptions for certain men.'

'I'm glad you do,' said Rory.

But Tom was looking straight at Kitty. 'You and Dave...?'

She shook her head.

'Kitty sent him back to the pound,' said Shazza. 'The one run by his mother, the dreaded Maureen.'

Tom looked at Kitty. 'So you're *not* marrying him?'

Kitty shook her head. 'No... too much has happened.' Her eyes met his.

'Kitty has finally come to her senses,' Shazza was saying. 'She's seen the light, halleluiah.'

Tom was smiling at Kitty. 'That's good to know...'

Kitty was smiling back at Tom.

'God, Kitty,' said Shazza. 'We almost lost you to Dave. No wonder you were so on edge... and unhappy. I would have been unhinged and furious if I was being forced into marrying those two...'

'Two?' Tom was still looking straight at Kitty.

'Dave's mother... they came as a pair. The gruesome twosome...' Shazza paused. 'You two! Stop staring at each other.

You can do all of that lovey-dovey stuff later. Kitty, don't you have your project to finish?'

Kitty nodded. 'Yes… I'd better get back…'

'I'll drop you,' said Rory.

'I can walk,' said Kitty. 'It's easier…'

'Well, then,' said Tom, 'I'll walk you home.'

Kitty turned to him. 'If you have time…'

'Of course I do. I'll just leave Juliet back inside and we can collect her when she's had all her shots. And I can keep an eye on Romeo for you.'

Kitty felt quite emotional all of a sudden. 'Thank you,' she said. 'That means a lot…'

They waved Rory and Shazza off and said goodbye to Billy and then went back inside to give Romeo a goodbye kiss and another for little Juliet in her special bed, ready for her injections, and then Tom and Kitty began walking home.

They fell into step with each other, Tom's long stride matching Kitty's brisk pace and they began to talk, not deeply, not intensely, but easily, as though they'd only been apart for a few hours, bringing each other up to speed on everything that had happened. She told him about ending it with Dave and how Annie had been in hospital and how sorry she was to have rejected him on her doorstep, and then he told her that he was ready to accept whatever the turn of events was, and that he had told himself that he was just happy if she was happy.

'But I would have liked to have seen where things would take us,' he said. 'If I'd had the chance.'

And even though she could feel a tangible energy between them, she knew she hadn't dreamed any of it. She wanted to put her hand in his or feel his body close to hers. Neither of them said anything more about that weekend they had spent together, and Kitty wondered if they had missed their moment and from now on they would just be friends. But that, she told herself, was better than not being friends with this gorgeous man.

Happiness, she thought, should be pursued. Heart and soul were always there, ready to wrap themselves around you if you only let them. She'd learned her lesson.

They slowed down as they neared the house, and she opened the door tentatively, just in case Maureen was ready to pounce again, like something out of a Stephen King novel. Tom was close behind her, taking it all in, silently. But thankfully the house was empty, denuded of everything Dave owned, including a few things belonging to Kitty. So, that was it, then, she thought. Her life with Dave was over.

'Are you okay?' Tom asked.

She nodded. 'Very.'

He smiled. 'Good to know.' He hesitated. 'If there is anything I can do, let me know.'

She nodded. 'Thank you...'

He smiled at her and she found herself suddenly wrapped in his arms, pressed against his chest, the smell of him, the feel of him and then, just as suddenly, he let her go. 'I'll see you tomorrow at the match. And I can bring Juliet over when she's had her injections.'

'Tom?'

'Yes?'

'Thanks... for being such a good friend.'

He looked puzzled for a moment. 'No worries... I'd better get back. Good luck with your pitch.'

She nodded, a smile plastered to her face but she didn't know what else to say. She didn't have time for anything except to concentrate on the pitch. But she had faith in life... what was meant to happen, always did. You just had to be in flow... everything sorted itself out at the end. You had to believe in the universe. What was supposed to happen would happen, even if that meant they weren't meant to be. Anyway, she had to focus on work. Nothing could distract her now.

48

It was 7.30 a.m., two and a half hours before the presentation, and Kitty arrived at the office and flicked on the lights. There was a stir from under Hughie's desk, making her jump. And there was Hughie, curled up under his desk, his head on his courier bag. He scrunched up his eyes against the light and then blinked at her.

'Hughie? You slept here?'

'I was working late,' he said, attempting to get to his feet but stumbling from being so stiff. He'd been in a sleeping bag, one of the ones which can pack away into almost nothing. 'I didn't think you'd be in so early.' He smiled that Hughie smile, then turned his back, pulling open his top drawer, and Kitty thought she saw a washbag, which he hid under the arm furthest away from her. 'Back in a moment,' he said, disappearing from the office.

Had he been sleeping in the office every evening? He was always the first one in, and the last to leave. He did always have that big bag in the corner.

'So,' said Hughie, re-emerging, hair artfully tousled, his face fresh, his teeth gleaming. 'Let's get down to business,' he added breezily. 'I finished what you sent me yesterday evening... what about the rest of the copy?'

'I'll send it over now,' said Kitty, handing him a croissant and her practically still-hot coffee, and putting another coffee and croissant on Mary Rose's desk. 'Hughie,' she said, 'have you been sleeping in the office?'

'No!' he said. 'I was just tired, late night... you know...'

'Hughie...?'

'Well...' His smile faded. 'I can't find anywhere to live. After John-Paul dumped me, I couldn't keep couch-surfing. And I kept thinking I would find a place of my own, but everything is so expensive. I can't afford even a box room in a shared house. And there are queues and queues of people for every horrific kip calling itself a *studio*.' He gave his head a little shake, and stared up at the ceiling for a moment. 'I didn't think it would be for more than a day or so... but...'

'You should have said something,' said Kitty. 'We could have helped you. And you're coming home with me this evening.'

Hughie shook his head. 'I don't accept charity,' he said. 'I have my pride. If nothing else.'

'It's not charity,' she said. 'You'd do me a favour. Now Dave is gone, I need a new flatmate.'

'Well...' he said, stiffly, 'if I'd be doing you a *favour*, then I accept. Just for a few days, until I find a more permanent place.' He smiled at her. 'Thank you. Just for a day or two...'

Fifteen minutes later, Mary Rose arrived. 'Kitty!' she said, looking relieved. 'You're here! Are you sure you want to give the presentation because—'

'I'm sure,' said Kitty, confidently. 'I think we're just about ready...'

She talked them both through her plan, carefully watching

their faces as she explained her thinking behind it, weaving a story around each image.

'It's wonderful,' said Mary Rose, when she'd finished. 'It's exactly what we wanted… simple, effective, impactful…'

Hughie was nodding, pleased. 'I knew your genius would return.' He gave Kitty a wink. 'Well done… you did it, just at the last moment.'

By now, it was getting on for 9.30 a.m. and nearly time to make their way to the conference room. 'Right, Kitty…' said Mary Rose, taking out her make-up bag. 'Bit of powder.' She dabbed some on Kitty's nose. 'Hughie, you're next…' As Mary Rose moved his bag with her foot, Kitty saw her spotting the sleeping bag. Mary Rose paused for a second before continuing to dab his nose with her brush. 'Right… there you go… ready for your big performance. Mr Mulligan says he will see us there.'

The three of them walked across Merrion Square to the Welcome Ireland offices. The black door in the middle of the building shone in glossy emerald green and inside the vast hall was a magnificent marble Georgian fireplace where a turf fire crackled with life, an original Jack B. Yeats painting above it. In their ears was taped traditional music, the plaintive sound of a lonely fiddle. And instead of the usual bored receptionist, there was a console table laid with brown bread and butter and a large urn of tea. 'Will you have a cup?' said a woman with ruddy cheeks. '*Céad míle a fáilte*,' she said. 'Here for the pitch are ye?'

They nodded.

'Now, I'd say not a one of you has eaten a thing today, have you? Try the butter. It's from a farm in Killorglin… but before you do, sign your names and I will give out the old name tags. Help yourselves to whatever you want.'

Mary Rose passed Kitty a mug of tea. 'We should have something,' she said. 'Settle our stomachs.'

'Ah, there they are!' It was Mr Mulligan, coming in behind them. 'Good morning, everyone. Mary Rose, Kitty. Hughie. All looking forward to the pitch? And yes, I'll have tea, Kathleen,' he said to the woman. 'And some of that brown bread with the caraway seeds. I think Welcome Ireland is the most civilised building in Ireland. Tea and brown bread.'

Hughie managed three slices of bread and two cups of tea in the five minutes they stood in the reception area, and just as he was about to go for fourths, their two rival teams trooped past them. There was Jacinta Boyle from DNG and her team, all looking calmly confident, and on the other sat Louella Murphy from Elevation and her team. Both DNG and Elevation all seemed to look the same, in matching heavy-framed spectacles, and sharply cut black clothes. They looked like members from a weird cult who worshipped at the altar of Scandinavian design aesthetics. Kitty and her team did not quite fit the mould. Mary Rose was wearing a floral dress, Hughie had on his trusty Rick Astley T-shirt and Kitty, having dressed quickly that morning, was in her navy jacket and smart jeans, her lucky pink glass earrings in. But without Alex, as a team, they felt smaller and less significant than the others, who seemed to glow with self-confidence.

Hughie drained the tea from his mug, one eye on the marching formation of the rival teams. 'There's something of the *Squid Games* commandant about them,' he said in a low voice to Kitty.

'Shall we go in?' said Mr Mulligan, clutching his hands at his chest. 'Thank you, Kathleen. Superb as usual.'

Kitty, Hughie and Mary Rose sat at the top end of the large conference table, Louella's team were on one side, Jacinta's on the other. Mr Mulligan took a seat at the back of the room, still eating his brown bread and drinking his tea.

Patrick O'Malley, the head of Welcome Ireland, stood at the front of the room, wearing an Aran jumper, a pair of itchy-looking tweed trousers and an old rope tied around his wrist. 'Good morning, everyone,' he said. 'It's an exciting day to hear all your pitches. We are hoping this morning we will choose the very best and most creative idea, something which connects with the national and international tourist trade. I know you have been working very hard towards this... and one team were up all night...' He smiled at Louella, who preened in his gaze. 'Well, why don't we start with DNG?'

'Thank you, Patrick,' she said, rising to her feet, and leading her team to the front of the room. 'I just want to say what an honour it is to be pitching to Welcome Ireland. I always say, that if you do a job you love, you never work a day in your life... and working at DNG is like being on holiday every single day.' She smiled a weird smile which looked as though she had eaten one of those evil pistachios that lurk in the bowl of nuts. 'Now,' she went on, 'Christopher is going to lead the presentation, aren't you, Christopher?'

Christopher was wearing a bow tie for the occasion.

'Thank you,' said Christopher. 'I am going to take you through our presentation now...' Up on the screen behind him flashed images of Dublin, people singing in the streets, a close-up of pints of Guinness outside a pub, a Jack Russell wearing an Irish rugby jersey, and a group of small children on a beach. 'This is Ireland,' began Christopher, 'and it's a land of saints...' A picture of St Patrick holding his crozier in what looked to Kitty in a threatening manner. 'And scholars...' Next, was a picture of monks working on what perhaps was the *Book of Kells*. 'We call this campaign "Rediscovering the old, again",' he went on. 'It's about seeing this ancient culture and country through fresh eyes.'

He went on, in the same vein for a long time, making Kitty

worry that their team's pitch was too short. Finally, Christopher finished to a round of applause.

Kitty and Hughie glanced at each other. How on earth were they going to beat Louella's team?

49

'Thank you, Louella's team,' said Patrick. 'What about team Elevation? Jacinta, are you ready?'

'We most certainly are, Patrick,' she said. 'I just want to say how much we loved this journey around Ireland, to really think and connect with this little country of ours, and we think we have come up with something very special indeed.'

Jacinta's team had decided to focus on a camper-van trip, very similar to Alex's initial idea, the van taking a family around the country, from north to south and east to west with a tagline: 'Ireland, where magical voyages await…'

'Thank you, Jacinta,' said Patrick O'Malley as Jacinta brought the presentation to a conclusion. 'Right, last but not least…'

Louella poked Christopher and said something under her breath and they both sniggered.

'We have the team from Mulligan O'Leary. Who is leading the pitch this morning?'

Mary Rose caught Kitty's eye. 'Showtime,' she mouthed. Kitty's nerves began building. *Focus on why you are here*, Kitty told herself. She had to change herself and challenge herself and put herself out there. Being part of the messiness and the chaos of the universe was what made life more interesting, not hiding away trying to be perfect and not getting inkblots on life's copybook.

'It's Kitty O'Sullivan,' said Mary Rose, as their team walked to the front of the room. Hughie nearly stepped on Kitty's heels, as they shuffled around to face everyone.

Deep breath. Right.

Kitty smiled. 'Good morning, everyone,' she began. 'It's a great honour to be pitching this morning. To be able to think about our wonderful country in a new way has been a real privilege.' She had to make this work. She had to do everything she could. She thought of her team members, Hughie, Mary Rose and Alex. She thought of Catherine and her constant bravery. She thought of Shazza and how she had handled her life. She thought of little Romeo, attached to the drip, his eyes closed. She thought of Billy and how much she'd learned about him over the last couple of weeks, and how she felt so much more accepting and forgiving of him, just as we all had to accept and forgive everyone. We were human, after all. And then she thought of Tom and wondered what he was doing. She was going to speak to him, she resolved. As soon as she had a spare moment, perhaps she could see if he wanted to explore something with her. Or if he didn't... if she had got everything wrong, if she had misunderstood what had passed or if she was too late... but she had to find out. The cracks were, after all, where the light got in.

At the back of the room, Mr Mulligan's cup of tea rattled on the saucer, bringing her to the present. And so she began. 'This morning, we'd like to pitch our campaign called Heartstoppers...' She smiled again, feeling the sweat trickle under her armpits and prickle all over her back. Had they turned the heating up? Why had she decided to do this?

'A heartstopper is something that stops you in your tracks,

something that takes you out of everyday life and makes you marvel at the wonders of the universe... We know how we feel when we see a rainbow, don't we? We point it out to people – look at that rainbow, we say. Isn't it beautiful? And, of course, it is. And Ireland is full of beauty, everywhere we go, from our magnificent mountains to the sea, our lakes, our uplands and lowlands... and how do these sights make us feel...?'

Behind her, Hughie began clicking through the images, some of those they had collected when Alex was leading the pitch, photographs of mountain walkers, of sea swimmers, of people eating an ice cream in Dingle or playing on a beach in Kerry. 'It's about soul,' went on Kitty, as the photograph of Rory poking out of his hatch came onto the big screen. Transformed by Hughie, the words 'Feed Your Soul' were emblazoned across the top, and Kitty's copy below. 'It's about connection, it's about people, it's about being transformed to something other than our ordinary lives.' Next, another picture of Rory's handsome and happy face popped up. 'It's about finding your real self,' went on Kitty, 'discovering who you are, knowing that this time you spend in Ireland, on this mountain, or walking in the rain, these feelings won't leave you as you board the bus or the plane or the ferry home. They stay with you.'

Next, the image of Tara, her ball in the air, her face laughing, her hands up and slightly blurred, and the words 'Mind your inner child'.

'Because when you connect,' went on Kitty, 'when you change your neurotransmitters, whether it's to take a moment to marvel at a rainbow or to play with friends, it's enough to sustain you.' Next, there was Edith, smiling, the light reflected in her eyes. She looked stunning. And the words 'Find your sprit'. 'There is only now,' said Kitty, 'we have only today to live as well as we can. Find love, find the things that make your heart skip, open your mind.'

And then there was the image of Tom, with tiny Juliet in his arms. He looked even better blown up to the size of a wall, thought Kitty, with the words 'Follow Your Heart – make your life shine'. 'Ireland is here, to connect you to your heart, your soul, the life you wish you were living. Ireland is…' She paused, glancing at Hughie, who smiled at her, and at Mary Rose, who was looking intently at her, with the kind of look on her face reserved for parents watching their child perform. 'Because Ireland is truly heartstopping.' Kitty paused again, breathed in, and managed to smile at everyone. Even the bespectacled DNG and Elevation teams were looking impressed. One or two were nodding. 'Thank you,' she said, 'for letting us share our pitch this morning. We've enjoyed every second of working on it.' She looked at Mary Rose again, who flashed her a big grin.

It was over. She breathed in deeply and sat down, feeling the sweat on the back of her neck, her hands hot.

Hughie felt for her hand and squeezed it. 'Well done,' he whispered. 'You were brilliant. My imaginary parrot couldn't have been more inspiring.'

* * *

Mary Rose insisted on taking them out for lunch. 'Champagne for all of us,' she said, when they sat in Gibaud's, starched white napkins on their laps, perusing the menu.

Hughie had disappeared behind his. 'I think I will have the oysters,' he said loftily. 'And a glass of the…' He peered closer at the menu. 'Cava…'

'We're having proper champagne,' said Mary Rose. 'You were both amazing. And I don't care if we don't win or if my probation isn't successful, I feel we've won anyway.' She looked up at someone coming towards them, weaving through the tables of the restaurant. 'Ah, here she is. I didn't know if she'd got my text.'

It was Alex. 'So? Is the champagne a good sign?'

'So far,' said Mary Rose, moving along the bench to make room. 'Kitty did a brilliant presentation. Mr Mulligan is going to text us when Welcome Ireland comes to a decision.' She looked up at the waiter. 'A bottle of champagne,' she said. 'We'll celebrate whatever the result. It's not about winning, is it? It's the taking part.'

'Mary Rose,' said Alex, 'it's always about the winning.'

Kitty thought about Tara and her need to win. And she thought of Tom, and that phrase he'd used about not wasting this wild and precious life. From now on, she was never going to waste a moment longer. She'd wasted a bit of time with Dave but it wasn't too long. Thankfully, they'd both come to their senses early enough. She wondered if Tom was going to be part of her future but whatever was in store for her, she was going to make sure she had fun.

'Have some more champagne,' said Mary Rose. 'Before Hughie polishes the whole bottle off.'

'I think I could get used to the expensive stuff,' Hughie said. 'From now on, I only drink vintage champa—'

Just then, Mary Rose's phone beeped and she grabbed at it. 'Hello? Yes, hello, Mr Mulligan... okay... yes, I thought so too... really?' Her eyes were shining. 'Yes, right, well... that's wonderful news! Fabulous news! I will, I'll tell them. And what? My contract? Of course! Yes... Okay. I will see you on Monday morning. Thank you. Thank you.' Her eyes glistened with tears. 'We've only gone and fecking well done it,' she said. 'We've won! Welcome Ireland loved it!'

The four of them cheered and began hugging each other.

Hughie's arms were wrapped around Kitty. 'You did it!' he said. 'You got us there!'

Alex was next to hug her. 'I am so proud of you,' she said. 'I used to think you were my protégé, but I think you've overtaken me.'

Mary Rose was next to squeeze her. 'You've been a marvel,' she said. 'The kind of person who rises to challenges, who treats life like a treasure hunt, you keep finding keys to unlock the next adventure. Don't stop the adventure, will you? Keep going.'

'Best of all,' said Hughie, when they were all seated again, a glass of champagne in their hands, 'we're not being dispersed. Well, as long as Alex comes back. Are you?'

Alex nodded. 'HR called me this morning to say Ben O'Leary has left the company. His wife contacted Mr Mulligan and informed him what was going on. I offered to resign, but they said that they wanted me back and Ben's behaviour is not befitting a manager. And apparently, there are financial irregularities...' She looked at Mary Rose. 'Do you have an idea what they are?'

Mary Rose gave a non-committal shrug, while Hughie and Kitty didn't dare look at each other.

'Anyway,' said Alex, 'having said all that, I've decided to take some time off. A friend of mine lives in Dingle and needs someone to help run his glamping site... so I'm leaving the rat race behind...'

'And rat-faced men,' said Hughie.

Alex laughed. 'Yeah... exactly. But I am so ashamed of what I did, I don't know how I will ever forgive myself.'

'You have to,' said Kitty, immediately thinking of Shazza and Annie. 'We all do things we're not proud of.'

'Well, I'm staying,' said Mary Rose. 'And I called Ailish last night and I told her everything. She was delighted to hear about

Sylvester and managed not to say she told me so. But, what's more, she's been miserable in Galway but has managed to get a new job in Dublin starting in September and she's going to move in with me!' Mary Rose looked thrilled. 'Which means...' She looked at Hughie. 'There's one room still available... I don't suppose... you know of anyone who needs somewhere to live?'

'I might do,' Hughie said, slowly. 'He's clean, tidy, and excellent company. He was very kindly going to go to another friend's. But this is a bit more permanent.' He gave Kitty a look, and she smiled back at him. 'He needs somewhere he can spread out and he's got a really big record collection. But he's really tidy. And a good cook. And his strawberry caipirinhas are to die for.'

'He sounds amazing,' said Mary Rose. 'Well, as long as he is also a Rick Astley fan, give him my number.' She winked at him before clutching his hands. 'You and Ailish are going to love each other. Now, more champagne?'

Kitty shook her head. 'I can't. I have a football match tonight.'

'Well, then, we're going to have to plan for another karaoke night,' said Hughie. 'And this time, Alex, you're coming too.'

50

It was a warm summer's Friday evening when Kitty, Shazza and Tara gathered in the changing rooms before their match.

'So, how are you feeling?' asked Shazza to Tara. 'Worried about losing?'

'I gave myself a good talking-to, internally,' said Tara, sitting on the bench, her football socks pulled up smooth, her long legs stretched out. 'Trying to tell myself that these matches aren't important, that it's not the winning, it's the—'

'Not being an arse...' finished Shazza. 'That's my new motto. Winning, losing, none of it matters, it's just try not to be an arse while you're at it.' Shazza turned to Kitty. 'Do you have a new motto these days?'

Kitty nodded. 'Don't force someone to marry you who doesn't want to...'

Shazza nodded. 'Sage advice. Or their mother might attack you. My other new motto is, don't tell everyone you're incarcerated in a virtual nunnery if you have no intention of staying in there...'

'Rory,' said Kitty.

'Rory?' said Tara, smiling. 'He's a very nice man. I approve.'

'Yes, he is nice,' said Shazza. 'And he's single-handedly transformed my feelings about men. Turns out some of them are actually quite lovely indeed. But my real motto, said by some clever philosopher, is life is a rollercoaster and you've just got to ride it...'

Tara stood up. 'Come on,' she said, 'it's time to play...'

The three of them left the changing room, arm in arm singing 'Life Is A Rollercoaster'.

Billy was standing at the side of the pitch. 'Just thought I'd cheer you on,' he said, smiling at Kitty.

'Thanks, Dad,' she said.

'Now, remember, what did I say about focus, about the ball...?'

'Be in the moment, the ball is just a representation of my energy...' Kitty replied.

'Exactly,' said Tara. 'That's exactly what it is.'

'Go on,' said Billy. 'Go and show the Glenageary Goers why Sandycove is the best...' He put his arms out to hug Kitty and she allowed him to fold them around her and he kissed the top of her head. 'Chip off the old block,' he said. 'All my good points and none of my bad.'

'Thanks, Dad,' Kitty said, smiling when he released her. 'But I don't think you have very many bad points. None that I've noticed, anyway.'

He grinned back at her, his face lighting up suddenly. 'Selective memory, eh?'

'Maybe...' She smiled at him, as the girls ran onto the pitch and joined Tom and Rory. Kitty turned to him, feeling slightly nervous. Perhaps, there was nothing between them? Perhaps they would just be friends. But he, for some reason, seemed as nervous as she.

'How did it go earlier?' he asked.

Kitty put her thumb up. 'Couldn't have gone better.'

'Brilliant,' he said, 'but I'm not surprised. And Juliet and Romeo are both doing well. They can go home tomorrow...'

Kitty was just about to answer when she heard someone call her name and over at the stand, sitting on one of the plastic flip-down chairs, was Catherine.

'It's my mum,' she explained to Tom. 'I'd better go and say hello.'

'Thought I would see my footballer daughter,' said Catherine, after Kitty had hugged her. 'Now I am no longer gainfully employed.'

'How are you feeling?'

'Like a weight has been lifted off my shoulders. I'm going to take a few weeks' holiday and then see what else is out there for me. Now, tell me, how was the pitch?'

'We won!' Kitty felt quite tearful. None of it had sunk in.

'That's wonderful!' Catherine hugged her again.

Tara blew her whistle.

'I'd better go,' said Kitty. 'Are you going to stay for the whole match?'

'Of course I am,' said Catherine, just as Billy came over.

'If you're staying,' he said, 'then maybe you would like some company?'

'That would be very nice,' said Catherine. And Kitty jogged back to her team, thinking how strange it was to have both of her parents, sitting together, as though they were old friends, which was, of course, what they were. Time was a great healer. Heart and soul were all you needed. Love was all around.

Right. Time to focus. Kitty took a moment to breathe, to centre herself, to listen to the sounds of cars far away, the sound of the voices from the other team, Shazza and Rory laughing, Billy's ball which he was kicking around while he waited, and her heart beating. *I am alive*, she thought. *I am living*.

The referee blew her whistle, and they were off, Kitty focused on the game. She couldn't remember the last time she'd enjoyed herself this much. And, by the way, they lost. The Glenageary Goers won 3-2.

After it was all over, Kitty ran over to Catherine and Billy. It was strange but also lovely to see her parents together, two old friends, comfortable in each other's presence. She smiled at them both.

'I thought you played brilliantly,' said Catherine. 'You had great... what's the word? Conviction?'

'She's someone to be proud of,' said Billy. 'I think your ball skills are improving. I think another few training sessions and you'll be scoring goals all the time. I'm going to write everything down, stop being unreliable.'

Catherine let out a laugh. 'Well, that would be nice to see,' she said.

'Wonders never cease,' said Billy. 'You'll see.'

And the two of them smiled at each other. It was quite nice seeing your divorced parents being kind to each other, thought Kitty, as she walked back to the changing room. And yes, he probably would let her down again, but her perfectionism and his unreliability might meet in the middle somehow and cancel one another out.

'I've got to rush,' said Tara. 'I've got a hot date... I'll let you know how it goes next time I see you both. Training on Tuesday?'

'Glad you're still going to score after all,' said Shazza, making Tara laugh again. 'We know how competitive you are.'

'Not as much as I used to be,' said Tara. 'I've learned it's not all about winning... I mean, I still *hate* losing... but you two have made me more comfortable with this alien concept.'

'Everyone should spend time with losers like us,' announced Shazza, happily. 'We're good for the soul!'

Tara laughed again. 'You two are,' she said. 'And you're not losers either. You are just more comfortable that not everything goes your way all the time. You're psychologically healthy.'

Kitty and Shazza preened happily. 'Psychologically healthy, eh?' said Shazza. 'First time that's ever been said about me.'

'Or me,' agreed Kitty.

'But you are,' said Tara, 'both of you. You know how to enjoy yourselves, you don't pretend to have everything perfectly sorted, you're open to new things, you don't mind embarrassing yourself or looking foolish...'

'Luckily,' said Kitty.

'And you're both great fun to be around,' added Tara. 'I've enjoyed losing with you two far more than I've ever enjoyed winning with the other teams.'

'That kind of sounds like a compliment,' said Shazza.

'It is,' said Tara, 'believe me.'

They walked out of the changing room and there was Rory and Tom walking towards them. Tom was smiling, just at her, and she smiled back, her heart and soul being as full as they possibly could be. Shazza ran up to Rory and Tom and chatted with them, while Kitty said goodbye to Tara.

'Good luck on your date,' she said.

'I'm learning to keep my ambitions low,' said Tara as she made her way across the grass, back to the car park.

Shazza, flanked by Tom and Rory, came over.

'I come bearing good news,' said Shazza. 'Go on, Tom. Tell Kitty.'

He looked a little shy, as though he wasn't quite sure what Kitty's reaction was going to be.

'Fergal texted earlier,' he said. 'He and Sadie are taking *Pansy-*

Pearl for an evening sail. Does...' – he paused and looked straight at Kitty – '...anyone want to come?'

'We'll come,' said Shazza, immediately. 'Won't we, Kitty?'

'I'd love to,' she said to Tom, looking straight at him, smile as wide as her heart at that moment. Shazza and Rory began walking towards the car park, to Rory's van.

'Good...' Tom smiled back at Kitty. 'Because I'm not going if you don't...'

'And I'm not going if you don't...' she said.

'In fact there's lots of things I want to do with you...'

'Me too...'

'And there's lot of things I don't want to do with anyone else but you...'

'Nor me...' Her throat was dry.

'Come on then,' he said. 'Let's go sailing...'

Kitty felt almost fluttery and breathless as they walked to Rory's van. Tom held out his hand, catching hers in his. 'All right?'

Kitty wondered if this was one of those moments in life when you were on the cusp of something new, that twist of fate, that turn in the universe when heart and soul are in perfect harmony and you found your flow. Whatever the future held for her and Tom, she was going to make sure she enjoyed every second.

'Yes,' she said. 'Completely. You?'

He nodded, smiling at her. 'Yeah... couldn't be better. My wild and precious life and all that.'

'It is,' she said. 'That's exactly what life is. Wild and precious. Not to be wasted.'

'Not a single moment.' He squeezed her hand.

* * *

Later, under that still-bright sky, which was only darkening at the edges, *Pansy-Pearl* made her way through the deepening navy-blue water of Dublin Bay, the wind catching her sail and tugging them out to sea. Fergal was at the wheel, peering through the sails, his eyes on the horizon, Shazza and Rory were at the back of the boat giggling and poking each other. Kitty sat at the front, her bare feet over the edge, the spray of the water splashing her toes, the breeze in her hair. She felt invincible, and Shazza had been right, you didn't need to have a perfect life to feel that you had enough. Just enough frills was more than enough. It was strange how bright the world was, from here, on this little boat. They could keep going and follow the sun. You need never run out of day.

'You look as though you are having deep thoughts…' Tom slipped down beside her, his feet dangling off the edge of the boat, his thigh close to hers.

'I was just thinking that we could keep on sailing,' she said. 'Go forward into tomorrow or back to yesterday?'

He laughed. 'You mean, cross the International Date Line? I don't think *Pansy-Pearl* is fast enough.'

'It's just the idea that we can do anything. We're not stuck,' she said. 'We can do so much more than we think.'

'We can.' He grinned at her. 'We really can.'

'Life is beautiful,' she said. 'Even the messy bits, the things you can't tidy up.'

'There is a crack in everything,' he said, 'that is how the light gets in…' He took her hand in his. 'It's been quite an adventure getting to know you. And to think it started with volunteering for a football match.' He put his arm around her shoulders, and lightly kissed the top of her head, as they sailed into the glittering sunset.

EPILOGUE

A YEAR LATER...

The ring sparkled on her finger and Shazza kept putting her hand to her face so no one could fail to notice. 'I think it's too heavy for my hand,' she said light-heartedly. 'I'll have to do weight training.'

Shazza was in flying form. Just that week, she'd been awarded 'regional campaign journalist of the year' at the National Media Awards, and Rory had proposed. Not with a diamond ring – neither of them was into that – but with a handmade Irish silver Claddagh ring with two hands holding a heart. It was so much nicer and simpler than the ring Dave had given Kitty.

'I love it,' Shazza said. 'And it's got our names on the inside.'

'It's a long way since you were off men,' said Kitty.

'I was never off all of them,' said Shazza. 'Just most of them.'

They were sitting in the garden of Roz's house, in the shade of the apple tree. Rory had built a pizza oven in the garden and was lighting the fire inside. 'Another hour,' he called out. 'Hope everyone is hungry?'

'Always,' said Shazza.

He turned and laughed.

'What did Mary Rose and Hughie say about you getting yet another promotion?' asked Shazza. 'You're chief copywriter now?'

'Hughie is more interested in working on his karaoke,' said Kitty. 'He and Mary Rose and their housemate, Ailish, are taking it very seriously. They are entering the Irish championships next week. If they get through that, the world final is in Prague next month.'

'You'll have to go and support them,' said Shazza.

'I can't,' said Kitty. 'Tom and I will be sailing around the West Coast, remember? We'll be on *Pansy-Pearl*.'

'I still can't believe that we're engaged to two brothers,' said Shazza. 'Does that mean we'll be sisters?'

'Sisters-in-law,' said Kitty. 'Although we've always been sisters...'

'Heart-sisters,' said Shazza. 'The best kind...'

Catherine walked over to them and sat on the deckchair beside them.

Over the last year, Catherine had been nominated to chair two boards, as well as being chairperson of a local homeless charity. After their children had moved in together, Roz and Catherine had become closer and closer and had been away on a few weekends. They'd just returned from a walking holiday in Galicia. Catherine had considered joining Annie on her trips abroad but had decided that the clubs in Ibiza weren't for her. She and Billy had continued their friendly conversations, and Billy was now a permanent fixture at all family gatherings. He was due to be here, right now, but he was always late and no one minded. Billy would be here when he arrived. And Edith was on her way, she was just going for a summer afternoon swim with her tribe at the Forty Foot. She never missed these family gatherings.

'I saw Dave earlier,' said Catherine. 'He and Maureen were

just coming out of the chipper with cod and chips. They looked very happy.'

'Good, I'm glad,' said Kitty.

'Who are Dave and Maureen?' teased Shazza. 'I mean, I vaguely recollect those names, but I can't quite put my finger on who they are.'

'People we used to know,' said Kitty. 'In the old days. The no-frill days.'

'Ah, the bad old days,' said Shazza.

Kitty had bumped into Dave a few months earlier and he was still working for the same company but he had Maureen catering to his every whim. And he did look happier and healthier. The arrangement suited them all. And as for Maureen's slippers? They were donated, along with some other unwanted effects, to the charity shop. Kitty still loved tidying and organising as a way of de-stressing, but she was quite happy to let a little bit of clutter build up. The slippers, however, were clutter that she just couldn't live with.

The football continued, the team becoming better and better and winning more matches than they lost, which made Tara very happy indeed. 'I can't help it,' she would say. 'I just like winning more than I like losing.'

Over the last year, Kitty and Tom had grown more and more in love and, just the previous month, he had moved into her house, joining her, Romeo and sweet little Juliet, making them feel like a family. The addition of Juliet had suited Romeo, he was looking years younger, and the two cats would curl up together, in patches of sunlight around the house. He never went night-time prowling any longer, having finally learned his lesson, but it didn't really matter because Timmy the tabby had. Kitty learned on the neighbourhood grapevine that he had passed to cat heaven. The streets were safe again.

Kitty was loving her work, and loving her new responsibilities as team leader. They had spent the last year working on new campaigns for Welcome Ireland, tailoring campaigns for different markets, developing the Heartstoppers theme, and playing ideas of heart and soul. They had employed a new junior copywriter, straight out of college, who looked up to Kitty and thought everything she did was impressive. *I was her, once upon a time,* thought Kitty.

Across the garden, Tom and Rory were carrying out the wooden kitchen table and placing it just outside the back door, where the wisteria grew.

'Do you need a hand?' she called.

Tom turned to look at her, his face opening into that gorgeous smile. 'No, you sit and talk,' he said. 'Catch up with everyone.' And then he gave her that look he always gave when their eyes met when they were out and about. His eyebrow slightly raised. A message from him to her. I love you. She nodded in return. *I love you too.*

Next month was the sailing trip with Fergal and Sadie. And in September was the wedding, to be held in the Sandycove Arms. Shazza, of course, was matron of honour. Annie was chief bridesmaid and had cried when Kitty had asked her. 'I'd be honoured,' she'd blubbed. 'I really would.' And now Annie was on a wedding regime of zero carbs and a full facial and body scrub. She was going to Gran Canaria the week before the wedding to ensure she was a perfectly rotisseried golden brown. And she hadn't borrowed a penny from either Catherine or Kitty over the last year. Sometimes, Kitty wished they could go back in time and she would willingly give Annie any money she needed. But Annie was happy, having met and fallen for Roger O'Reilly, a smartly dressed, moustachioed used-car salesman who liked sun holidays just as much as Annie. Kitty had bought Annie a brand-new silk faux-fur-trimmed robe and matching slippers, in pink and orange for her last birthday. Annie had begun crying all over again when she'd opened it. 'I can't accept this,' she said, through her tears. 'It's too nice. Proper silk and everything.'

'It's for the best auntie in the world,' said Kitty. 'She deserves it.'

And she did. And everyone deserved love and fun, heart and soul, thought Kitty. She'd woken up the last year and reminded herself to spend the day wisely... happily and joyfully. And, although not every day lived up to this idea, on the whole, they had. Annie was going to cat-sit Romeo and Juliet while they were away. Romeo surely was a contender for Ireland's oldest cat, and Juliet definitely for Ireland's cutest.

Rory was topping up everyone's glasses, the sun was shining, the smell of pizza was in the air, and she was surrounded by everyone she loved.

'What are you thinking about?' Tom was walking towards her, smiling.

'Just about life,' said Kitty. 'My wild and precious life.'

Tom sat down, took her hand in his and brought it to his lips. 'It's been lovely, hasn't it?'

She nodded. It had, it really had. When you stopped trying to control everything and just let the universe do its thing, it was then that the world seemed less complicated, as though you were part of some big and wonderful plan. That is when the light gets in, that is when life starts to make sense, and that is when you know all is well.

ACKNOWLEDGEMENTS

Thank you so much...

To the best agent ever and the loveliest person, Ger Nichol... and to the wonderful team at Boldwood, particularly my editor Caroline Ridding, Nia Beynon, Niamh Wallace, Jenna Houston, Jade Craddock and the brilliant and meticulous Ross Dickinson.

ABOUT THE AUTHOR

Siân O'Gorman was born in Galway and now lives just along the coast from Dublin. She works as a radio producer alongside writing contemporary women's fiction inspired by friend and family relationships.

Sign up to Siân O'Gorman's mailing list here for news, competitions and updates on future books.

Follow Siân on social media:

- facebook.com/sian.ogorman.7
- x.com/msogorman
- instagram.com/msogorman
- bookbub.com/authors/sian-o-gorman

ALSO BY SIÂN O'GORMAN

Friends Like Us

Always and Forever

Mothers and Daughters

Life After You

Life's What You Make It

The Sandycove Supper Club

The Sandycove Sunset Swimmers

The Girls from Sandycove

For Once in My Life

Printed in Great Britain
by Amazon

43445999R00178